SOUL AND BLADE

Tara Brown

SOUL AND BLADE

**BOOK 3 IN THE
BLOOD AND BONE SERIES**

Text copyright © 2015 Tara Brown

Published by Montlake Romance, Seattle

www.apub.com

Amazon, the Amazon logo, and Montlake Romance are trademarks of Amazon.com, Inc., or its affiliates.

ISBN-13: 9781503950443
ISBN-10: 1503950441

Cover design by Kerrie Robertson

Printed in the United States of America

1. EIGHT-SIX-SEVEN-FIVE-THREE-OH-NINE

ANDREA!"

I glance back, searching for the person calling me. The voice sounds familiar, but I can't place it in the second it takes to turn and recognize Rory's smile. Straightaway I return the favorable look and shout, "Did you have to run to catch me?"

My question surprises both of us. I don't understand how I didn't know it was him, and he looks puzzled as he answers, "I did. Ya got some pace going there!" He speeds up. His Irish accent sounds thicker with his huffing and puffing.

I continue walking, clicking my heels on the dry concrete. I know he'll catch up. He's more than a foot taller than I am and runs just because he enjoys it.

"How do ya walk so fast for someone so short?" He nudges me when he catches up, sucking wind.

I stare up into his blue eyes and grin, lost for a second on the details. I'm always missing the details. There's a sea of knowledge in my head; I can feel it, but I don't know how to tap into it when I need to. My memory is such a mess.

I know I walk this same treed street in Manhattan all the time, from our apartment to my small office in the Village.

I know I love where my office is. The location seems a little less hectic than uptown, and the streets feel old, like they have a lot of heritage. The brick buildings and old row houses are a comfort.

I like being surrounded by them.

But I do wish it wasn't here where the whole world seems to be, always buzzing around and constantly moving.

Rory is the other thing I am certain of. My heart tells me that he's mine and I'm his and this small piece of the world is ours. The rest has always been a haze of uncertainty. Looking at him, I realize I don't need certainty about anything else. I have love and that's more important.

He links his fingers with mine, making my small hand appear childlike. "Do ya have an early appointment?" he asks. "I made ya a bit of breakfast before I realized ya were gone."

"Sorry, I do. I looked at my calendar and realized I had rescheduled one of my regulars for the morning instead of the usual lunch appointment. She likes to pretend she's having lunch with friends instead of seeing me. Anyway, you were sleeping when I got up. I didn't want to disturb you. You looked peaceful." I nod, but I don't remember the fact he was sleeping. That fact's just part of the knowledge cloud I have. My rotten memory should hinder my work as a therapist, and yet it doesn't. I keep meticulous notes and a rigid calendar.

"I think I was peaceful. When I woke I felt great and I made pancakes, so ya can have the leftovers tomorrow," he says as he swings our arms.

—We swing arms.

—We dance.

—We like scotch and cigars.

—We like this street with the trees overhead and the old feel to the neighborhood.

All of this I know. But I only know it because I repeat it. Usually when I am alone so I can speak the list. It helps me remember better.

I hate that I have to list the facts—that I have to remember this way.

I hate it more that he endures it and doesn't complain.

Instead, he lifts my hand, pressing his soft lips into the back of it, and offers a look that tells me what's on his mind. He lingers, kissing it a second time before speaking, almost like he's talking to my hand. "I made reservations for us at that Thai place ya like."

—We like Thai.

—We like traveling.

—We have seen the world together.

—We like spy movies and the news.

—We are happy.

I can hear my inner voice repeating it over and over, like I am trying to convince myself. It's almost like I'm trying to force long-term memories into my new reality, but it's harder than just repeating something over and over until it becomes more than just a chant.

The problem is, those words aren't the only ones I chant. I catch myself doing it most of the time, but it's not easy being rid of the old feelings and memories. Especially the ones that don't fit, but also feel right.

"Dinner? But we have the pottery class later."

He looks annoyed as I say pottery. "I had hoped ya would've forgotten it," he sighs, and I wish it was closer to my face; I love the feel of his breath on my cheek. "Of all the terribly important things ya might remember, this is the thing that sticks? Pottery?"

I ignore his bitching. "It's at that old dance studio on East Third. They closed down and now it's pottery. Don't be late, okay?"

He winces. "Will we have enough time to eat if the dinner res is at seven?"

I contemplate it before I speak. "Just, but I'll preorder anyway."

"All right, yer lucky yer cute." His Irish accent thickens when he pouts, which is whenever he doesn't get his own way.

I nuzzle into him and inhale the mix of deodorant and laundry detergent—a clean, yet somehow sexy smell. "I'm lucky to have you."

He kisses the top of my head, taking a long draw off my hair. "Naw, *we're* lucky." He smacks me on the butt softly. "Yer going to have to leave work early, eh? If ya need to be clear across town at six, ya have to leave early."

"I'll work it out." I nod, searching my brain for the moment where I agreed that him taking the job at the UN in Manhattan was a good idea. I think I love my practice and I know I love our apartment, but I suspect I'll tire of the city—of the noise. It never dies down. It's never peaceful. It all seems appealing when you see those scenes in movies where two people stroll around Manhattan in a pocket of silence and serenity. But for some reason I don't ever seem to be on the right street for those moments. I'm always stuck in the crowds or the moments the cars are passing by.

But he's the good part of it all. And that's probably why I'm here, in this noisy city. Because he is it—all that matters. I give him a soft smile, contemplating where I would have been if it hadn't been for him—still sitting in the hospital with the other brain-injury patients.

With a sideways glance, his eyes catch me staring at him, and while he does blush, he doesn't look at me completely. "What?"

"Nothing." I smile wider now that I've been caught. "Just thinking about the brain-injury center."

He rolls his eyes. "It was years ago. How does it still linger in there for ya like it was yesterday and then ya forget yesterday?"

"It's the first thing I remember. You were the first person I saw. You're my first memory. Your eyes looking down on me and your mouth moving, but I couldn't hear your voice, not at first." The memory hurts for some reason.

He blushes and glances down. He doesn't have a smart-ass response for that.

"I won't ever lose that memory. The world became clearer and my eyes ached, but I forced them to focus on the thing in front of me. Your dark-blue eyes were the first color I saw. You blinked, and all the color left the whole world for a millisecond. And when you opened them, it was as if the entire place lit up, and I saw everything in front of me. The monitors and the walls and the faces of the people behind you. Then you spoke again and I heard it."

He swallows. It's the same every time. He looks like a snake swallowing a mouse the way he gulps. He jokes his way through everything, but he can't joke about this, it's too serious. He offers up a sideways glance and tries not to grin. "I don't like talking about it. Ya know that." He's not the sort of doctor to brag about the effort he puts in, but with me he says he hates remembering me that way.

"I know you don't like talking about it, but I do. I like remembering. It's good perspective. When my clients—patients—" I pause and wonder what it could mean that I said *clients* instead of *patients*. It's a strange way to refer to them.

"What were ya going to say?"

I blink and stare at him, almost feeling like a whole life passes by my eyes in the second it takes for my brain to grasp what I was saying. "That when they complain, it's easy for me to see their problems for what they are and easy for me to explain my perspective and how things can always be worse."

He grimaces. "Ya share your private life with them now?"

It takes me a second to answer. "No." I know I don't, and yet I paused.

"Feeling fuzzy?" he asks as we near my office. His tone is the one where he's trying to be playful, but his eyes reveal his lies. He's worried.

"No. I'm good, I swear." I kiss him, just brushing my lips against his rough cheek. His dark whiskers are slightly longer than they should be for work. I lift my hand, running my fingers across the bristles. "Are you working today?"

"Aye." He scratches the dark hair, offering a crooked grin and half laugh. "I am. I have some paperwork to do. It's nothing too formal today." He leans back, narrowing his dark-blue eyes. "I thought ya liked my scruff."

"I do."

He lowers his face to mine, brushing a wet kiss on my mouth, sucking my bottom lip and dragging his teeth. "Maybe I should come inside to check and see if yer couch is as comfortable as I recall it being."

I shove him, offering back the wry grin on his face. "I feel like you remember just how comfy it is."

He drags me to him, encircling his arms around my back and pressing his wet lips against mine. His tongue caresses mine as his hands knead my back and butt. I give him a slight push, wiping my face. "You are so naughty." I offer a wave and turn away, skipping up the steps and unlocking the door to my office in the row house. When I step inside and look back, he's walking away backward, holding his hand to his heart. I blow him a kiss and wave again.

I can't stop myself from noticing the cute butt in his dress pants as he turns to flag a cab. I am a lucky girl.

His steps turn to a jog to grab one, and something about the back of him jogging away from me in the city is off. It disconcerts, but I can't pinpoint why, so I close the door and put my bag down on one of the armchairs in my window by the old fireplace I have converted to a plant holder. I haven't ever lit it for fear the ancient thing might cause a fire in the building.

It's exactly the sort of cozy office setting I saw myself in. My desk is across the room with a set of comfortable chairs in front of it, and in the back there is a kitchenette and a bathroom and a small storage room. Above me there are two residential apartments, rounding out the three-story row-house building.

Glancing about the space and admiring it, I see the clock and wince. I have half an hour before my first appointment of the day, with a regular client, which is not enough time.

Hurrying to the back, I start the coffee and mix my breakfast shake and guzzle it as I check my appointments and start the computer. Being a therapist always seemed like it might be glamorous in my mind. The reality is far less. It regularly consists of me parenting adults and soothing bruised egos.

The office seems dark, so I walk back to the front, and as I'm opening the blinds, I have the funniest feeling I have missed something important. I glance at the stairs next door and wonder if I am meant to be feeding the cat there.

I tap my fingers against the window and try desperately to see if the memory pops back into my brain, but it doesn't. So I hurry to my agenda and check for the name Binx. He is the cat who lives in the townhouse next door. I do love feeding him and pretending I live there. His owner's townhouse is quaint and cute, exactly the sort of place I see myself in one day—not that I could afford one in Manhattan.

And if I am meant to be feeding him, I know it'll be on my agenda. I always add important things to my schedule to help me remember them. But as I drag my finger down the day, I frown, seeing his name isn't there. Regardless of that fact, I feel like I've missed something about him.

I hurry out of the office and down the front stairs, knowing I won't rest until I make certain he's had food and water, on the off chance my hunch is correct. I'd die if he was right next door to me hungry and waiting for his breakfast.

Mrs. Starling, my neighbor, is the owner of Binx the cat. I hate admitting it, but Binx is pretty much my best friend. I wish he could come and be my cat, but Rory is deathly allergic. It's about the worst thing in my life, aside from living in this godforsaken city.

I must look crazy running down the stairs, and then up hers right next to mine. But I don't care; I put the key in and turn the lock, opening the door. In the hallway, as I step in, I see Mrs. Starling in her robe looking back at me with a cup of coffee in her hand. "Next Tuesday, Andrea. You feed our dear boy next week. Remember, I'm going to see my sister in Detroit." She gives me a grin through tangled gray hair. She knows me too well.

I pause and nod, feeling heat on my cheeks. She gets it and I hate it.

"You might as well come in now; you're halfway in. And you know if he sees you he's going to be upset if you don't say hello." She chuckles.

"Well, maybe a quick pet and a snuggle." I close the door and walk in, laughing and shaking my head. "I don't know why I thought this week."

She pats my back as she leads me to the living room. "Come in." She might be older and sort of eccentric, but she's my friend too. I like the closeness of someone else next door, their wall touching yours, but they aren't so close they can see you or hear you. It's comforting to know they're there if you need them.

The moment I see him and his black-and-white fur, I drop to my knees in my work clothes, not even caring. He scampers to me, looking like he has Russian pants on the way his fur is puffy halfway up the leg. Our love and devotion were instant, a spark like soulmates might experience. Not a lady with her work neighbor's cat. It has always been this way with us.

I pet his soft coat, scratching deep in the places he likes. I'm always ready for the moment when he's done and he's about to get feisty. He'll tense, and if you don't stop petting, he will scratch.

"I have never seen him take love off a single person the way he does with you. He genuinely adores you."

"He's my man. I love his little face and his name; it just rings a bell with me. Right, Mr. Binx? You're a Binxy bear. My Binxy bear." I beam at him, but speak to her. "I love being near him. He just makes everything else feel like nothing." He assumes I'm speaking to him and meows back in perfect timing.

We both laugh, and I catch a glance of the clock behind her. "Crap, is that the time?"

She nods, laughing like she already knew I was behind schedule again.

Giving one last pet, I jump up and dash for the door, waving. "See you next week, Mrs. Starling."

"Bye, Jane!"

Her words have me instantly stopping and turning. "What?"

"I said 'Bye, Andrea.' You better hurry." She waves me off, but the name Jane seems like such an odd mistake, considering . . .

I wave again and hurry out the door, uncertain whether she'd said my dead sister's name, or if I'd misheard and somehow subconsciously imagined my sister's name.

When I get back in the office, the coffee is just finishing. I pour a cup and drop into my chair, preparing for the appointment I am about to have. I don't even have a second to stretch my neck or even just sip my coffee before she's slamming the door and greeting me with her sunglasses still on. "Hi, Dr. Spears. Sorry I'm late." Her name is Maria Bentley, and we've been working on her inability to relate emotionally. She complains, but she never stops and thinks or feels. I think she comes only so she can say she does.

I don't even bother to tell her she's early; she'll cut me off. I take a breath and let her continue her rant. It has become a bit of a routine for us. "The babysitter was late and the van was out of window wash, and I couldn't even find my yoga clothes for my class after this. It was a brutal morning. I swear, God is against me ever just relaxing for a minute." I feel myself put a wall up against her roiling ball of madness and energy. "And last night I was in the shower and I heard him talking to someone. He was on the phone at ten at night. When he climbed in the shower I asked him—I said, 'Ted, who were you on the phone with?' But he denied it. He said I was going crazy and the voices in my head were having conversations now. So I got out before him and checked his phone."

Our session continues with her tense routine of suspected adultery and powerlessness, until she picks her things up—almost in the exact opposite order of how she entered—and departs. I have never agreed with their marriage. She always comes across as his doormat.

Sitting back, I take a deep breath and a sip of my cold coffee, feeling a bit overwhelmed by the pace of that fourteen-minute session. We always do fifty-five minute sessions with loads of talking about nothing.

The phone rings, flashing a number I don't know. "Hello, Dr. Andrea Spears's office." I answer like I have a receptionist, but that would mean having someone else in my space constantly.

"Jane!"

I wrinkle my forehead. Jane again? "I'm—I'm sorry, you have the wrong number."

"Jane, it's me, Andrea. You have to find your way out. The box is the key. Find the box. You know it's hidden somewhere safe." The confused woman on the other end of the line stops as if she's midsentence and breathes a few breaths softly, almost obscenely. "You know you kept it somewhere he won't see it. Try to find it."

"Are you a patient of mine?" I ask as she hangs up. I call the number on the call display, but it goes directly to a recorded message explaining that it's missing the area code. I look at it intently, wondering where I've seen the number before: 867-5309. I whisper the number, but it doesn't ring any bells, except one that's bugging me, one I can't place.

With no answers coming to mind, I open the client files on my computer and enter *Jane*. No names pop. I don't have a single client named Jane.

I sit back and wonder who she might have been and how likely it is that she has the name of my dead sister.

2. LET'S TALK ABOUT SEX

I tap my fingernail against my lip as I watch the Lower East Side pass in front of me. Heading north in the taxi to my dinner date gives me time to contemplate the number of the woman who called me.

The cabbie rattles on about something, but his voice is muted compared with *The Howard Stern Show*, playing loudly on the radio. The driver honks and waves his hands. "Pick a lane, asswipe!"

My mind is stuck on the numbers. I can't even stop adding them to my chant. They form a tune almost, taunting me.

The cabbie shouts at the radio show and slaps the top of the dash. "You're a fucking moron!" He changes the station to a song and nods his head. "A classic."

I hear it and remember something. The lyrics are numbers and the numbers are lyrics—"867-5309." I remember the song and where I was the first time I heard it. Sung by a woman with different-colored eyes. She was twirling and telling me she almost called me Jenny but she didn't. She liked Jane better. "867-5309/Jenny" was the name of the song.

Jane?

My insides clench as I contemplate the possibility that my memory is actually my sister Jane's and I am remembering her telling me the story. I know she did. I know she told me she was wearing overalls and her shoelaces were untied. She told me the story or I watched it, before they died.

It's unsettling thinking of one's family as gone, but after so many years passing by this way, I don't feel unsettled about them being dead. I feel unsettled because I remember something. It's not major, but it's something, almost tangible it's so real.

I am an amnesiac. I don't remember anything, ever.

The tune sticks with me as the cab stops and I toss cash and dash for the restaurant in a sudden rainstorm.

Rory is standing waiting for me in a peacoat, smiling. I stop, scared to continue to him as the rain pours down on me and soaks me. My feet won't move. They are stuck to the concrete of the sidewalk. He waves. "Hurry! Yer getting soaked."

I part my lips with a word sitting on them, stuck the way my feet are. I want to say something, but I don't know what it is. Something about seeing him under the awning in a peacoat is disconcerting. Was he wearing it when he left me this morning?

"Andrea!" he calls to me, looking confused or worried. I force my feet forward, walking to his embrace. "Did ya get a wee bit fuzzy?"

I nod and snuggle into him, taking a long draw of the smell of him from the coat.

"Let's get inside and warm up with some Thai. You'll come around. What do ya say?"

I glance up, and for some reason I can't smile, so I nod and walk to the door.

When we get inside the fuzzy feeling goes away. The smell of the food gnaws at me, reminding me I haven't eaten in hours.

We sit in the window, my preferred seat, and the server offers us a smile. "You want tea or soda?"

"Water for me, please."

"I'll take a Coke." Rory smiles back at her, blinking and staring for too long. He says he does it to make patients feel better, more comfortable, but he doesn't have the best bedside manner as far as doctors go.

As she walks off he grins and speaks in a low tone, "Her accent is thick. Always a good sign. I hate eating ethnic and having a North American working there." I give him a look, making him glance down and shake his head. "I don't mean it like that. I just think ethnic people should work with the ethnic food."

"How are you even racist? You're Irish. You're the underdog of the entire United Kingdom, including Wales. You can't make fun of anyone at all."

He chuckles and reaches across for me, making me feel normal for the first time since the day started. "Tell me about yer day."

I open my mouth to do that, but as I have been doing all day, I close up. So I say the first thing that comes to mind. "A client suspects her husband is having an affair with someone from his office."

He raises his eyebrows. "Wealthy people?"

"Yes."

"It's always the same with them. Let me guess—the wife is from the wrong side of the tracks, not rich like the husband, and he's getting bored with her after a few kids have come along and she's not tight like she once was. So he screws around on her with a girl from the office. Someone young enough that it won't actually become a situation for him because she won't want him to leave his wife."

I sit back, a bit stunned. "Did you bug my office?"

"What?" His answer is abrupt. "Naw. It's always the same with those people. Rich men grow up with too many options; they can't help themselves. They always stray."

The subject feels like a tender one, so I shrug and leave it at that. I don't agree, even if my work is mostly with rich women who are miserable in their marriages. Poor women are miserable too. It isn't just the upper classes. Maybe it's monogamy. "How was your day?"

He sighs, but it turns into a yawn. "Besides being exhausted all day long, it was fine. We went through files of patients we have in foreign countries—we've had a few doctors, nurses, and aid workers contract serious illnesses. So we have to ensure they're getting the best treatment from their fellow colleagues at the United Nations World Health Organization. We have to care for our own and we have to assess need based on critical illness." He yawns again. "Quite boring actually."

"It does sound a bit boring, but at least they're getting the care they need."

He rubs his thumb into the palm of my hand, caressing it like a deep-tissue massage. "Go to the bathroom."

I glance up, shocked.

He offers a sly grin, but it doesn't mask the dominating tone that suggests he wants to fuck. "Go to the bathroom."

I get up as if on autopilot; I don't even think about it further, and walk to the ladies' room. It's a strange request, but he doesn't look like he's in the mood to argue.

When I get inside I look into the mirror, pausing and staring at my eyes. The pale blue of them matches almost exactly. It reminds me of a saying I heard once about your eyes being sisters and not twins. They would never be the same color. I like that saying and I don't even remember who gave it to me.

I wonder if there's a saying about exhausted eyes. The door swings open—I jump but not nearly as high as I would have at seeing a strange man. It's just Rory. "What are you doing? We can't do it in here!"

He pushes me against the counter, lifting me slightly. I don't fight him, regardless of the fact I'm clearly not comfortable with sex in a public washroom. His kisses are too wet with saliva; he's too excited. He has an overactive salivary gland that acts up the moment he gets worked up, so I avoid the kisses. Talking won't do anything but put him in a bad mood. When he's decided something is a good idea, anything counter is pointless.

He invades my mouth, undoing my pants and dragging them down.

He kisses my neck, and then bends me over the sink's edge so we are both looking at ourselves, or each other, in the mirror.

He drags my underwear down sharply, scraping my thighs. I wince, at both the pain and the expression of it on my face.

He shoves himself inside me, instantly looking calm again. The rage and impatience are gone and slowly he slides himself in and out of me. He doesn't notice the lack of lube or the look of shock on my face. He doesn't notice anything. He's in his own world, with his eyes closed and his mouth open.

I rock into the counter, my face inches from my reflection. I can't help but look at myself, no longer wanting to see the bliss on his face as he violates me. My jerking and swaying reflection makes the room spin a bit, but I focus on my eyes. I stare so hard I swear my eyes turn two different colors.

I look into the dark-blue eye, noting the hint of purple that's there. My reflection glances up, but I swear I am still looking into my own eyes. She wrinkles her nose and then looks back at me. Her lips are moving, or are they my lips? She's talking but I can't hear her.

I think it's a result of the vertigo from being shoved into the counter, but I swear my lips are pressed together in hate and despair.

She moves her mouth again and I catch a word. *Four.* She's saying *four* over and over. So I say it. "Four?"

"What?" Rory looks confused in the mirror.

"Harder."

He grins and ups his pace.

I glance back and her cheeks have flushed red, but she doesn't look embarrassed and I know I'm not. She looks angry. Angry that my boyfriend is doing this here, maybe.

She looks straight at me and mouths words, but I understand her as if she is speaking. *The four-leaf box. Find the four-leaf box. You hid it somewhere he won't look.*

I pull my brows together as he ruts and finishes with twitchy jerks.

A moment later my reflection is again just my face, annoyed and bewildered as he pulls himself from me and walks into one of the stalls, leaving me bent over the sink.

In the reflection of him and me I see something else—a stage. We are playing at something, and he is an actor and I am too. This isn't real. The world we live in is fake, and I don't know how or why. If I said that aloud, I'd need to check myself into a mental institution.

I pull up my pants, leaving whatever mess he made, and walk out of the bathroom, heading right for the exit.

I'm halfway down the block when he catches up. "What's wrong?" he shouts.

I turn, exasperated and spent. "You just assaulted me in a bathroom. Really? What's wrong? I don't know, how about the fact you ruined my night on purpose because you didn't want to go to pottery." It feels like the most brazen thing I have ever said.

His eyes cloud over with fury. "Are ya kidding me? Not two weeks ago ya asked for us to spice things up. I figured bathroom sex and some Thai before yer silly pottery class might be just the ticket." His accent is thick, ridiculously so.

I roll my eyes and stalk off to hail a cab. My underwear is soaked and my patience is gone—to the point that I'm hallucinating.

Essentially I think I need some sleep.

The lyrics to the song slip back into my head as I walk, the digits of the phone number.

867-5309

867-5309

867-5309

867-5309

I chant it and make my steps match the beat in my head.

If the answer to what it all means would just pop into my half-crazed head, I'd be able to shake this feeling of artificiality in my world.

3. RADIO NOWHERE

Rory's snoring. It's so bad I can feel the vibration in my skin. I roll away from him and wrap my pillow around my head. But that doesn't help. The moment I close my eyes, I hear the numbers again and again, on a loop, and somehow it incorporates into his snoring, making a song.

I might kill someone if I don't get some sleep.

Finally, defeated and dejected, I get up and slip down the hall to the bathroom. I sit on the toilet and listen to him snoring. Even peeing doesn't mute it.

I think he is an animal.

Thinking about him evokes Maria, my client from earlier. I can't help but wonder how she's doing.

The strangest feeling washes over me as I think about her—one of envy. If she divorces him, if she says no, she wouldn't have to do all the things he requires for his life to run smoothly, and work on top of that.

Her life would get very uncomplicated.

The notion is enticing.

867-5309

The stupid numbers are stuck in my brain. I stare at the bathtub and then realize, they might not just be numbers. I count it out on my hands, getting *hfg-ecoi*. If it was a word scrambler, I would replace the *o* with an actual *o*. So the letters are *hfgecoi*.

I rearrange them, realizing there isn't a single word in the English dictionary that comes from using all those letters.

Drumming my fingers on the tub, I space out.

Fiocheg, gif-echo, hc-fogie . . . there is nothing.

The letters mean nothing. I get up and walk into the kitchen, picking up my phone and entering the title of the song in Google, "867-5309/Jenny." That has no significance to me other than that memory of the woman singing it.

My brain makes up a hundred word combinations, but none of them works. I happen to glance back at my phone and smile at the name of the artist.

I whisper it, almost wondering what a silly name like that feels like on the tongue: "Tommy Tutone."

A flash instantly hits me like a ton of bricks. I heard the song on the radio awhile ago. I was in the bathroom looking for something. Yet I can't recall it clearly.

Movement catches my eye, but what I see has no explanation. A vision of me is walking down the hall, holding something and looking all around the house. I step back, expecting the air to go cold or my heart to leap from my chest.

But I'm not scared. The thing in my hands has me mystified or entranced.

She/me walks right across the room in front of me and out the door—through the door.

I hurry back to the bedroom and pull on clothes and a sweater. I slip on shoes and rush out the door and down the street.

I run to catch up to her. Rory's right; I do walk fast. I run my hand through the air the ghost of me is in, but this version of me must be made of my dreams and exhaustion and walks like she is in a different world. Somehow the two worlds are crossing, like she's a ghost reliving her version of our death as it happened wherever she is from.

Or a foreshadowing of my death?

Will I die tonight?

I laugh at myself, concluding that the ghost is more likely to be a reflection of my day, based upon the varying clients and the lack of sleep. Or even more likely, I am in my bed sleeping at this very moment and it's all a dream.

But she walks exactly where I think she will. She doesn't knock on the door but walks right through it, proving she is indeed a ghost or a dream. I grab the hide-a-key and open the door quietly. Binx comes running to me, weaving in between my legs.

"I never thought you would finally understand it all."

I jump when Mrs. Starling speaks into the dark hallway.

"Understand what?"

"How you came to be here." She lifts a flashlight to her face like we're at camp and she's trying to tell me the end of the creepy story about the man with the hook hand. I wince and step back.

"Why am I here?" I can't tell her that I followed a ghostly version of me, but my eyes dart around, looking for me.

She opens her mouth, but the song comes from her lips instead of an explanation. My scientific mind tries to explain it all, and I haven't got the fancy words I expect. I should have theories as to what's wrong with me. I am a therapist after all.

Binx purrs and snakes my legs, weaving in and out of them as Mrs. Starling sings softly, as if doing an acoustic version of the song that has been plaguing me all day.

I'm having a dream. I need to go with it. The dream will lead me to the answers.

My head jerks to the right, as I notice the stairs to the second floor. Binx runs to them, standing on the landing and meowing at me. I follow him without asking her. I know I've cat-sat for her more times than I can count, but I don't ever recall going up the stairs before this moment.

They creak with an unfamiliar sound. When I get to the top of the stairs, only a small night-light plugged in near the floor illuminates the landing. I creep past the closed doors, inwardly telling myself I need to go home.

When I open the door to the bathroom, it matches the one from the memory I had, just before I saw the ghostly version of me. This is the bathroom I was searching.

In the dark shadows I cast, I miss her at first, but when I step back, the light catches her—me. She's kneeling on the floor in the dark. She lifts a finger to her lips and pulls the grate off the heating vent at the bottom of the cabinet. She puts the box, which I now see was the item in her hands, into the vent and puts the grate back over the top. She smiles at me and even in the dark I can see that her eyes don't match in color.

She puts her finger back up to her lips and vanishes. I jump, looking around, but she isn't there. I turn, jumping again when I see Mrs. Starling in the hallway, casting a shadow over me. She smiles, still whispering the friggin' song.

Binx rubs himself against her bare ankles, getting lost every couple of seconds in her nightgown.

I panic as I look around and the light flickers. Finally I can't take it anymore and I scream.

I blink and realize I'm in my bed naked and covered in sweat.

Rory is gone.

This was easily the worst dream I have ever had.

"Rory!" I call out, but no one answers.

My heart is racing and my mouth is dry, but my mind is reeling.

I get up, flinging the covers and skidding along the floor to the bathroom, slamming the door when I get inside. My back is pressed against the cold wood, but I'm still coated in sweat—cool sweat—the worst kind really.

I drop to my knees, my eyes avoiding the mirror. If she's there in the reflection, I might actually stroke out on the floor, and no one wants to be found naked.

Behind the white grate under the bathroom vanity, I see it. There's no mistaking what I see. My left arm tingles, no doubt from the heart attack I am actually having. I ignore the warnings from my body and scoot forward enough to drop to my elbows and stare straight.

Behind the grate there is exactly what she said there would be. A four-leaf box—a box with a four-leaf clover. I know the box; I clearly hid it in some fugue state. But I don't want to touch it.

It feels like it's more than just a box. It feels like a memory filled with joy and sadness. I was unhappy for the clover being trapped forever, but she was pleased that it was always going to be perfect, trapped there.

Who is she? Who is the voice in my head that says the clover will be beautiful forever, protected?

The mystery woman is one baffling notion, but the other is why I hid the box in the first place. Why am I dreaming about it and yet not remembering any of this?

My fingers creep forward, tiptoeing along the tile like legs might walk it—miniature legs. I loop two of my very expensive gel-tipped nails into the grate and use them to pull it forward.

I can only pray Rory doesn't come home and open the door to find me bent over naked.

I tilt my head to the side as I drop the grate to the tile and stare at the ominous little box. There must be some meaning to it beyond the strange image it pulls up in my mind, the one of the lady with the different-colored eyes smiling at me. She laughs, tucking one strand of my hair behind my ear, and she helps me stand up. Her arms encircle me, but it isn't her that's clinging, it's me. I'm clinging to her in my mind. I open my eyes, hardly aware that I closed them, and reach for the box.

A noise in the house stops me from reaching. I turn back, staring at the door. Rory's back.

I don't relish the thought of him finding me. Not because I look insane, but because there's something about the idea of him in my mind that's changed.

I turn the lock and stuff a towel under the door so he can't see in.

His footsteps vibrate, but I ignore it and look at the box. As I do, I drop back to my knees, and the handle turns, clicking and jerking against the lock. "Andrea?"

That's not my name.

I don't remember everything, but that is not my name—I know that.

My hands shake and my thighs tremble as I lean forward and clutch the small wooden box.

"Andrea!" The door rattles and the lock clicks, but I drag the box out, focused solely on it.

"What are ya doing in there? Are ya all right?" His body slams against the door, shaking the entire house. "*Andrea!* Bloody hell!"

I tilt back the lid and instantly I know it all. There's a face with green-gray eyes and perfect lips inside. I lift the picture and know him. Dash!

I glance at the underside of the lid and whisper the words that seem foreign and familiar at the same time. She was the sugar and I was the spice. "Tell me about the swans, the way the swans circle the stars and shoot across the sky."

The cupboards blow up and away from me. The walls of the house where I am become nothing more than debris and particles, making dust in the air. I step into the nothingness, the black and swirling vortex. I don't float like the particles or the cracked mirror that reflects things to me. I drop and fall into the blackness, where I see and feel nothing.

"*Jane!*" he screams, but I blink and leave the screaming there inside him. Something beeps and something swirls, and my blinking eyes convey still images as if in a flip-book, trying to give me a moving picture.

I cough and gasp and stare at the white-tiled ceiling of the bright

room. Everything is moving too rapidly, but I now know where I am—
just barely.

I'm in Rory's head because he abducted girls and kept them in cells.
He used them in a brothel built for powerful men around the world.
Leaders. I am on a mind run trying to find answers and to see if he has
other secrets he isn't sharing with us. The memory of the girls in their
cells and the torture Rory inflicted upon them gives me chills. He is a
rapist and a murderer, and, worst of all, the best CIA agent I have ever
met. And likely the better mind runner.

I reach for Dash, the one who will bring it all back.

His hand closes around mine, but when I look, it's Rory, not Dash.
He's smiling and holding me. *"Get away from me!"* I scream in a cracked
and croaking voice.

He drops to my side, patting my hand and shaking his head. "I only
want to love ya, Jane. Let me love ya. Only you can save me."

I try to swat and fight, but my hands are restrained and my muscles
are weak, atrophied from my lengthy stay on the bed. He stands and
nods at someone I can't see. "Take her to the ward."

I scream and cry, everything coming out in dry pieces as my throat
feels like it's bleeding. I need to wake up. I need to find Dash.

I chant the things I need to remember.

"I am marrying Dash. I am happy. This isn't real. None of this is
real. I don't live here. I live at 1707 Girard Street North in Washington,
DC. I am Jane Spears. I am military. I handle mind runs and special
ops. I am not Andrea. I don't live in Manhattan. I am not married to
Rory. I am not in love with Rory. The love of my life is Binx."

Angie walks to me, glaring with her cold gray-blue eyes. "Shut yer
yap, ya wee harlot. Going after my man like that. I know it was ya who
corrupted him. Yer Jane Spears all right. Yer the reason Rory is a bad
man. It's all yer fault."

"No!' I scream, but the bed is already rolling, the walls flying by.
The ceiling. The ceiling indicates the distance I am going. I count the

tiles, seventeen. A door opens and the light changes, turning gray and dank with a smell of something I can't quite discern—musty but sweet. We are still in a hallway.

A woman in an old-fashioned nurse's uniform walks to me. She has a clipboard and a pen. She clicks it and glares at me, pursing jammy pink lips that remind me of a B-movie villainess. "Dr. Dash will be here any second. He will want to assess you."

At her words, I blink, and the world gets hard to focus on. When I tilt my head to the right, it tilts with me, twisting and roiling like I do.

She transforms from Nurse Ratched into a sweet older woman the moment I hear his voice from behind us. "I want her in a private room, fully restrained. I will examine her before I administer any meds."

The nurse nods her head, batting her lashes at him. She turns to me, again becoming something frightening. She snaps her fingers and my bed moves, as if by magic. The ceiling lights are gapped between several tiles, telling me we are going a much longer way this time. I count fourteen lights and seven tiles before we stop and turn to the right. The bed scrapes and knocks into a room with only one light, hanging from a cord by a crack in the concrete ceiling. Water drips in the background, and I don't know what to make of it all.

The room is more cell than room.

I lift my head, in time to see the door close. I'm left staring at a slot-like gap in the middle of the door. Something you could peek through to check on patients or hand meds and food through. It looks like a mail slot.

I am alone long enough to realize what it is.

I'm still inside.

The clover box was a trap. Rory is running the show.

But at least I know that now.

I am stuck inside his mind, with no way out on my own. He somehow hijacked the mind run Angie and I had planned, turning it into one he ran himself.

He is better at this than I am. If a mind run can be compared to playing a video game, then he's winning.

Feeling a cool breeze tickle across my skin, I shudder under the swinging light. In the stillness of my room I can't stop hearing its wires creak ever so slightly as it sways in the breeze.

That sound could make me crazy, but the next sound I hear makes me scared.

I would know his footsteps anywhere. He drags his left leg subtly from an injury during his time in G2, Irish intelligence. His ACL went in a hard landing from an airdrop.

When his key turns in the lock, I expect it. The squeal of the door doesn't shock me. I don't even flinch when he closes us in here together.

"I will need ya to tell me how it felt to be fucked by me when ya were in the cells with all the girls. I need ya to tell me how much ya liked it."

That surprises me. I grimace at the disturbing man he really is. A man I never saw inside the colleague I had liked, maybe because I always saw the damage and respected it—as kindred spirits might.

But as his hand lands on my foot and he rubs it, chuckling to himself, I see it. I see what he is.

He laughs like he's reliving it, squeezing my foot in a rhythmic fashion. "I loved that cave of cells. I even loved those girls. I cared for them. It was my idea to put the medicine in the water bottles and vitamins in the food. I loved those bloody girls." His voice cracks and I realize his laughing is shredding into tears and the gripping of my skin is out of desperation.

I look at him, hardly recognizing him.

His dark-blue eyes find their way out from under his heavy brow, seeking out my stare. "But you didn't see it that way, did you?" His grip tightens to the point that I wince and then his nails dig in and I cry out.

I'm softer here. I'm weaker. He's controlling the script and running the show and I can't be me, Jane. I can't be strong and trained and ready to fight him. Somehow he's changing who I am in the story too. His sick and twisted version of Andrea, my poor dead sister, is weak and pathetic. She needs him. She's malleable.

But I am me. I will find a way to be Jane.

I struggle against the restraints and bed, but he doesn't relent.

He doesn't care that I'm struggling or crying. I don't even know if he's consciously in this room or if his mind is somewhere else, imagining we are somewhere else. Someplace where I am enjoying his affections and not writhing and crying.

His hands work their way up my legs. He rubs and massages, getting so deep into the tissue I'm sure I'm bruising. He moves his hand between my thighs, lifting the hospital gown I didn't even realize I was wearing.

I jerk when his fingers make direct contact with my bare lips. I'm not wearing underwear either. It's his dream and his fantasy.

Maybe it's the way he sees my relationship with Dash. He is wearing a DR. DASH name tag.

He glides a finger inside me, still staring off to the back of the room, absently thrusting his finger in and out of me.

I look up at the ceiling and scream, "Tell me about the swans, the way the swans circle the stars and shoot across the sky!"

He looks down at his hand and my bared body. "Why can't I see it? Why can't I see what it really looks like? Show yerself to me! Let me have ya."

I don't know what he means, but I imagine it perfectly: the room with the old French decor and the lady, my grandmother, sitting at the couch.

She holds up a cup of tea, but the distraction of a second finger being inserted inside me blurs the room. He thrusts harder, keeping my attention span.

The swans aren't working. Dash isn't working. The clover box isn't working. But I know there's one thing that will. One thing Rory can't change in any world. "Binx, come to Mommy! Come and find me, Binxy bear!" I squeeze my eyes shut and relax into the jerking sensation, leaving it behind. I need it to fade away, but Rory's doing it to keep me present. He is trying to make me his victim and his prisoner, but I refuse to be either.

The first meow echoes like a miracle. I laugh, both relieved and combative. "You can't stop him or my love for him."

My beloved Binx jumps onto my belly, his little cat feet kneading. He comes to my neck, nuzzling himself there. He curls around me. When I open my eyes, I meet his as he purrs and stares at me. His green eyes glow. Tears stream down my cheeks suddenly, unexpectedly. Binx turns and hisses against Rory's snarl. He spits his disgust, but Rory doesn't stop thrusting his fingers in and out of me.

"That cat isn't here, Jane. But I am. I know you feel me." He sounds angry, maybe because he can't seem to get the cat out of his scenario.

Binx is my part of this horrid world.

Binx turns back to me, overtaking my gaze with his. It's mesmerizing.

His eyes swirl, making my lips turn up. Everything fades, except the shoving motion, but I don't care. I know it isn't real. Rory isn't touching me. He's abusing me in his head; it's his pleasure and pain and twisted perversion. I am not here.

Binx's purring gets louder, bringing me back with him, like the rabbit leading Alice. I fall back into the swirling vortex, still jerking from the fingers inside me, making me raw even if it's not real.

I blink and the room is the one I went to sleep in. The lab where Rory is next to me. I don't need to look at him to know he's there with me. There is one face, and only one face I need to see. And he is here. Dash gives me a worried look. "Jane?"

I still jerk like there are fingers moving in and out of me, but I don't look away from the green-gray eyes bearing down on me.

"Jane?" Dash repeats as he reaches for me.

I clear my throat, recoiling from his touch. I swear I can still hear my cat purring and feel the weight of him on my throat. I close my eyes and focus on that, still moving like the fingers are jabbing me.

I turn my head away from the heat coming off Dash, opening my eyes to Rory lying next to me. His fingers move like he's inside me.

I wince and realize the doctors and lab techs know what is happening. The movement stops, yet Rory continues jerking as if he is inside me. As if I am still in there with him.

"It never was me," I whisper and close my eyes again. "He was never touching me."

In that moment, hands touch me. I flail and curse at them. The people talking, trying to calm me, say they want to help. They say they need to take off the monitors. I don't believe it. None of this is real.

I am still inside.

I scratch and claw, punching someone in the face and kicking another in the stomach.

In only seconds of fighting, I have my hands around Rory's neck, choking the life from him. Someone grabs my arms, but I head-butt him or her, and continue squeezing as hard as I can. I hit them and him in the face, each as hard as I can from atop Rory's chest. When I manage to fight them all off, my hands find their way back to his throat, and within heartbeats, his eyes are bulging from their sockets.

A stabbing pain hits my arm and all my strength fades. The floor doesn't fall away, even though I prepare for that, because I am still inside. I can't get out.

"I can't get out! I can't get out!" I panic, losing my grip on his neck even though I want to squeeze.

Dash is there suddenly, in my face. He lifts his hands, and the worry in his eyes makes me wonder if he is just trying to take off the monitors. If I'm out of the imaginary world and free of it all, even though I'm still moving like I'm inside.

Even when they shove me in the cell, saying it's for my own safety until I come down from the run, I know it—I am still inside.

4. I SAY A LITTLE PRAYER

The bed smells creepy-familiar enough that even dragging the sheets from it, I have to hold my breath. It's been four days and I can't shake the leftovers this time.

I am not inside, and yet I doubt my every move. I doubt everything I see. I doubted when Dash and the team put me in the cell at the end of the run. I screamed and raged and fought, and even when I realized it was all over and I was out of Rory's head, I still couldn't feel safe.

Mind runs always come with leftovers, but this time they are affecting me worse than ever. I can still smell the dank air all around me. The dank and dark places where Rory lives.

"It's the third time you've changed them since you got home." Dash's tone isn't purposely mocking, but I feel it sting just the same.

"You could help instead of judge." I look back with daggers. Dr. Dash, the real Dash, leans against the doorframe with the strangest look on his face. I refuse to let his look soften me. "Or stand there weighing in with your psychological opinions," I add. Being back in our townhouse hasn't been easy for either of us.

"Jane, come on. I have been bending over backward here, waiting for you to snap out of it." He sighs and walks to me, wrapping himself around me. I shudder, instantly too hot, and the smell of the sheets I hold crowds me, so much so I swear I taste whatever that dank scent is. I push him off, clutching the very sheets that are ruining my life.

I turn and storm to the laundry room, stuffing them in the front-load washer, but the machine carries the smell too. I dump bleach in, right on top of the sheets. "Where is Sirius?" I ask, suddenly aware the dog isn't here. Was there a dog? I swear there was.

"He's at my mother's being cared for by the staff. He's in good hands. I wanted to wait until we were adjusted and everything was normal again. He and Binx didn't see eye to eye."

I swallow, not sure if that's true or not. "Binx and he met?" I wasn't there, I don't think.

"They did. I brought him here and their meeting became fur and nails and hissing. Poor Sirius is a baby, so I had my mother come and get him. She said everyone loves him."

I pause, racking my brain for any of this. "Was I here when this happened?"

"No." His disapproving sigh behind me is like nails on a chalkboard. "I need you to see a friend of mine, someone not related to the team."

I look back. "You just want to make them lock me away!"

He cocks an eyebrow, fighting a grin. "You know I don't. Perhaps I'll lock you in our bedroom, and we can do something else with those sheets."

I slam the washer and put it on whitest whites before stomping to the linen closet. The moment I open it I smell it. The smell has invaded the closet too. "Do you smell that? That dank smell?"

He comes to my side, leaning in, getting too close to me. "No. It smells like those little scent things you make me put in after counting out exactly seven of them for each wash." His refusal to buy into my concern overwhelms me. I turn to shout, but he grabs my face, planting a firm kiss on my lips. I struggle and shake, but he doesn't stop.

We kiss until my legs have buckled and I'm on the floor sobbing. "I don't know what's wrong with me."

He lifts my chin. "This is what happens after too many runs." His eyes are filled with concern. "You are bringing things back with you. Things you can't shake. It's why I want you to see someone." He kisses the tip of my nose. I don't recoil, not because I don't want to; I do. I force myself to stay and tolerate the affection.

Binx walks up to me, weaving himself around my legs and purring with his pathetic attempt at cat love. He's not the most snuggly cat, but he knows when I need something. I wrap my arms around him, pick him up, and take a long draw of the smell of his fur. He chases away the dank smell and the dirty feelings. He chases everything away.

There has never been a love like ours—mine. It's fairly one-sided, but I don't mind. I know he loves me in his own way. Selfish and difficult, maybe, but I don't care.

He stiffens, possibly about to attempt his escape, but then goes limp again, resigning himself to the fact I need him. Probably sensing by my behavior and grip that I won't let him go without a fight.

Dash wraps around me too, bringing the smell of deodorant and sweat and him. I lean into my boys and breathe them both in.

"I hate where he took me."

"I know. I read the debrief. The president isn't very happy that you didn't find anything out. He was hoping you would know if Rory had betrayed the country in any other ways."

"The president can suck it."

"That's treason."

"Only if he hears me."

He chuckles. "Our house is likely bugged. Let's be honest."

I nod against him, certain it is. "Sorry, Mr. President. But I'm not going back in." I give him a weak smile. "I'm sorry my cat hates your dog." I close my eyes and stay here, huddled on the floor and wrapped in love, even if one participant is being forced to endure it.

"Binx and Sirius will learn to like each other. When we move to the big house, they will have a yard to explore together and plenty of room."

I lift my face. "The big house? Which one of the many you own? Is there one that's larger than the others? Is it like your parents' place?" I tense, not even wanting the answers to the questions. "It doesn't matter, I don't think I can move. I need to be here where it's familiar."

Dash strokes my cheek and kisses my head. "We don't need to discuss it now."

I lift my face to Dash. "It's been too many runs, you were right. I can feel the walls of my sanity crumbling away. And let's be honest, they weren't sturdy to start with." I laugh, but he sees the truth.

"You are perfectly sane, Jane. No one can do that many mind runs. No one."

"He had all the control, Rory did," I mutter, contemplating the fact the nanobot installed in Rory's brain, identical to the one installed in mine, was set to run the hijacked op in his head. "I know I set up a run where I was a doctor and he was my boyfriend and we were in love. I know I set that up. But I was meant to know who I was in his head. I was supposed to know what was happening. No mystery. I just needed to trigger the memory of how he came into the possession of that cabin with those rape cells and then the larger brothel itself. But I wasn't given that opportunity. I was lost and all of my memories were gone. Even in his forced coma, he is in control."

"I think we need to disengage his nanite for the next person going in. I don't actually know how to do it without killing him." He kisses the side of my face, and I can tell by the way he's breathing that he's hoping for more than an awkward floor snuggle.

But I can't, so I continue on about Rory, a subject that turns us both off. "He's better at mind running than I am."

"No. He's not better. It was his head. Home-court advantage."

I nod and try to push it all away. "Well, whoever goes in next will have to be prepared for that if you can't disengage the nanobot."

"Nanite."

"Whatever." Binx struggles from my grip, but after an indignant shake of his fur, he turns and starts to nuzzle me, writhing against me with love and purring.

"He missed you."

I glance up at Dash, nodding. "I've never been in a run for a full week before."

"I suspect he trapped you inside, using the programming in his nanite to override the information in yours. He let you in, but then somehow he managed to gain control. It wasn't a mind run, as much as it was a mind hostage situation."

"That's about how it felt too." I can still feel his fingers inside me and his wet kisses and the weird sex in the Thai restaurant.

I officially will never eat Thai again.

"How's Angie? I never saw her when I woke."

He looks troubled. "She resigned actually, the day before you woke up. She's gone home to Scotland. Gave no notice and told the team she was ending it while she was still remotely close to sane. She'll be taking a long sabbatical before starting up with a position in a clinic just outside Edinburgh. It's some spot that is doing research on nanite technology in coma patients and unresponsive people—what the research was initially created for before we used it to solve crimes."

I can't help but be sad that my friend left without a good-bye, but I understand. I imagine her dating life with Rory gave her a thousand memories like the one I experienced—being violated in a restaurant or tied up for Rory's pleasure. "I'll miss her."

He cocks an eyebrow. "She'll be at your fitting in two weeks."

It's my turn to look confused. "Fitting?"

Dash leans back, examining me for something. "You're joking, right?"

I laugh and lower my face, completely baffled about what a fitting is. "Yeah."

"After the week we've had, that's not even funny." He gets up and hands me my cell phone. "I've taken the liberty of updating your schedule with all the wedding information. The dressmaker needs eight months from the time you try the dress on to the time it's ready. And you can't gain or lose any weight."

The wedding dress. No wonder he's feisty. I never remember the crap that goes into planning a wedding, and for some cracked-out reason he takes it personally. "I haven't gained weight in ages."

He cracks a grin and I see the force behind it. He's being pleasant. We're being weird.

The silence that was once calm and relaxing turns awkward.

There are too many things fitting in the silence now. Too many lies. So many I don't know if we will ever work them all out. I know he told all of them to protect me, but it doesn't change the fact he lied.

Underneath his cool doctor exterior, he's actually quite rich and very British, contrary to the lack of accent, unless he's angry, of course. He's completely snobbish when he's being honest, and his parents are insane and pretentious. Of course the one tidbit of it all that makes me really cringe is his brother, Henry. The man who is currently in jail awaiting trial for crimes against humanity in the International Criminal Court. Along with many other prominent political figures. His time spent at Rory's brothel has earned him a special place in history, shaming his family and friends.

God, I hate Rory.

All I want is to call Antoine and tell him how bad it all was—is. To call the last member of my team. What we had before Rory went rogue was amazing. Antoine was the brains and me and Rory the brawn. He and Angie are the only ones who really understand the weight of all this betrayal, and there is no way I would ever talk to Angie about it.

Instead of that, I settle for some loving and lift Binx into my arms, forcing another struggle snuggle—the one he hates, where I pretend to kiss him, but am driving my nose into his fur, sniffing him. He lies in my arms, his body stretched further than a cat should stretch as I carry him to the bed. Without any sheets I wrap myself around him and sit, hugging and sniffing.

"We have chicken Parm from Mrs. Starling. She wanted to make sure she made you dinner for your first night back, but I told her to wait a few days. I tried to explain, but—"

But.

It is an epic *but* that contains images and horrors flashing behind my eyes.

Images of me getting off the table and then screaming and fighting the team who are clearing me of the monitors.

Images of me shoving everyone away while trying to strangle an unconscious Rory as his finger still gyrates inside what he believes is me.

Images of me throwing everything and being forced into a cell for my own safety and the safety of others.

Images of Dash's eyes through the window as he watches me sitting in the corner rocking back and forth with slight twitches from the drugs I never even took.

Images like the one of Dash finally risking coming into the cell and wrapping himself around me while I sob and cling to him, weak and exhausted. I didn't believe it was him or that I was really out.

It's a big *but*, a huge *but*. One we won't ever discuss again. I whisper silent prayers to that effect to the gods I don't completely believe in.

"I love chicken Parm."

He smiles and it's real, thank God it's real.

"We're okay, right?"

"Always, Jane. No matter what." He nods.

I don't know if it's true or not. I don't know how I feel about anything or what will happen, but I know as long as he still loves me, I don't care. He has always been the right kind of dark for me.

There is a place inside me that is damaged from everything. A life without family or memories of love. Years of being a soldier and seeing too much and feeling too little. Years as a mind runner who feels my emotions plus the victim's, and stumbles blindly in the brains of others. Years of PTSD that I don't even want to scratch the surface of. But he matches the damage. I can't figure out how—he's so perfect—but he does. He somehow matches me and I him, and we round all the bad things off.

There is a reason Dash is the way he is, a reason he fucks and doesn't make love. A reason he doesn't talk about things.

And I doubt that reason is entirely his upbringing.

There's more and I don't care what it is. He doesn't ask to see my issues, even though I know he wants to, and I won't ask to see his. I would rather not see mine, so adding in anyone else's is scary.

"Do you want to eat now?" he asks, snapping me out of my thoughts.

"Yes, please." I put Binx down, smiling when he sprints from the room, from my needy mood, his least favorite.

Dash walks to me, lifting me up and hugging me tightly. "Let it go. It doesn't matter now anyway," he whispers and carries me from the room. He hasn't started heating up the chicken, but I swear I can already smell it.

We eat. We shower. He tries to touch me and I cower like a rape victim. We each go to bed dissatisfied and annoyed.

It's not the evening the chicken Parm deserved. It deserved wine and kisses and maybe a soak in a deep tub followed by a massage.

But it isn't what I get.

I get heartburn and heartache and memories that aren't real about things that have scarred me.

5. S-A-T-U-R-D-A-Y NIGHT!

"Ya ready for this?" Angie nudges me, grinning from ear to ear. Since Dash and I picked her up at the airport in New York for the blessed weekend with Dash's family, she's been grinning. I'm almost scared she's forcing it, even if she flew all the way here from Scotland.

I frown but nod, making her laugh. "Ya can be excited, Jane. Yer about to marry the best man in the world. A girl should be excited on the day she tries on her wedding dress." Maybe she is genuinely happy for me and not faking it at all. Maybe I'll be alone in the faking it. Lord knows I had to fake it the entire drive up to New York from DC.

I swallow, but my mouth is dry and my throat is oddly sore. Even the walls of the town car feel like they're closing in around me.

She rolls her wide eyes. "Just get it out then, ya awkward wee weirdo."

"I'm sorry. I know it isn't mine to be sorry for. I know I didn't do anything. But I feel sick all the time when I think about it."

She winces, her eyes glossing over for half a second. But she shakes her head, swallows, and squeezes her eyes shut until the tears are gone again. "He doesn't deserve a single moment more of me time or me energy. Not a minute of it. He was a wanker and a scumbag, and he was never mine. I see that now. I was a means to an end." She opens her eyes and smiles through the pain. "I am better off. I've joined a dating site and I have three hundred hits."

"A dating site?" The skeptical agent inside me screams this is a bad idea. I always assume the worst, which in the case of dating sites is abduction and possibly being made into a skin suit.

"Och, ya don't expect me to spend the rest of me days pining after some Irishman? Bah, never happen. From now on I only date Scots, and I only accept men with beards."

My nose wrinkles involuntarily. I don't like the idea and I can't hide it.

"Don't make that face. Ya don't know." She leans in so close I can smell her coffee breath. "Ya have never actually lived until a man has rubbed his beard on your cunny."

I lean back, horrified and unsure if I should mention the article I saw about the germs in beards.

She closes her eyes and relives something naughty before sighing and nodding. "Tell Dash to give it a try. Even a wee beard is some kind of special on the girlie bits."

"I'll take your word for it."

She nudges me again. "Yer so awkward. Just show him a picture and point and say, 'Jane likey. Jane want.' And then grunt. He'll get the point."

I finally laugh at that—the kind of healing laughter I haven't had in ages.

"Ya missed me, didn't ya, Janey?"

"I did. But I understood too." I nod and lean into her, still laughing. She is exactly the comic relief I need at this moment.

"How weird is this going to be with Dash's mom, since ya basically put her golden Henry in jail?"

"More awkward than before, which was unbearably awkward. So I'd assume, more awkward than any single thing you could compare awkwardness to. He's Dash's brother. And she loves him the best. It'll be bad."

Angie looks like she might try to calm me down, but the car pulls up to the shop, and she smiles. I don't smile. Instead, my insides tighten and I feel a little nauseated.

Through my partially open window, I can see the arrogance and snobbery flowing from the bridal shop. I am nearly crawling backward to escape it when Angie sighs and makes an "och" sound as she grabs my hand and drags me from the car.

Now I'm leaning against the car, wondering what my chances are like if I run and wishing I had a paper bag to blow in.

But I change my mind the moment I see it.

It isn't a white dress and it isn't the frilly shit in the window.

Instead my gaze snags on a suit with a top hat on the mannequin in the window. I pause when I see him. The doll has a slighter build than Dash, but the general idea is pretty clear.

I want to see that on him. I lift a finger and point at it. "Jane likey. Jane want." I offer my best grunt as Angie laughs and drags me to the shop.

"Dash will be dressed to the nines. It's your tomboy ass we have to worry about. He probably already owns a top hat." Angie misses seeing an evil sneer when we walk in.

But I don't.

Dash's mom, Lady Townshend, laughs. "Of course Benjamin has top hats. He has plenty of them. How lovely to see you both are on time."

Angie stops and smiles. "Lady Townshend, how are you?"

"Very well, thank you. Lovely to see you, Angela." Dash's mom steps to Angie, fake-hugging and fake-kissing, but her eyes stay on me the entire time. "Have you gained some weight since I saw you last, Jane?"

I hate that her greeting is what I expected. I wish I could find a greeting card that says, "Sorry I'm the white trash marrying your rich son. Oh, and double sorry I locked your other son up."

But I can't.

And as punishment for never finding that greeting card, I see Dash's ex, Melody, standing in the corner of the room. The unknown I hadn't planned for. I shake my head as if to clear it and his mother takes that for an answer.

"Well, perhaps ease up on the salt for the next eight months so the dress remains perfect." His mother fake-hugs me, oozing fake love all over me. "No one wants to spend thirty thousand dollars on a dress and come out with a bride looking like a stuffed sausage."

I would strangle her, but the way she says *sausage* tickles me. I love her British accent and wish Dash would actually use his for more than angry and drunken moments.

Angie knows them well enough. She cocks an eyebrow, offering me some silent support. To add insult to injury, I feel like I'm in a forest surrounded by tall trees. They're all in huge heels, but even in flats they would be towering over me.

"How are you?" I ask with an extremely polite smile for Melody Astor, the mother-ex of all exes.

"I am doing well. How are you and Dash?" She beams with rosy cheeks complemented by her pin-straight blonde hair and bright-blue eyes. Her little accent is perfect, just like the rest of her.

Lady Townshend wrinkles her nose. "I do wish you would all call him Benjamin. This Dash business is a remnant of his childhood and I dislike it."

Melody gives me a sparkly-eyed smile. She doesn't seem fazed by the comment.

We don't have a chance to correct ourselves, because a woman enters in a very intense dress for a Saturday afternoon—she's too shiny, too polished, and too made up. Her forceful smile precedes her through the arched doorway into the main room.

Still, even Angie has lipstick on and some blush and her unruly red hair is locked up tight in a beautiful bun.

I look homeless compared with them all.

"You must be the bride." The intense lady strides toward Melody, arms outstretched. Melody smiles and lets the woman take her hands before she corrects her with a nod in my direction. "No. Jane is the lucky girl," she says with a hint of bitterness.

To quash my urge to flee, I conjure the look on Dash's face when I forgot about the stupid dress altogether.

The shop lady looks at me and musters as much courage as she can before coming over, her smile at half wattage. "How lovely." She turns and points at the doorway she has just walked through and the hallway behind it. "We are ready for you now."

Where are we going? The room we are in is filled with beautiful dresses in glass cases. If this is simply the foyer, then it's impressive.

"Just follow me," she says and turns, clicking with hip-swaying strides back down the long hallway.

I swallow and Angie clears her throat as she takes my hand, squeezing.

But as we turn the corner and clear the doorway to the right, the room before us explodes in lace, silk, and taffeta. Mannequin princesses extend as far as the eye can see in gowns of a thousand colors.

"Now Lady Townshend has told me the theme is actually lavender and lace, which I feel is just divine for a proper English wedding."

I don't know what "theme" means in this case, but I'm not completely clueless. "I am leaving all the details up to her. She's just telling me what to wear and when to be there." I laugh, alone.

The shop lady looks affronted, but Lady Townshend steps forward with her best unintentional Julie Andrews impression. "We are very pleased with the dresses Georges has found for her."

The dress bitch with the obvious hate-on for me gives Lady Townshend a slight bow. "And he is over the moon about being the designer chosen for this. It will be the event of the season."

My stomach turns.

"Quite." Dash's mom nods and turns, giving me a look that tells me throwing up on the Tiffany-blue rug would be a very poor choice.

"Would the lady follow me, please? We will put you in with the dressers and start the show!" She nearly sings the last couple of words. Angie's grip tightens as she subtly forces me forward.

Three girls stand in a giant dressing room that's the size of my first apartment. They are all brunette and all tall, slim, and pretty, but unlike the women I'm with or the shop owner, these girls look polite. Or at least they can fake it better.

In my mind I am repeating the ways I could incapacitate all three of them as the doors close, the ways in which I am trained to escape a moment like this one. I could knock them all out, and everyone in that room, and be down the block before I even got winded.

"I'm Jenny, this is Sasha, and that is Margolis," the brightest of the three beauties offers.

"Jane." A whisper creeps up my skin, not liking that her name is Jenny. I don't like that name anymore.

"So lovely to meet you, Miss Jane." They curtsy, of course, making me glower.

"Shall we prepare, then?" Margolis asks with a slight hint of an accent—Romanian, if I'm not mistaken.

I nod, removing my coat, but they grab for hangers with lingerie. Straightaway, I start to sweat. "Is there a bathroom? Is that stuff used?"

"Of course not. It is the lingerie you will wear under your dress. After you've tried it all on, we will have it dry-cleaned and put with your gown." Jenny points to the door behind her. "This is a bathroom here."

I rush past them, closing the door the moment I am in the small space. Flashes of being in the bathroom on my hands and knees, fishing the box out from under the vanity, haunt me. The smell of the dank cell lingers, even in here. It fights the lavender scent pervading the room.

I can't escape the feel of the concrete and the swaying light. I drop to my knees on the marble, breathing hard and deep.

It passes.

But only because I hold my arms close to me and take deep breaths with the image of Binxy in my grip. He isn't struggling or scratching or meowing. He just lies and lets me love him. The images of him bring Dash's face. His smile, his perfect features, his laugh—they encircle me, comfortingly. I pull my phone from my pocket and press his name.

"Hello?"

I sigh, breathing into the phone. "Your mom brought Melody as her special guest."

"Fuck." He sighs. "I'm so sorry, Jane. I will speak—"

"No! Don't! I'm stronger than that. I have to stop being such a pussy about your mom hating me. I don't know why I care so much." I'm still out of breath.

He chuckles with a sound that feels like delicately placed kisses on the back of my neck. "I love that you do, though. You never show your vulnerabilities about things, and it's so sexy."

"Meet me." The words come out before I even think them through.

"Two hours and I will be at the door to that shop." He hangs up before I can change my mind.

I don't want to, but I think I might change it. I don't want to be intimate and I can tell from Dash's tone he does.

I'm still trapped in that concrete room in a lot of ways. And the caves with the girls in the cells.

Rory's got a hold over me that is unlike anything I have ever experienced.

I force myself up to stare at my reflection. The difference in my eyes stands out today. The light one sparkles like it has a funny story to tell. The dark eye is the exact opposite. It appears to have secrets and deceptions, things it hides from me.

I splash cold water on my face and dry it with what I will forever recall as the softest towel I have ever used.

I push Dash to the forefront of my brain and turn to the door. I lived in an alley once, eating stolen food and pretending to be an urchin, all for the right moment to assassinate three men walking from a restaurant in Belize.

If I can do that, I can be dressed and fluffed and made to feel pretty. It's a different role to play for a different mark. I just happen to love this one.

The moment I leave the bathroom, it starts.

"Please, remove your shirt so we can get the appropriate items for underneath."

All the strength I have just mustered vanishes. I relent, taking the weird corset thingy they're holding and drag it back into the bathroom. I rip my shirt off, catching a glimpse of my scars, and pull on the corset, wincing when I drag it across my nipples. With my hair down and the corset on, most of the bad stuff is covered.

I go back out and let them take off my pants and hand me things I don't recognize as clothing—stripper apparel at best. For each item my only response is a wrinkled nose. They laugh and attempt to put me at ease, but I have seen it before, when people catch a glimpse of the horrors under my clothes. It's always the same, pity and worry. They never think military. They never think I am stronger because of every scar.

So I avoid instances like this—being naked in front of people who could never imagine the places I have been.

To their credit, the three girls do try to hide it.

The underwear they force on me is more comfortable than it looks, but it's overly puffy to be under a dress.

"Is she ready?" the mean shop owner snaps from outside the doors. A robe is wrapped around my shoulders as Jenny squeaks, "Ready!"

The doors are thrown open and the dresses parade in.

I don't realize I'm holding my breath until I blink and start to sweat again. Angie rolls her eyes at me and storms the changing room. She smiles as patronizingly as I have ever seen and says, "We 'ave this, 'er an I. Why dinna ya girls go and rest yur wee feet fer a half an hour." She really lays on the Scottish accent.

They part their lips but change their minds on whatever they're about to say when they see the gleam in her eyes—it's the crazy gleam that only Scots are able to use against the rest of us. To a Scot, it's a look of power and pride, but something the rest of us fear—mostly because it resembles instability.

The three girls scuttle out and Angie closes the doors, sighing and slumping into the overstuffed armchair. "This is some misery, this is." She sounds about half Scot with it just being the two of us. "She has ya changing into ten dresses of differing styles and fluffiness and she's got all sorts of plans. And we don't eat for another three hours."

"What do we do?" I ask, not certain of the plan, but liking where she might be going with it all. She sounds like she wants to escape.

She raises her eyebrows and nods at the dresses. "We're gonna try them on and see which one the old battle-ax likes, then we're getting pissed. And Dash is fucking well buying enough booze to float me back home on." She pulls her feet out of her shoes and gets up, grabbing the first frock.

I back away slowly, as if she were wielding a knife. "That's a lot of lace. Maybe we can start with the others. They look less lacy. The back is see-through on that." I cock an eyebrow and point.

She winces. "Right, which would be why they put the corset on ya. The scars are going to be covered, Janey."

I wrinkle my nose and she puts the dress back, chuckling and calling me something like "little bitch" in Gaelic.

She grabs a princess gown with a tight corset bodice and a huge skirt made of the stuff that sounds like where the Russian president has his offices and all the tourists go—Kremlin—but not.

I think of ways to wiggle out or protest but remember she's here for me, to help me. So I nod and sigh and think bad thoughts, but keep them to myself.

She holds it open for me to step into. Honestly, it looks like I might fall into a magical hole and end up in Neverland or Wonderland, if I step into it. But not wanting to be a little bitch, I lift a heeled foot, not even recalling when they got the stockings or heels on me, and step in. She lifts with an ooooomph and barks, "Hold it up, ya ninny! It weighs a goddamned ton, Janey. Lift her up and hold her tight so I can get the clasps and hooks at the top, then we worry about the eight billion snaps."

I do as she has ordered. She steps back after a second and says, "Nope! The scars are fully visible. This fucking corset doesn't hide a damned thing." She looks at me in the mirror, cocking a dark eyebrow. "I think they're fucking with ya out there. I think she wants everyone to see them scars."

I sigh and tap my fingers against my thighs. "Is there one that perhaps has some sort of mesh on the top? One that might cover the worst of it? I don't want the entire world to look at my back and think Dash rescued me from some kind of sex slavery."

"Not if Georges says it's not in style. He's all about the haute couture."

I don't even know if Angie knows what she's talking about, but I am getting annoyed. "He's going to be all about digging out whatever I shove up his ass if he doesn't make me a fucking dress that fits and covers my shit and makes that wing nut happy." I point at the doors, possibly speaking too loud. "I was in a terrible accident, where my whole family fucking died and then I went to war. I fought for my country. I am covered in the proof and I don't need everyone thinking I am some sad little orphan. It's bad enough my side will consist only of you, Mrs. Starling, and my partner in crime, Antoine, but to be blasting my scars everywhere is just too much. Maybe he can make me a midriff *I Dream of Genie* dress and we can talk about how I can't have kids—cause my family died!" The words leave in a panicked rant, and I'm pretty sure I have spit on both of us during it.

Angie laughs, accustomed to the way I get when we do things like shop or involve Dash's family. "Well, why in the hell are ya so beaten up all over, ya wee brat? Who even has this many scars from war?" She winks and chuckles before nodding. "All right then. Ya better be ready to play some Little Orphan Annie for this." She shakes her head and steps out, closing the French doors. I can't make out what she's saying, which gives me hope they haven't heard us this entire time.

The shop owner follows Angie in, cocking an eyebrow at me in the monstrosity of a dress. "She's actually an orphan," says Angie. "Her entire family was killed in a terrible accident and she's the sole survivor. But her body is battered. Scarred, if ya will. She canna wear a dress showing all her injuries to tha world." Her accent is so thick I barely make it all out.

I lay my own act on thick, lowering my brow in shame, with my voice breaking a tiny bit as I speak. "Perhaps more coverage won't humiliate Lady Townshend."

The shop lady, whom I had believed to be the owner, swallows, clearly uncomfortable, but I bet not nearly as uncomfortable as I am. "I will speak with Georges and see if we have something. Give me a moment." She turns and leaves.

"I love when we get to do the *Cagney and Lacey* thing."

Angie snorts. "The fact that we know who Cagney and Lacey are proves we both need to worry more about getting married and less about how."

"Classy." I laugh and lean against the wall, sweating in the dress made of pain and hate.

The door opens, but a snooty shop owner doesn't come in; instead it is a very old man. He's got white hair and thick glasses. His fingers look like they are all callused on the ends and his skin is nearly see-through, it's so thin. "You vant a special dress?" he asks with a thick accent, French and German, if I'm not mistaken. Alsace perhaps. "I do not make zee special dress for just anyvone. My line is my line. Vere are zeese scars?"

He comes around the back of me, and as he lifts his hands, I lose all the fight in me. I let him see them. The serial numbers on his wrist tell me that there is not a scar on my body that he has not seen on another and the ones inside him are ten times worse.

Angie sees it too. I can tell by the way she flinches and swallows like there's a whole potato in her throat.

"Yes, zeese are wery bad. You have been vipped, no? And zis one here, it is a mess. Zee person zat stitched you vas an amateur. You are a soldier? Zis one vas done in a hurry."

I nod slowly.

"Vat is your rank?"

"Master sergeant," I mutter and turn, looking into his eyes, his old blue eyes. "So you understand the delicate nature of this?"

He nods once. "You vill have zee greatest dress. I need eight months." He turns and leaves, shouting in French that he wants everyone out of the shop and that he must have silence. The woman I mistook as the shop owner gives me a look. "What did you do?"

"Nothing. He wants to make me a special dress."

Angie scoffs, "None of these will do for her." She steps out over the dress's train and closes the door, undoing me in a hurry.

I pull on my clothes and sigh when my poor battered nipples relax into my comfy sports bra. The dragging off of the corset instead of unbuttoning the damned thing is about the least of my issues, but it hasn't done my poor boobs any favors.

I leave the dressing room to find Lady Townshend is gone, as is Melody. The shop lady gives me a snooty glance. "We will be in touch when Georges believes he is closer to the finishing date and needs sizing."

"He never took my measurements."

She laughs an almost perfect maniacal laugh. "He's been doing this since the fifties. He can assess your measurements in a glance."

I take a breath; it's the one that I need to take so I don't strangle her. Angie grabs my hand and drags me from the boutique. The air on the street is remarkable. It's crisp and cool but fresh and cleansing. And the open space, even in New York, is a better feeling than any.

"Jane!"

I turn to see Dash jogging up the street.

"You're early," I shout back, with a wave and an instant smile that he always puts on my lips.

"I got worried. My mom and Melody and the dresses—it made me think you might not be doing so well. That maybe this wasn't the distraction you needed."

I laugh and look at Angie. "It was exactly the distraction I needed."

Angie laughs with me. "Aye, me too. Those people in there are terrible, and yer mother, Dash, was in prime form, a real ballbuster today. Even Melody took a couple hits."

I wished I had seen more of those. The only one I really saw was when she got bitchy about Dash's name.

He winces as he walks to us, kissing me on the cheek and quickly hugging Angie. "Well, for all that, I am sorry. I have heard Georges is a fairly amazing designer."

I can't help but smile. "He's amazing. Sort of sharp and spicy, but impressive. He's making me a dress."

Dash looks concerned. "You didn't find one, then?"

"They don't work." Angie nods. "She's small and shaped funny. So he is just going to custom one up."

He isn't fooled. "My mother tried picking dresses that would show your scars, didn't she?"

I bite my lip.

He sighs and covers his eyes. "I told her there were scars from the accident on your back and stomach that you didn't like showing. I was hoping she wouldn't use them as her modus operandi for torturing you."

I shrug. "It didn't work. But it doesn't matter. If I end up telling them I was a spy and an assassin and a master sergeant, then I do. I don't care. And besides, Georges has endured far worse and he's a much better man for it. This won't kill me. Nothing else has."

"I heard he was in Alsace as a boy, only ten when the Germans took it. His family was Jewish, therefore they were sent to Natzweiler-Struthof. Somehow he managed to stay alive, but his parents died there in the camp. An uncle took him in and raised him as a dressmaker. He came to America when he was thirty and now runs both this shop and the one in Paris that his uncle owned."

Angie cocks an eyebrow. "Look who's a wealth of knowledge! Does yer mother know all of this as well?"

"I'm sure she's been told the story. Whether she cares to recall it is another matter. My mother doesn't bother about anything but herself, Henry, and me. And in that order I'm afraid." He laughs, but only lifts one side of his lip, revealing that sharp incisor I love so much. "I, on the other hand, enjoy getting to know people. It's another thing we disagree on."

I wince at the name Henry. I hate that Dash's brother was part of the disgusting crimes Rory committed in the brothel. I hate that the family is humiliated by the outcome of my work. I sigh and lean in, letting his warmth seep into me. "It's one of the things I like about you."

"Okay, I can take a hint. You two need some alone time." Angie waves her hand at him. "What time is dinner then?"

Dash winces, making me groan. "Noooooo."

He pleads with his eyes. "It's one meal. They're very excited about the wedding. Please, one dinner and maybe a brunch and then we are back to DC and you can start your resignation letter as well."

Angie looks shocked. "Yer leaving the team as well, then?"

I realize I've held it together remarkably for her. "I am. I need some 'me' time."

"Too many runs and too many crazy people." She sighs. "I feel that." A forced smile spreads across her face. "My new gig will be a lot less interactive. There's going to be a great deal of 'me' time to be had. If I wasn't already there, I might go crazy from all the aloneness."

"I think we will all need a little break from reality when this is finally over." Dash chuckles as he glances at the ground. He looks like he might say something else but doesn't. He just reaches for my hand and squeezes. "We will meet you for dinner at eight. Can I get you a car?"

Angie shakes her head, still forcing her smile. "Naw, I'm grand. I'll see to myself, maybe do some shopping. I never brought anything fancy enough for dinner with yer parents."

He scoffs. "I never have anything fancy enough for that."

She waves as she turns, disappearing into the crowds when she gets to the crosswalk.

We don't speak. He about-faces suddenly, jerking and dragging me along the sidewalk. He doesn't say a single thing, not even when we reach the car he has parked. He opens the back door for me. I'm almost afraid he's angry with me for something, but I can hardly think what that would be.

I climb in, realizing the partition between the driver and us is closed. It's black and thick, and I don't know who's up there. It feels like a mind run again.

My breath hitches as my fingers graze the partition. It feels cold and real, but there are so few places inside me that believe in real anymore.

Dash climbs in, slamming the door and pressing himself against my back. He pulls my coat off, kissing my neck while drawing me into his lap.

My eyes are stuck on the black partition, wondering if whoever is up there can see us. Wondering if this is some kind of cruelty Rory has planned. I can't fight the urge to lift my fingers again to the partition and touch it. It's still cold and it still feels real, but I have a terrible feeling it's not. That none of this is.

The dress shop and the scars and the shame all feel like things Rory would torture me with. I can't breathe and the walls are closing in on me.

My mind forces me to recognize this for what it is. It's the direct result of too many mind runs.

I get a chill and shiver, maybe at again staring into my own eyes as someone pulls away my sweater and shirt. That it's Dash this time doesn't quite make it better.

I close my eyes, forcing myself to like it. This is something I like. I even tilt my head to the side so his reach is better and his kisses get deeper into my neck.

His greedy hands grab and massage, as the car takes off from the curb.

I almost make him stop, but I force myself to stay with it, to let it happen. I need this man and I need to remember how much.

I start to participate, lifting my hands up to his cheeks and cupping his face, contradicting the haste and pressure of his movements. He grabs roughly as I smooth my fingers along his neck. He jerks his pants open, fumbling for the zipper and button as I softly place kisses along his jawline and suck his bottom lip. I am slowing the pace and fighting him on his attempts to be rough with me.

We don't do this. We don't do slow.

"Open your eyes," he whispers into the small space between us. I shake my head. "Open them, Jane. I mean it." His tone is soft, but I can tell he senses something is wrong.

I force one eye open to see disapproval on his face and quickly close my eye again, blocking it out. I can lie to myself, to us both, in most areas, but not about our intimacy or the passion we share.

"What's going on?" His words even sound disappointed.

"Nothing. I just want soft."

He sighs. "Can you not bring him in here with us?" His words bite into me and before I can really think about it, I slap and thump on the partition. The car stops and I hop out, pulling on my sweater and stomping down the road.

"*Jane!*" he shouts after me, but I break into a run, hurrying around a corner and getting lost in the crowd.

The street is busy, so busy you feel alone. The honking and crowd conversations create a sea of noise that hides his voice from me.

I wave down a cab and jump in, leaving him on the road yelling at me.

I don't look back.

6. CUPID'S CHOKEHOLD

Angie gives me a once-over before nodding. "Ya look fine, but I don't understand why he wanted ya to go over with me. Is Dash all right then? Or you two having a row?"

"He's fine. I think he wanted to talk to his mother," I lie, smoothly and evenly.

Her I can lie to. It's to protect her anyway. I cannot bear the idea of telling her why I froze up mid–limo sex.

She shrugs. "His mother *is* a bit of a twat." The word forces a grimace from me and my face forces a laugh from her. "Ya know what I mean. She can't even help it."

"I feel like she can. No one needs to be that rude."

"Right, hence the twat."

"Right," I confirm and spend another half second staring at myself. My reflection tells me I look great, perfect even, with my dark hair pulled into Angie's half-assed knot that somehow looks classy, even on me. Even my eyes are Angelina Jolie's—those cat eyes from *Mr. and Mrs. Smith*.

A Google search taught us that red lips and a black cocktail dress are about as good as it gets on pale brunettes. All that is helped out by my heels, boasting an extra four inches.

But my eyes hunt out imperfections. It's my way of seeing myself in there. The flaws are me.

My heart hurts just a little and my insides ache from the way he said what he did. I have to push it all away to make it through the night. I need to be me to do that.

My lack of relationship experience has me curious if this is me acting like a giant baby again, or if what he said was as off base as it feels. There's a large part of me that thinks I might have the dress and shoes to go with my dramatic girlie tantrum and sudden lack of self-confidence.

I sigh and give Angie a once-over. She does look perfect. The idea of a redhead in a red dress seems like it shouldn't work, but it does. She's got one frilly strap on the right side and her entire left arm and shoulder are bare. She even has side boob. She catches me focusing on the creamy flesh and scoffs, "It's acceptable. I'm single. In society only single ladies are allowed a little side boob."

"What about a lot of side boob?"

She sticks her tongue out before smearing on more of the lipstick that matches the dress. "We look smashing," she says in a perfect English accent.

"I like your *ochs* and *twats*."

She wrinkles her nose. "The Queen's English is fun for a piss, but that's about it." She loops her arm in mine and I forget about everything else. "Now, shall we venture down and see if there's a car waiting for us?"

In that moment there are no Rorys or Dashes. There are no evil mothers-in-law and no British Barbie waiting in the wing to steal my man. There's not even a man. It's just my friend and me. All the other things are swept away and labeled as unimportant.

We look beautiful. We are both safe from the man who had us fooled. I am free of that prison, and even if this is a mind run, I don't care. "I wish we were going somewhere fun instead of out for dinner."

She gives me a sidelong look. "We can."

The mischief in her eyes tells me she's serious, but I can't do that to Dash. "No, and you know it. Standing them up would never go away. That one act would haunt us the rest of our days. Or not, because Dash would never speak to me again."

"That's a true story if I ever heard one. And we are nearly late, look!" She points at the clock and I grab the door handle.

We hurry to the hotel elevator. I nearly pause when I see it, wishing we could take the stairs as I did on the way up. But that had been in comfy shoes, not heels that were trying to murder me. If I had some intense adrenaline I might be fine, but I'm not feeling either frightened or alert at all.

When we get inside the small space, I take deep breaths and push away all the walls that try to close in.

"Ya have been looking off since ya came out of Rory's head. Ya all right?"

"No." I swallow the lump in my throat. "It was a tough one."

"I don't want to know, I'm sorry." She says it looking up, avoiding the mirrors and my eyes. "I wish to tha gods I could help ya, but I canna." Her accent thickens when she's emotional.

"I don't blame you. I don't want to know either."

Her response is a squeeze of my hand and that is all. She's there for me, but she wants this one kept silent. She wants her clean start from that world.

When the elevator lands on the main floor, we step off into a crowd of people. Even through them, all I can see are his eyes, hunting for me. I have seen the face he's wearing, the "angry, but sorry he was such a dick" face, a few times. Yet never have I observed it from a hiding place. His green-gray eyes are dark now, not lively. Worried. We're late and he thinks maybe not coming. He's been blowing my phone up since I ran from the limo, but I've ignored it.

When he sees Angie, that face fades away and he offers a wave and a smile. I can actually see the tension fade when his gaze meets hers. There is still something lingering behind his eyes, but he's hiding it, even when he finally sees me.

"Guess Dash's meeting us here and riding over to the restaurant with us. His family must have gone on ahead." We walk to him, but when he offers me his arm, I stay next to Angie.

She remains oblivious, chatting on. "The reservations said they were for eight, but I had hoped we would be a wee bit early. Yer mother likes to make everyone feel late, even when they're on time. Have ya ever noticed that?"

Dash nods, smiling a little. "I have. She's the master of making you feel bad. It's why I like showing up a bit late. She's already going to make it hard on you." Dash walks to my side, taking my hand in his. The grip means we are going to be talking far sooner than I imagined we might be. I figured he would try to keep it in his pants until after dinner.

He leads us out to the car, the very same one I ran from. The valet at the entrance to the hotel gets the door for us as we all climb in.

Angie looks around the backseat, offering Dash a disappointed look. "No champagne?"

His lips attempt a grin. "There will be plenty, you know that."

She shrugs coyly. "I suppose that will have to do."

Dash focuses on me. "How was your walk?"

"Fine."

And there it is, *fine*. I've said it without thinking. Immediately Angie gives me a look. "Walk?"

"I wanted some fresh air. So I grabbed my dress from the shop I was picking it up from and brought it to your hotel room. I needed to get ready with you anyway. Dash isn't great at makeup."

She gives me a look that tells me she understands now that Dash hadn't asked me to get ready at her room and he didn't ask me to meet him at the restaurant. I hope she'll forget and not ask me any questions about it.

"You both look lovely." Dash offers his best attempt at the American *lovely*, a normal *lovely*. It is one of the few words he doesn't manage to pronounce without some inflection from the British accent he's tried to shed while living in America. When he shouts, that accent comes through, fully. He is an angry British man and a calm American. It's quite distinct when he's drunk as well.

My phone buzzes in my purse, almost scaring me. I pull it out, not expecting anyone, since the person who has been ringing me all day is with me, but when I answer, I get the person I expect the least. "Hello?"

"Jane?" The voice belongs to Henry, Dash's brother and lover of underage prostitutes.

"Hi." I don't know what to do or say. What do you say to a man who is in jail because of you?

"If my brother is right beside you, please don't pass him the phone. I need to speak with you. I need you to ask my father to take some of my calls. He's avoiding me, as is Dash."

"I'm not interested, thanks."

"Wait." He pauses. "I'm cut off without a penny to my name and no one will touch me as far as barristers go. I need some help. Can't you just ask them to at least hear me out?"

"Um, no thanks."

"Jane, I am begging. I know a strong girl like you gets off on that."

I squeeze the phone as if strangling Henry, but keep my comments to myself. I don't even know how he got my number.

"Please, just ask my father to hear me out. I have got something of a defense here. I just need some funds to cover the barrister. We have been given one through the special UN courts, but I need one who will make this go away for good. I was there as a guest—I didn't traffic the damned girls, Jane! I went because I was invited. I assumed it was regular prostitution. I didn't know it was human trafficking and slavery. I never would have gone to a brothel like that, ever."

"Sorry, I don't think I'm interested." I press "off" and put the phone back in my bag.

"Was that a telemarketer on your mobile?" Angie asks with her brows lifted.

"Yeah. Weird." I wonder how he knew I would be seeing his parents tonight, though I know he knows about the wedding.

The car stops before I can even really give it much thought. Angie climbs out, even though Dash should climb out first. He stays, pinning me by blocking the door. "We need to talk."

I have a thousand things to say, but I don't want to talk. I want to slap him around first. I turn with an annoyed sigh and climb out the other side—the wrong side, where I have to open my own door.

The driver looks affronted and Dash looks pissed, but I don't give a damn.

I click away in my heels and tight pencil skirt of the dress, thanking the men who get the doors for me as I step inside the restaurant.

Dash is right behind me when we get to the maître d'. He presses himself against me obscenely. "The Townshend party is expecting us."

The man smiles and offers a subtle bow before turning and leading us to our table.

Dash's parents are there, beaming and laughing with their friends. It isn't the intimate dinner I expected. Melody is there, along with several people I have never seen before in my life. For some reason even a family meal during this trip is enough for his mother to create an event. I doubt they ever just sit and read the paper and eat potato chips from the bag.

The men stand and Dash's mother offers a smug grin.

"Mother, Father, Melody, nice to see you again."

His father points at the people beside him. "Benjamin, my dear boy. So glad you could make it. These are all old friends of ours from Cheltenham, actually. Lawrence and Clarice Underhill. Surely you recall them. They are across the pond looking at a venue for a wedding in Nantucket."

"Of course, lovely to see you again."

They both nod as Dash's mother laughs in a way that makes me want to stuff a dinner roll in her throat. "A wedding in Nantucket? It sounds like a murder mystery weekend."

The woman, Clarice, who is clearly Dash's mother's age and equally snooty, offers Lady Townshend a look that tells me she doesn't fancy a stay in Nantucket. "It is positively uncivil to ask one's relations to travel such a distance and then offer only mediocre accommodations. We have been greatly disappointed by what we have seen."

I can't even stop myself. "Where did you end up deciding on staying for the wedding?"

She squints her eyes at me, no doubt annoyed, as we have not formally been introduced. "The Wauwinet. It's not open yet, but they let us have a look."

"That's a five-star hotel, isn't it?"

She sniffs at me. "We found it adequate, though I do not understand how it can possibly be a Relais and Châteaux designation. There was a man with a large white beard and a flannel shirt sitting on some sort of scooter on the deck, in the cold."

Her husband's movement to meet my gaze is the only thing that suggests he is even alive and breathing. "He was a beast of a man. No one ought to grow to that size." His jaw barely moves with his words.

Angie grabs my hand, squeezing it once. I remind myself I need to see this as a mission and I need to keep my cool.

"I'm sure the wedding will be lovely, having the ocean on either side of you." Dash tries to end the conversation.

"That is some wind they get there," I add. Silence falls at my comment and we sit, letting the staff push our chairs in for us.

"And of course this is Silas and Darlene Noble. They've come to escape the rain for a few weeks." Dash's mother points at the couple at the other end of the table, a younger and more posh-looking couple than the old snooty ones to my right.

I wave awkwardly as Angie extends a hand. "Very nice to meet ya."

"And this is my future daughter-in-law, Jane Spears. And her very dear friend Dr. Angela O'Conner, a colleague of Benjamin's. We have known Angela for some time."

Everyone greets us as warmly as they are able.

I don't know what to expect from any of them except Dash's parents, so I don't say anything else.

His father decides dinner for us all. We drink the wine he orders, but only after he spends ages discussing the entire event with the sommelier. It feels like something they could have discussed before we all arrived.

Dash laughs and jokes, getting more British as the wine is served.

Angie fits in perfectly, even keeping her *fucks* and *twats* and *ochs* in check.

I am the odd man out, as always. I almost wish Henry were here to sneak me red wine so I didn't have to suffer through the courses of wine I am being served. Of course then he would make weird passes at me but at least it would have filled the time.

Henry?

How odd that he called my phone.

I excuse myself to the washroom after the palate-cleansing lime sorbet following the third course.

As might be expected, even the restaurant's bathroom is posh, filled with luxurious items for the use of anyone who might need them. I can't help but shake my head at them all. The face cream on the counter costs more than the rent at my first apartment.

I look at myself in the mirror and wonder if I will ever fit in.

My brain doesn't even whisper the no; it screams it and begs me to run away as fast as I am able in the huge heels. I suspect every version of me worries this is a mind run and not real. No orphan ends up the way I have.

But my heart whispers about hope and Dash being someone else when he is away from them. It whispers that if I'd had a family who loved me all, I might have ended up in a life like this one. Maybe it's destiny.

Unfortunately the words Dash spoke in the limo haunt me. They are the ones telling me that this is not my life.

When the door handle rattles, I jump, realizing I must not have locked it. "I'm in here, it's occupied." I reach for the door, but Dash pushes his way in, closing it behind him and locking it. "We need to talk."

I look beyond him at the door and plot the ways in which I can get past him. Reaching behind me for the fifty-dollar hair spray seems like the least painful way to do it. I don't want to kill him, and probably not maim him. Maybe just stun or knock him out.

He steps forward carefully, maybe checking to see how angry I am. "I didn't mean what I said."

"Yes, you did."

He winces. "I did, but not in the way you think."

"Yes, you did." My words are a whisper and not nearly as brave as they ought to be.

"No, Jane, I didn't." His green-gray eyes have gone darker, the way they always do when he's upset about something, and he furrows his brow to shade them. "I honestly just said it like a jerk and didn't mean it. The moment I said it, I froze. I couldn't believe I could be so rude to you."

"You're angry with me." I say it so he doesn't have to; he might never. He is English, after all.

"You're right." He admits defeat and lays it out there. "I don't understand why you couldn't have pretended to go in and act like it was dead in there. Like Rory was shut down and you didn't find anything. I don't know why you didn't even fight to not go in there. You could have helped finish training someone else and sent them in. It's been months since Rory was put under. He isn't going to die waiting a couple months longer for the runners who are nearly done being trained."

"The president sent me in. What did you want me to do?"

"Retire."

I sigh. "You want me to stop being me so I can play house with you in the mansion?"

He doesn't even try to hide it. "We could have a good life. It could be amazing, just you and me and our pets and kids. We could have it all."

I don't even know who he is anymore, so I say it. "Who are you? Why don't you want to be the people we are now? I like working. You like working—why would we stop? And I said I don't want to talk about kids. Why are you doing this?"

He comes forward. "I want a future. Not a shell of a girl who is half stuck in some pervert's brain."

"You helped create this girl! You were part of the research!" I am beyond exasperation.

"I know, but this program can never work the way they have forced it to. It was intended for good people. So doctors and specialists could find their way into the minds of those who couldn't talk—patients with ALS or stroke victims who are still functioning, but unable to speak. We create the world inside the mind; it could be based on what the family says the patient loves. So those who are dying could spend more time with their families. Think of the applications, Jane—if it was used for good and not for evil."

"I know, I know!" Dear God, I know. I have heard the stupid rant several times from him and Angie. When they get going on the subject, it's hours before they surface.

"I'm so sorry." He offers me the look, the one that melts my heart every time.

"But you have to see it my way too, Dash. You made all of this. You let the governments of the world take your work. You forget that people like me are a dime a dozen. We are expendable. Property of the government. So we can't even fight back and say we don't want to do it. We are told to do it, so we do. That's how the military works. That's how the Navy works. We do our job. In some ways I wish I had never walked through the door to the facility."

"But then we might not have met."

The fight starts to leave me. "Right, but you science types give the government all the tools to do something terrible and then bitch when they do the terrible thing. It's really annoying for us minor folk."

"You count in all of this. You count." He takes another step. "I'm so sorry I said what I said. I'm sorry I want to sweep you up, broken and battered, from the thing I made you do, and protect you and take care of you. And most of all, I'm so very sorry that you cannot see that my intentions are honorable. That I only have your interests in my heart." He steps even closer, taking my hands in his. "I love you, Jane. I love that this has made you weaker and more human. You were once a very hard girl with a very hard heart. This has taken away so much of that and I wish you didn't see it as a flaw."

I melt.

"And I see your need for softness," he continues. "I don't love it when we are soft, but I get it. He let you into his mind and he used everything he knew about you against you."

I sigh and breathe him in, feeling more myself than I have in ages. "Thank you." I open my eyes and look at the reflection of us in the mirror of the bathroom. It's very different here in the real world with him. This reflection is real. It's me and it's Dash, and this is the response a person needs when they are sad or broken or haunted. This is the reaction a woman needs from a man.

He lifts my chin, placing a soft kiss on my cheek. "Now, let's get back to dinner before my mother comes and bangs the door down." He takes my hand in his and leads me from the bathroom, earning a look from the lady waiting outside the door.

"She thinks we had sex," he whispers, but not subtly.

"I know." I nearly roll my eyes at him. I can't believe I ever imagined he would have been at the brothel. A normal brothel would be a stretch for him, even with all his lies. But that brothel . . . I can't even make him that evil in my mind.

7. I'LL MAKE LOVE TO YOU

The moment we sit back down at the table, a knowing look crosses his mother's eyes. She smiles at me, and I can't help but see the evil stepmother in *Cinderella* every time. "I was just telling everyone how you somehow managed to win over the heart of the designer today."

"He was very kind to me."

Her gaze alights only long enough to make me uncomfortable, and then her eyes turn to dazzling emeralds as she laughs and leans into the table. "He is a strange little man, from France. A genius with fabric and design, but a complete recluse."

"Actually, Mother, he's a survivor of the Second World War. He was in a concentration camp in the forties. His entire family died there, and he was raised by an uncle when the Allies freed him. So he's earned the right to be a recluse, and he makes enough money to be eccentric."

Dash's father nods, lifting his glass. "Rightly so." The table awkwardly drinks to the man they do not know.

I barely know him either, but I raise my glass and sip, wondering how long this will all go on. Will I be in my fifties and Dash's mom in her eighties when she finally accepts this marriage? And that I am who I am.

The crowd sorts themselves back to their original chats. I'm socially awkward enough to know not to speak unless spoken to. It never ends well. And thus I am again the only person not really talking or joining in.

Dash's mom glances at me from time to time, checking on me. I realize she doesn't intimidate me the way I thought she did. She's mean and rude and snooty, but I am not afraid of her or her opinion of me. In her eyes, I will never be free of the fact that I am somehow guilty of the crimes her son, Henry, committed. That I got him arrested because he went to a brothel where human trafficking and slavery were on the menu.

As we are leaving the restaurant hours later, I lean into Dash and mutter, "Dinner with them is an Olympic sport. This should be considered torture." I rub my food belly and moan.

He laughs. "You don't have to finish every piece of food on the plate for every course. You can put the fork down."

I give him a look. "Where I was raised we finished our food. Don't put it in front of me if you don't want me to eat it."

He rubs my belly. "Now you look food-pregnant and uncomfortable."

The feeling of his hands rubbing the mound of my belly makes me recoil. He pauses, realizing what he doing. "Sorry." His hand lowers and the joy fades from his face.

"It's nothing." I take his hand again and squeeze as we stroll to the car. Angie catches up, jumping in the car after us and groaning. "Och, I ate too much. It was too good. I couldn't stop. I dinna want to."

I laugh and sit next to her. "Look at my poor dress. It's about to burst and injure everyone with shrapnel."

Angie scoffs, "I am actually making myself sick when I get back to the room. I need a Roman lunch."

"Women are disgusting." Dash grimaces.

"I can't go to sleep like this, Dash. I'll die in the night—explode like the guy on Monty Python."

Dash snorts and she giggles and they both lose me.

"You've seen *The Meaning of Life*, right?" Angie gives me a sideways stare.

"No."

Her eyes dart to Dash. "She hasn't seen Monty Python."

"I will have to rectify this, Jane. I cannot marry a girl who doesn't understand what it means when I hop about the yard clapping coconuts together."

I cock an eyebrow, but Angie explodes in laughter. Dash giggles; it's weird to see. Strangely pleasant is the way I would describe it. He runs a hand through his dark-blond hair and makes his dimple pop. His eyes are sparkling green-gray and full of humor and relaxed joy. They take off in a tirade of movie quotes, each speaking with a perfect English accent.

They make me smile, afflicting me with their contagious grins and giggles. I have no clue as to what is going on, but I can't stop myself from wishing I did know.

Before we know it the car stops and the door is open. Angie laughs and points. "Ya better watch them." She gives Dash a grin. "Thank your mother again for a fabulous meal. See ya tomorrow for that bridesmaids' brunch then, Janey!" She climbs out and waves, nearly tripping. She spins and staggers into the hotel.

He laughs and offers her retreating back a wave. "Night, Angela!"

I laugh too. "I didn't realize she was drunk."

Dash gives me a look. "I didn't realize *I* was drunk." He bends his face forward, grazing my lips lazily and whispering, "If I promise to be the most gentle lover under the sun, can I ravish you when we get back to the hotel?"

I nod and slide against him as the door is closed.

But a switch turns in my mind. As Dash nibbles at my ear, I remember just how fragile I am not, regardless of how feeble I have been acting.

The girl I am is not the one from the mind runs.

The girl I am survived war and abandonment and too many things to list.

I am brave and strong and in love with the man tempting with me kisses and caresses.

And we don't do gentle.

My hands become greedy, unable to touch every bit of his skin. I grab his biceps roughly and then smooth my hands over the spot I've gripped. My lips leave a trail of kisses along his jawline to his lips.

Our mouths meet again without restraint.

It's a frenzy.

The sound of my skirt ripping up the side joins our ragged breath and kissing noises. The feel of his fingers prying at my underwear makes my very full stomach tingle. He drags them down my thighs in jerks, to the point where I have to sit up on my knees so he can rip them down past my heels. The taste of scotch still on his breath fills my mouth as our tongues slide against each other, massaging and sucking.

Those are the only slow-moving parts.

Buttons from his shirt ping from their various tethers as my head lowers to his flawless skin. I suck his nipple and clamp down on the tender flesh. He sucks his breath as his fingers tug at his belt and trousers. The warmth of his freed cock hits my inner thighs, bringing me down on him. I grip his chest with one hand and grab his rigid erection with my other, slowly lowering myself, bobbing slightly so he can enter me with ease.

His hands slide up my thighs, gripping my ass and moving me the way he wants to, the way I want him to. The car makes turns and stops, becoming part of our game and rocking sea of movements.

He kisses my neck, burying himself inside me. He maneuvers my hips, rocking and rolling with the car. I arch my back, leaning a little so I can control the motion slightly. My hands slide along the soft roof, pushing so I can use him the way he uses me.

His hands travel to my waist to accommodate my leaning back as I work his cock. I pump rapidly, feeling everything start to fuzz out as the sensations build in my stomach. He wraps an arm around my back and thumbs my clit with his other hand, just at the right moment.

Everything tightens and I cry out, not even noticing we are in a moving car as I roll my head back and jerk my body against his. The second I'm done he pulls me back to him, back to his realm where he controls me like a fuck puppet. His fingers dig in, grabbing too hard and too much, but I love it.

He moves me, lifting me up and slamming me down, thrusting in and out violently. He lowers his face, kissing along my neck until he climaxes. Then his teeth bite down, clamping as he moans softly, jerking and thrusting as hard as I can take.

We tremble and cling to one another, shaking and twitching for several moments.

"I love you, Jane," he whispers into the tender spot he's made on my damp skin.

It's exactly the sort of thing a girl needs to hear after doing what we just did. Especially in the back of a limo.

When the car stops I start to laugh. "This should be interesting."

He gives my outfit a once-over before pulling off his jacket and sliding it around my shoulders. It's still warm from his back, but his shirt is ripped right open. He pulls me in, kissing me on the forehead and whispering as the door opens for us.

"Just walk in like your outfit was made this way." There's a subtle hint of his accent when he says it.

I climb out, nodding at the driver, and stroll up to the front door, waiting for the doorman to get it for me. My heels click across the marble floor as I head straight for the elevator, desperately trying to ignore the dampness of the semen running down my thighs.

The elevator door opens, and I catch a reflection of us both in the mirror on the back wall. A blush creeps across my cheeks.

My eyes stay down, but when I look over at Dash, I start to giggle under my breath. He's standing completely tall and proud, shirt ripped open and bite mark visible. He puts his hands in his pockets, looking ridiculous, but for some crazy reason the only person the guy working the elevator stares at is me.

When we get into the room, we strip and head straight for the huge walk-in shower. He envelops me in the hot water, encompassing me with his body and laying soft kisses along my neck and back.

We don't talk about anything, and I can't help but find bliss in that.

8. PILLS AND POTIONS

Lady Townshend had decided a bridesmaids' brunch might be a good idea—mostly because I don't know a single one apart from Angie and, of course, Melody.

Meeting the rest of the ladies is like preparing for a mind run, but I can't be bothered with this one. I'd barely thought of it until Angie mentioned it last night.

At one head of the table is Lady Townshend, in a hat one might wear to the beach, only fancier—much fancier. It's white with a huge wide brim and a black band around the middle. All the Englishwomen wear hats—at the table.

It's beyond the scope of what I consider reasonable. Any orphan knows not to wear a hat at a table. I avoided hats for many years after leaving the orphanage. They hadn't been allowed in church or in classes or at the table.

Next to Lady Townshend is Melody, who spends the entire brunch acting like she is the one getting married. It bothers me until I realize that sends all the questions right to her and away from me. Everyone sort of assumes she and Dash might have rekindled their relationship after college.

She constantly waves to me from the other end of the table, but I'm not sitting at the opposite end. I'm placed next to Angie somewhere in the middle as if I'm a regular guest. I don't know if I'm being slighted or if Lady Townshend is taking into consideration that I know no one and don't like the spotlight.

Next to Melody are horse-faced girls, who must be in their mid-twenties. It's a sin seeing them next to Melody, who could be a model.

I have the unfortunate experience of again sitting near Clarice Underhill, the terrible snob from dinner the night before. She sits telling the same horrible story, bashing the Wauwinet and all of Nantucket.

The rest of the ladies all seem the same as Clarice, British and snooty. I think it's the true wedding theme here. But then Angie is here and she's not snooty at all. Unless it's about her dating anyone—then she's insanely particular and strange.

I could gag on my mimosa listening to them all talk, but I might need alcohol to get through this. In fact, I might order a scotch.

The only woman I seem to understand is Darlene, the other moron we met the night before at the restaurant. She's the one with the severe lack of personality, but I suspect it's drug induced. She doesn't even try to talk to anyone, just stares and drinks and smiles at nothing. It's rather restful.

I can't believe this is my bridal brunch and the only bridesmaids I have are Dash's cousins and Angie. I suck back my drink, and, as if by magic, another appears. The server offers me a wink and he's gone again.

Angie leans in, whispering, "I want some of whatever Darlene is on. That woman is crackers. She's high as fuck."

I snort and do my best to not stare at the obviously stoned look on her face.

"Can we get high on yer wedding day?"

"Yes. Or drunk, but something is happening. Xanax. You're a doctor, you could get some."

"Yeah, I can do that. I never even thought of it."

Darlene gives us a grin. "I'll take a pack too."

"Absolutely." Angie laughs, not having realized Darlene has super-hearing.

She slides her small navy Burberry clutch across the table at us. "The pink ones," she mumbles.

I almost return the bag, but Mrs. Townshend cackles and says, "Yes, well, we have been rather busy caring for Benjamin's new hound. He's a handful. Too much for Benjamin to care for on his own, what with work and all." Her mean words raise every hair on my neck. I drag the purse into my lap and hand Angie a pill before taking one for myself. We slip them into our mouths before handing the bag back.

"Love the detail. Burberry is so nice," Angie smiles and says loudly in case anyone gives a rat's ass what we're up to.

Darlene laughs—a lot and loudly.

I sip the mimosa in my hand and wonder what my liver will look like in an hour, and how much I truly care.

After about fifteen minutes Angie leans in, whispering so quietly I can barely hear her. "I think that was Ecstasy."

I sigh, loving the feeling of the air rushing past my skin. "I think you're right. I haven't done drugs since I was forced to as part of training. It's been years."

She starts laughing, sort of like Darlene did. She snorts a bit, earning a look from Lady Townshend. I lean in. "She is on to us, tone it down."

Angie giggles instead of chuckling, but it isn't much better. When breakfast comes, it lands like an eagle swooped in and dropped it off. I know then I'm really fucking high. Whether my lips are chapped or just dry, I can't stand the taste of the booze, and am forced to drink the too-cold water. It slithers down my throat, tickling and squirming.

"I think that was acid," I mutter, hating the feel of my insides burning with cold water.

Angie is too excited about the eggs Benedict in front of us with smoked salmon from Norway on it. She takes her first bite, moaning like we've just smoked a lot of pot.

Darlene nods; she knows.

I cut in, moaning and sighing into my food. We look like idiots; I'm aware of it, and yet I cannot stop myself.

Darlene leans fully across the table, as if the three of us are having brunch alone, and starts talking so loud I swear she's shouting, but no one else is looking or noticing. "When I was seventeen, I met a Frenchman who was so beautiful. We went to the banks of the Thames and drank a bottle of wine that he had put Ecstasy into. We lay there, feeling the poke of every blade of grass touching our backs. When the sky got dark we could see the stars, even though I have never seen the stars in London. We saw them that night." She points with her dripping knife before cutting into another bite.

I don't even care that I have hands or lips or there are stars in the sky. My breath is my life force.

I'm sighing again, making myself stronger with the force of the air, when I look up and see Dash. He waves and walks to us. All of the ladies at the table jump up, gushing and hugging him, greeting him in some way, but he's locked on to me.

He comes and kneels next to me, holding up a small blue box, and kisses me on the cheek. "I wanted to come and say hello. Father and I and a few others are in the private dining room next door."

I stare at the box, smiling. "Thank you." I think it's the most beautiful thing I have ever seen.

"Open it," he whispers.

I turn, our noses touch, and he smirks and looks at Darlene. The disapproving stare on his face makes her look down at her plate and mutter something, but I don't know what it is. My super-hearing isn't working yet.

I pluck at the white ribbon on the box and open it, smiling at the necklace with the black-and-white cat made of diamonds—of course, black and white diamonds.

He kisses my cheek again. "So you can wear him on your heart, and he can be at our wedding, as your family."

I close my eyes as tears start to fill them. "You're wrecking my high and my record for never really crying in public like this before. Ever."

He pulls it out of the box and slips it over my head. The chain is long so it slips down into my blouse, lying exactly where my heart is. He bends and kisses me once more, waving and laughing. "Enjoy breakfast, ladies." He leaves and suddenly the entire table is staring at me.

I just grin. I don't have a single other response.

When my gaze travels the table, it meets a different sort of look from Dash's mom—not mean or judgmental. It's something else. Maybe awareness. Maybe she sees how much we actually love each other, even if we don't show it. Even if no one else sees it the way we do.

I lift the necklace so they can all see. "It's my cat." The words emerge matter-of-fact and plain, despite the effect of the drugs.

They don't seem excited, apart from Angie, who completely gets it, and Darlene, who would have been excited if I had a lump of crap.

"How lovely. He's so thoughtful, my boy," his mother says with force. She cocks an eyebrow. "The cat you brought to our house? The one who has made it hard on Benjamin's new dog?"

"Binx."

Their faces all tighten for half a second and then turn into smiles—terribly phony smiles.

"It may seem silly, but my entire family died in a terrible accident, and I am an orphan. Angie and that cat are my only family. This means I will have them both at my wedding." I choke out the last sentence and pray they feel like shit. It's wrong to work the orphan angle so hard, but I hate being just the ridiculous girl Dash is dating.

There are two sets of dry eyes at the table—mine and Lady Townshend's, although she wipes like she might have shed a tear.

Melody sobs, quivering just a little bit. I hope it stings her to know she has been laboring after my boyfriend and treating me like a second-class citizen. Wishing evil on her makes me the second-worst person at the table.

We finish brunch with each woman turning remarkably kinder:

"We are so grateful to be able to welcome you into our family."

"Benjamin is so lucky, he really is."

"You are the bravest girl in all the world."

"May I see your cat again?"

It doesn't stop and even Melody hugs me. "I am so pleased to see his heart in such worthy hands." She whispers her blessing. With that white flag, I suspect Mrs. Townshend has lost her ally.

I feel dirty for cheating and using my dead family, but it is the truth, and a little kindness from them all on my wedding day will make it less awkward, considering it is meant to be the event of the year.

I wave and take the small box out to the foyer of the hotel attached to the restaurant.

Angie walks up, giving me a weird look. She sighs, looking down. "Go back and kill him."

"What?"

She looks at me again, confusing me with the look on her face. "If ya kill him in his head, he could stroke. Before ya go in, I'll terminate that nanite, taking his control out. Meet me in two days at the lab. I'll get the clearance and figure how the feck we can do it."

I wince, knowing she will suffer brutally going back there. "Dash will leave me."

"We won't tell him." She gives me a pleading look. "We both need the closure. Ya won't ever be free of him and the cells if ya don't do this. If that doesn't matter to ya, do it for me."

I nod, hating that I am agreeing when I know Dash is going to flip his shit. She grips my hands and squeezes. "I love ya, Janey." She leans in and plants a real kiss on my cheek before she walks off.

9. SHE BLINDED ME WITH SCIENCE

I lie back, wishing I'd told him I was doing it, because Dash is going to kill me when he finds out.

The laboratory bed lies cold and hard beneath me for a moment until my skin starts warming it up. I look over at Rory in his bed. His chest barely rises and falls. He's been under for a long time, living in his made-up realities. It might be part of why he's so strong with mind runs. He's grown stronger at creating the world he's in from being trapped in a state of mind run for the last few months. While I have been taking drugs and having brunch.

If they continue to keep Rory this way, he will not live past the next mind run. Coma patients are weak. Forced coma patients are less weak, but still not strong enough to fight even the flu or a cold or atrophy and fluid buildup in the lungs. Or I might kill him.

Lying there, he looks peaceful, even if I know he is not. His sins have prevented him from ever finding peace. I will not let them stop me from finding peace.

Angie comes to my bedside, touching my wrist with a sensor. She attaches all the other monitors and clips the two pads to my temples with the verbal plan inside of them. They sit there, sending signals to the nanobot in my head, coinciding with the headset I will be wearing. The pads tell the bot to use the biochip attached to it to send in the story. I will be given a shot to put me into forced sleep where I will hover in a state of semiconscious REM sleep. It is only attainable in this lab.

The biochip administers drugs to create the perfect environment for the mind run. The release of the neurotransmitters norepinephrine, histamine, and serotonin is curbed while melatonin is used to induce the sleep.

The prefrontal cortex is inhibited, tripped by the biochip, and cortisol is added to the system, creating a slightly more stressful environment in the dream world. It's why they use spies and military personnel to do the mind runs—we already have fight-or-flight mastered and this system tends to leave the dreamer feeling the pressure of fight or flight in their dreams.

Reason and logic flee while the body believes it is in REM sleep, but being in a semiconscious state, the mind is more susceptible to subliminal messaging and repetition.

Once REM sleep occurs and the story is linked through to the system, it starts to play over and over. Soft speech—repetition of names, dates, and places. Creating facts inside the sleeping person's mind.

Then the mind runner is hooked up to the patient, added to the same information as the dreamer. I never actually enter his mind, but we play together as if it were a video game.

We live the same dream, so to speak.

Angie hooks me up, getting me ready in silence until the other techs leave the room. Then she whispers, "I gave Rory an injection which sent another bot into his brain, like we did on the last run. This one is meant to search and destroy his old bot."

"What happened to the last bot you shot in there trying to kill his old bot?"

"We didn't try to kill the last bot, just override it. But he was somehow able to refuse the override. So now the last bot is a dud, just floating about, unable to receive or send anything, and his original bot is still running the show."

"How do you know this one will work?" I can't help but be dubious.

"Took the engineers two days with an entire team working the full forty-eight hours to come up with the little guy. It is programmed to take yer frequency to Rory's bot so he doesn't know there is a difference, but while it does that, it'll also wrap itself around the previous bot and take over. It's all delicate though and time consuming to kill that other bot. If we do it too quickly, he could go into shock or shut down. So this time the bot is creating an illusion like ya are not there and he is actually just dreaming about ya. It might give ya some time to sneak around. The bot will create the world around him; ya won't have control over where ya go, but yer reactions will be yers. And its purpose is going to be to create a world where he triggers other memories and a new playing field each time. We are trying to get him to lead us to the place where ya can learn how he came to know of the lodge. Once ya do, get out."

"This is a terrible idea. Genius and terrible." I give her a look. "Does anyone else know you did this?"

"The one person who needs to know."

She means the president, given that he's got the ultimate authority over our operations. "Does Dash know?" I whisper my question, scared of the answer.

She winces. "No." She's lying.

I bite my lip. "How bad?"

"Worry about it when ya get back."

I lie back and close my eyes, taking a deep breath. "He's going to kill me."

"Me first. It was all my idea. Oh and if ya get in there and it's just black with nothing, it means the new bot accidentally fried his brain so come back out," she says, and it's the last thing I hear before the whispers of my own voice fill my mind.

I'm falling, just for a second. It isn't like landing in the mind of a person who doesn't expect me; it's much more turbulent this time, like an invasion.

Walking down the torchlit hallway the new bot is programed for me to see is not something I'm excited about. It's dank and it smells. It's always dank here. His world stinks.

I walk to a door with a light making an outline around it, like the other side of the hallway is bright, compared with this place. I press against the door, pushing it open slowly and peeking around the edge. I'm exactly where I expected to be.

The photos Angie showed me have made a perfect picture and hopefully he doesn't know I'm here.

I slink past the door, stepping into the light of day in a slum-like place. It's something I haven't seen in a long time. I glance at the street, wondering where to start, if he has seen me yet. Or sensed the game is afoot.

This isn't a regular mind run. I'm alert and aware of who I am, not trying to convince Rory I'm him or to persuade him to let me into his world or share memories with him. This is all meant to trick him with an interactive bot that will change the scene we are in, in response to Rory's memories so he will take me to the brothel in the mountains.

I creep from the shadows and down the road. His house should be here, on the right. He showed it to her once, Angie. He took her here and let her see his house, above the cleaners on Clowney Street.

The name makes me think of pedophiles picking up kids.

The houses are rather small—row houses, with one window on the main floor and one window up top. They have small doors and tiny gates. The alleys have barred doors on them and everything is so little I feel a bit lost.

Northern Ireland was not peaceful when I became a spy, but it was peaceful enough that I didn't ever spend much time here.

Clowney Street shows the parts that weren't quite peaceful enough in murals and graffiti on the brick walls. The hunger strike of '81 is depicted in a mural and the riots of '69. There is an old mural with something about 350 years of occupation and 350 years of resistance. It's about the strangest thing I have ever seen.

I hurry along the concrete of the narrow street, passing the UPS storefront and another before stopping at the cleaners.

It's at the end, the shitty end.

But the door is locked.

I stand there, waiting for a moment, before a small boy appears. He's skipping and licking a lolly. He stops when he sees me, looks back behind him, and then at me. "Who are ya?" His accent is thick, but I would recognize those dark-blue eyes anywhere.

"I'm a friend of yer ma's." My accent is not so amazing. I can speak many languages, but mimicking the Irish accent always turns to Scottish for me.

He cocks an eyebrow. His little face is dirty and sticky. He hasn't changed much, apart from the fact he's a boy and still innocent of the evil I know him to have. "My ma died." He says it matter-of-factly.

"I know. I'm sorry."

He is dubious. "Ya know the sisters then?" He turns and points at a church. "My ma always loved the sisters—maybe not these ones, though." The second part is whispered.

I close my eyes a second and instantly I am a sister. My costume is a nun's habit, but one of the ones for younger women with the shorter skirt and all-white headdress. "I am one of them, Rory. I came to take ya back home. To the better sisters."

He lifts his hand, trusting me straightaway.

That frightens me a bit. No child should take the hand of a stranger. I take his small, sticky hand in mine and squeeze gently. "Ya must be getting hungry. I'm fairly glad it was ya I found."

He scowls. "Who the heck did ya think ya might find?"

"The other you. The one who scares me," I whisper, hoping my nun costume is putting him at ease and not triggering a ripple so grown-up Rory senses anything. "I was hoping I would just find you. So I could ask you some questions."

"After we eat?" he asks, like every street urchin might.

"After we eat," I confirm and lead him to the convent. I imagine it's filled with nuns, all kind and sweet, but I don't control the memories here. I control me. It's a different sort of run. "Where is the other Rory? The older one?"

He turns his little face up to mine and he shakes his head. "He never comes here." I open the door and find that inside is what I feared it might be. It's not nice or homey. It is most definitely not the place I grew up, with people loving you and caring for you. It's gray—like everything, including the furnishings, is indifferent to you.

This is a special place for children no one wants in the land of no birth control or abortions, but heaps of judgment. Add to that the fact Belfast is incredibly impoverished, and you have a perfect storm. Too many children no one wants and no money to feed them.

A red-faced woman storms to him, taking his ear in her hand. "Where did ya steal that lolly from, ya little brat?" She tosses him aside, making him drop the lolly. She kicks it to the corner, shouting at him and whacking him in the side of the head. "God is watching you, Rory. And he will never forgive the sins you have committed."

I want to defend him but that might make a ripple.

So I stand there, watching her hurt him.

"God doesn't love boys who don't live his word."

Rory sobs and stares at his broken lolly lying on the dirty wooden floor. "I got it from the lady at the cleaners. I swear to ya. I never stole it."

He has just finished the sentence when the lady hits him again. "Yer mother was a sinner and yer father was a sinner and you won't ever be anything but a sinner." She hits him until he's sobbing and then storms off to "deal" with another kid.

I cannot believe the difference between this and the life I lived.

"Thank you." I look up to the ceiling and smile. God and I have differing opinions on a few key items, but we both agree he took care of me. I believe in the part of the story where God carries you. And I believe the people who work here are Godless.

I hurry to Rory's side, taking his hand. "Let's get ya cleaned up." I turn and pull him to the bathroom, hoping he's going to feel better with a wash and a kind word.

He sniffs and shakes a little, but he isn't scared of me. It's weird. He should be. I'm one of them. But he isn't. He wasn't born an orphan like these kids. He had parents at one point, like I did.

The bathroom is dirty, everything is gray. Ash and soot sort of gray. Like they burn coal right in the rooms to heat them all. I don't know what to think. I never saw it this way. The place Angie told me about, Rory's orphanage, was wonderful. The pictures were bright and cheery, not desperate and scary like this place. But he is a liar, so maybe his good childhood was also a lie.

I grab a crisp paper towel and dampen it, softening it. I rub his face and wipe his tears, all the while looking in his eyes. "God loves you, Rory. He loves all children. The sins of the father are not the responsibility of the son."

"What about the sins of the mo—mother?" He sniffs.

"No. That is all wrong. She doesn't know what she's talking about. I know God very well. My ma and pa died when I was yer age, and I lived with the nuns and the priests and they were kind to me. They treated me with love and respect and taught me that God loved me, and that even a silly little orphan catches the eye of God. Just like the sparrow."

"Ya believe that?" His eyes are still filled with tears, but there is hope behind it all.

"I do."

He smiles and I can't help but laugh at the goofy grin on his face. He is not a monster yet. He's a baby still.

We sit in the old decrepit bathroom, me hoping for a moment of lucidity from him. "Where is yer room?" I ask.

He frowns and scoffs. "I sleep in the room we all sleep in. It's a bunk room."

"Do ya like it, being with all the other boys?"

"Naw. They're all mean. It's not like home here. I miss my ma and pa. I miss every bit of our old house. It was over a couple streets, where I met ya. My ma had a little garden and there was grass in the backyard. I had my own grass and a fence."

"How old were ya when they died?"

"It was last year. I was seven."

I know they died in an IRA-related incident so I don't ask about it. "I'm very sorry, Rory."

He shrugs. "It doesn't hurt me as much as it hurts him." He nods at the wall. I turn back, scared Rory is there, but he's not. No one is. "Who?" I ask.

"The other me. He's too sad to come here, ever." His eyes darken almost as they widen. "Wanna know a secret?"

I nod.

"Promise not to tell anyone?"

"Cross my heart and hope to die."

He swallows and looks around. "He found something that makes the hurt go away. A bad man came and showed him how, and he never comes here now."

I was sort of expecting the bad man but still not liking that I have struck gold. "Where is the bad man?"

He puts a finger to his lips. "We can't talk about it. Ya can follow me tonight, when the sisters are sleeping. I'll take ya."

I lift my pinky finger, and he wraps his tiny digit around mine. I shake and get up, creeping from the bathroom and back out onto the street, leaving him there until later. There are still no people milling about or even walking up the roads. As silent as a grave.

10. BELLE OF BELFAST

Walking around the streets, I get a bit turned around. Firstly, these memories are linked directly to Rory's memory from when he was little, so they are old. And secondly, they are based on the mind of a child, so they repeat. His world used to be quite small.

I pass the same chocolate shop three times before I even realize each shop looks more than just similar to the last one.

He's being led through a flash of his childhood that he once revealed while under hypnosis. Angie was the only person there, so she remembered it perfectly, and fortunately had a recording of it. Of course he spoke highly of it all.

Either way, it works to our advantage. Angie believes that if I can persuade "Rory the little boy" to help me stop "Rory the monster," then we might find out exactly what went wrong. Where he went astray in his life.

She has created what she considers the most intense dreamscape ever. It leads from his childhood to his teenage years in the gangs of Belfast and eventually the IRA.

She explained to me how his parents' lives had changed everything for him. They had believed in the IRA's cause, participating in the bombings in the '80s, resulting in the deaths of many innocent people. They themselves died during their terrorist activities, leaving poor Rory an orphan.

Rory himself had been part of the Manchester bombing in 1996. I vaguely recall the details of the day. I know more than two hundred people were injured, but luckily none died. When he got caught for being a terrorist, he became a narc for British intelligence at only sixteen. He ended up in the British military and then MI6, where I met him.

Angie is hoping she can trigger the memories using subliminal messaging and repetition to change the scenery in his mind, giving me a couple of days in each part of his psyche.

I am not so hopeful.

I have a terrible feeling Rory was never much of a good guy except as a little boy, but Angie has to have hope. She spent a lot of years in love with him.

The road ends and I turn around to go back, when something catches my eye. It's a boxing ring. I walk to it, taking the side path to the dusty old windows. I peek inside, seeing boys boxing. None of the few rings is clean or nice. It's part of the gray that is Belfast in Rory's head.

"Don't go in there," a voice whispers from behind me. I turn, expecting something scary like Rory as an adult, but I see it's only little Rory. His eyes are wide. "That's where the bad kids go to learn to fight. They train so they're ready to fight the English for the next uprising." He looks from side to side before he whispers again, "All the bad kids from the boys' house go there."

I offer him a hand. "Then we won't go inside." I feel like a character from *The Sound of Music*. I even speak softly when I talk to him, like a Disney princess would.

"We have to hurry. I saw some shadows, and that's always a bad thing," he says and runs down the road, dragging me with him. "The shadows are always watching me. They're with him, the bad one. They peek around the corners and scare me."

I don't know what he's talking about. I haven't seen anything.

We hurry along the silent streets to an old burned-out building, looking more like a skeleton or a husk than something a little boy should play in. We run across rubble and old bricks until he gets to a sheet of plywood. It's got some graffiti on it saying the rebellion is coming. He pulls it back for me and nods. "Inside with ya, then."

I hesitate, scared he's actually scary Rory and this is where he traps me and hurts me until I'm crazy too. Or crazier.

"Hurry," he whispers and looks back. He looks too scared to be faking, so I climb through into the dark room. He comes in right behind me, bumping into me.

"We have to go this way." He wraps his tiny hand around my middle finger and pulls me down a dimly lit corridor—about the creepiest place I have ever been. The old paneling is coming loose; some of it is burned and the rest of it is flaking away from the wall. The lights don't stay on. They flicker, making my insides tighten.

The floors have holes and the wallpaper nearly touches them as it flakes off. It smells dank and horrid.

When we get to the steps, he pauses. "The stairs always fall away when I try to climb them. I don't think I'm supposed to come."

I look down on his little face and smile. "Ya have been so brave. Why don't ya wait out front, and if I don't come back right away, it doesn't mean I won't ever. I will. I'll find ya again and I'll take you to the good people. Deal?"

He lifts his pinky and shakes mine. "There's an elevator too. But I don't think it works." He turns and bolts, leaving me standing there in the condemned building.

"Shit," I mutter and walk around, looking for the elevator. If I know Rory, the stairs will be a trap. If he is aware of me, he will make the stairs something terrible.

I have not been inside a person's mind like this before, not completely. When we started out, we did mind runs with the engineers and doctors, letting them lead us and show us the clues we leave ourselves. Memories we install into the run to stop from getting lost or stuck. My run was with Dash—simple and straightforward, unlike our relationship.

The minds are linked, so letting ourselves get lost can mean not finding our way back out, even after we are disconnected. It's why the testing was so stringent, with only two people passing—Rory and me.

But I haven't been in a changing mind like this one, where I am not pretending in order to create comfort and stability. I am me, and he is aware of how mind runs work. Tricking him wouldn't work: firstly, I'm a girl, so I can't pretend to be him, and secondly, he's a master at this. If the new bot doesn't kill his old one, he will be in control when he finds me.

The moment he becomes aware of me being here, he will control the game and I will end up in a cell again—or worse.

I walk in circles, passing the same flaking wallpaper and broken doors until I see a hallway that's new. I turn down it, listening for the sound of him.

When I get halfway I see the glisten of two metal doors. My stomach does leaps and hops, warning me like that robot on that show with the Robinsons, begging me to turn around. But I don't. I walk straight up to the rickety-looking piece of junk and press the button. It creaks and groans, shaking the whole building.

"Shit!" I whisper and look around.

The doors open, no ding. Of course no ding. I sigh and step in, waiting for the bottom to fall out and for me to go sailing through the dark into whatever hell he has planned. But the doors creak and scrape, closing slowly. The jerking start of the machine makes me jump, and the pace feels like the cables are vibrating from corrosion, but the elevator goes up.

It stops on the first floor, opening slowly. Opening onto a street. Clowney Street, cementing the idea that this is just a construct in Rory's mind. A bunch of boys with rickety bikes ride hard. They are chasing a boy who is running for his life. I'd know his face anywhere. He screams until they land on him, diving from their bikes like uncoordinated ninjas. They scratch and hit and tug until they turn him over, and then the pummeling starts. He screams and I slam my back against the wall of the shitty elevator, pressing the button for the second floor. I don't know if I love Angie's method of getting me through the timeline of his life.

The elevator creaks and groans in a plea to be put out of its misery, but when it stops on the second floor, I am stunned at the transformation in Rory. He's in the boxing ring and maybe fourteen. He's fighting with the agility and strength closer to that of the man I always knew.

A man is screaming at the boys as they fight—creepy on a different level of creepy, but Rory is eating it up. He is fierce and focused.

The doors close and I start to feel like Bill Murray in *Scrooged*.

The third floor does not hold what I expect—it's Rory tied to a chair and being lectured by an Irishman, surrounded by inspectors from Scotland Yard. The old man shouts, "You have a choice in life, Sonny. Be a loser like yer da was or man up and join a worthy cause. We found drugs on ya, we have enough to put ya away fer a long time. Ya need to think on that. Ya wanna be a washed-out drug junkie or a military man—something to be proud of?"

Rory winces; his jaw is set.

One of the policemen walks over with a folder. He places it on the table. "This is what happened to your mother and father, Rory. They were IRA. They caused this bombing. These are the faces of the innocents. Is this what you want too? Is this who you are?"

Rory's eyes lower and his jaw clenches so tight I swear his teeth are going to break. He lowers his face in defeat, as silent tears stream down his cheeks. I step back. I know where he ended up. I know he ended up in the military and he was young when he got there.

The doors squeal shut and I feel sorry, sorrier than I ever have for him. I skip the next floor and press five. I know where the fourth floor leads—right to the military. I know what he did there. We had a similar career.

The doors open on the fifth floor and my memories start to blend with Rory's. We were both here on the day this scenario played out. This was the first day we officially met, though we both knew who each other was before this.

It's the first day of testing for the mind runs.

I step out onto the floor, stunned at how much I have forgotten about how the room looked.

Dash is there. He walks across the foyer, nodding his head at me. His lips toy with a grin, the naughty one, and his eyes catch my ass as I walk past him. He *was* into me right from the start. It's just too weird.

I plunk into my desk, the one I sat in that first day.

Rory walks in, taking my breath away a little. He's strong and young and handsome and fresh from the military undercover units. His eyes are still clear, that evil isn't there yet. I thought I might have seen it in the boxing ring, but it's not there now.

He offers a sarcastic grin and sits next to me, just as he did when this moment really happened. "Ya think it's going to be like those drug tests where we see the future? Or pick the right card? Like *Ghostbusters*?"

I stare and look back at the front of the room. A younger Angie is there. Her eyes are on Rory straightaway. She noticed him right off the bat. I wonder how much that influenced their choices in picking us: Dash gluing his eyes to my ass and Angie tugging at her collar while staring at Rory. Surely that changed outcomes.

"All right, settle in. We know yer curious, and once we have all the confidentiality reports done, we will begin," Angie shouts at us all.

Dash dips to speak to her and she beams, shrugging and lifting her fingers up into her long red hair. His eyes draw toward me, but he nods at her, returning the smile and folding his broad arms across his chest. He's flexing.

Holy shit!

Are they flirting?

They totally have a thing and I missed it?

My chest tightens.

I glance down at the desk, wondering how many other things I've missed. Have they been having an affair all along? She is always there. His family likes her. They know her so well. For a colleague, that's so strange. She isn't a friend, she's a workmate.

Oh my God.

She's an ex-girlfriend and he didn't tell me to prevent it from being weird.

Oh my God.

I feel sick.

I am an idiot. Of course she sent me back into Rory's brain. She's trying to turn me into a mental case. Now that things aren't working out with Rory, she wants Dash.

I glance at the desk, seeing the box carved in it with the four-leaf clover. I know that means that inside the desk is something to take me home.

But there's a niggle of a whisper that tells me Rory is onto me and is setting me up. If he's onto me, he's making this what it is. Angie and Dash were never more than friends, and rarely hung out until I came along—as far as I recall. She knows his family because of functions his family has put on.

Or is that what they told me so it wouldn't be weird?

Fuck!

I cover the box and stare at the head of the class.

Angie smiles and nods. "All right, we have to congratulate ya all for making the cut. Dr. Dash and I are both very excited about this trial. We think this has some amazing applications in the world of coma patients. But until it's safe enough to use on the weak, we want to mess around with yer heads and try it out on you—the strong." She laughs and everyone laughs with her.

I want to hold her down and make her confess to loving my man and tricking me. But clearly that is not rational. And it would make a ripple.

She looks at Dash and continues, "We are hoping some of you, at least two, will be able to make the headway we need to get this program off the ground. Ideally we'd like to see a man and a woman proceed."

"But as this is the preliminary process, let's move to the most important part." Dash clears his throat. "We give you the director of this program, the vice president."

We all clap, even I do. I might not laugh at the jokes, but I'll be damned if I don't clap for the man who got me my job and stepped into his own as the president after the brothel scandal.

"Thank you all. I am excited to be here today, where miracle meets innovation. We have clearly made some exciting advances in science that we can't yet share with you, but we can share some of the ideas we are throwing around. Essentially I need you to imagine your body has all but shut down on you, and your mind is left alert and sharp. Your family is devastated at not being with you cognitively and you are frustrated at being stuck in a lifeless body. Or imagine being the victim of something absolutely terrible and having no way of telling the authorities what happened." He paces the room, before holding a hand up to a screen as faces flash. "These are all people without the ability to tell us what happened or what is happening." He holds up a finger and offers a grin. "Until now." He looks back at Angie and Dash. "These doctors are a special type of neurologist. I won't bother us all with the big words that won't mean a lick to you or me, but just know that they are skilled in a way most neurologists aren't. They are also engineers in robotics. We took them fresh from school and started them on this path, choosing only the best, just like you."

"What a windbag," Rory whispers and leans in. "Ya wanna get a drink after this?"

I pretend to scratch my cheek, but instead offer up my middle finger. He leans back, chuckling.

I glance around the room, a bit stunned that there are only three girls and the rest of the dozen are guys. I don't recall that at all. But I don't think I paid attention the first time.

As the VP finishes his lengthy explanation, I realize I don't know exactly what he's said, but it doesn't matter. Angie again speaks and clears it all up, "We are separating boys and girls. Ladies, you are with me. Gentlemen, you are with Dr. Dash."

She walks from the room and we follow, just as we did last time. I remember this part.

The three of us end up in a lab, where we are tested for strength, energy levels, patience, aggression, skills in combat, and much more.

I pass the tests applicable to the military with ease. But the think-tank stuff is harder. So I work harder.

Exhausted at the end of a long day, I saunter into the mess. We have barracks, a mess hall, and a lounge set aside for us and the doctors and techs. I sit and open my sandwich, yawning and then stretching my neck before I take my first bite.

"Intense, eh?" Rory asks as he sits.

"Yup."

"Ya think yer doing all right?"

I shrug. "Maybe. I am the last girl left. The other two went home today." I realize I don't know how long it's been. Just that I am tired in a way I haven't been in a long time.

"I think I'm doing all right too. I have an in," he volunteers with a wink as he eats a chip from the tiny bags we are allowed one of. They have cut our calories to allow for the lack of exercise we are doing, in comparison to what we are accustomed.

"An in?"

"Yup." He chuckles and gets up. I notice as he walks out that his left leg has a slight limp to it. I would guess a torn ACL at one point, but that the surgery wasn't completely successful.

I finish my meal, ending it with another yawn, catching a flash of something in my peripheral. It's little Rory, the boy. He waves at me to come with him and then vanishes around a corner.

I get up and hurry after him, catching just a glimpse of his legs rounding the next corner. I don't catch up to him until I round the following corner. Then I nearly bump into him. I stop, skidding. He lifts a finger to his lips. "Shhhh." He nods his head at the open crack of a door. A noise draws my attention. I glance in, realizing it's a storage room with boxes of computer paper and other office supplies on shelves. The noise happens again.

I turn toward it, jumping back when I see Angie. She's bent over the spare copy machine, with her leg up on it. Rory is behind her, thrusting inside her. His hands are around her, cupping her breasts in her shirt.

She moans and he slides a hand across her lips. She starts to push his hand away, but he's caught up in the moment. His grip is tight on her lips and his head is back as he slaps his balls against her, pumping wildly.

She spins, pulling his cock right out with the turn and slaps him across the cheek. He laughs and pushes her back onto the machine and lifts her leg again, pumping hard the second his cock head reaches her slit. His hands wrap around her throat as she moans. It's about the most disturbing thing I could have imagined for Angie. She seems so normal.

I close the door and step back, not even certain what I just saw. Little Rory is gone and I'm a Peeping Tom. But at least seeing, even for that brief moment, helps me start to recall the mission. I'd nearly forgotten him, for example.

11. BACK IN THE USSR

My head feels stiff with all the sensors and things taped to me. It's my first run and the patient is actually Dr. Dash. He turns and offers a soft smile. It's not authentic. If I've learned anything in the last few months, it's that he has a smile filled with promises normal people don't discuss. "When we get inside the dream I've created, I want you to try to change your outfit or your hair. I'll show you the triggers I have. Then we can talk about yours and the ones you think you might want to create."

I nod, taking a deep breath. I feel like I'm about to be launched into space, not a video game made up of the thoughts inside someone's head.

I close my eyes, and prepare for the words to start filling my mind. They are prerecorded subliminal messages intended to pull me in and force my brain to focus on certain aspects of my past. Or, in this case, his past.

I take a breath and suddenly the floor falls out. I'm falling into the blackness, screaming and flailing.

"It isn't real, Jane." His voice fills the void.

"Dr. Dash!" I call as I land with a thump in a huge yard. The sun is bright, and the garden is greener than anything I recall seeing in a long time. Everything has been gray for weeks, or months, I don't know how long.

There's a large pool with a statue of a boy jumping over another boy's back. I wrinkle my nose. Movement across the pool catches my eye. When I glance in the direction of it, my jaw falls. Dr. Dash, wearing beige pants and a white dress shirt, is walking along the edge, offering me a wave.

His dream is a resort?

I think my dream is *him* at a resort. Maybe we share this dream.

I wave back, not sure how it feels to walk in this world—if the gravity is the same. But the moment I take a step, I see it is our world. I see how you could get lost here. How you could make it so fantastical you wouldn't ever want to leave. It is real and yet it is made up of the things you want.

"Change your clothes," he says.

I look down at the hospital gown I'm wearing and blush, groaning quietly. "Great." Closing my eyes, I imagine I'm wearing a white dress. Something someone would wear to a resort—strapless and floor length, with some flow to the skirt. I don't normally wear dresses, but it just feels right here. In here I don't have those scars.

My pale skin almost matches the dress when I open my eyes. I need a tan. I can't help but notice he's got a much more Californian look to him. His white shirt stands out against his golden skin. I almost wonder what it feels like to touch it. I swear I know already.

"You feel how real this all is?"

I nod, noticing the sparkle in his green-gray eyes. He offers me a hand. I stare at it, confused and out of sorts. Do I touch him? Is that inappropriate?

"So you know how it all feels. This is just practice."

I take his hand, squeezing and holding. He feels warm—real and fleshy—and there's a tingle inside me. When I glance up, he offers a dazzling smile, dimple and all. I sigh, actually aloud, earning a grin instead of a smile. It's the grin he gives when I think he's promising something neither of us is ever going to explore.

He smiles. "See that?" He points at the small dog, a beagle I think, sleeping next to the bushes. "He's one of my triggers. He reminds me of being a small boy and being happy." His look turns inward, like he's reliving something amazing and heartbreaking all at once. I yawn, stretching and blinking.

"Shall we?" He nods at the small house that's there behind the bushes. I didn't even notice it before. I shrug and follow him, still letting him hold my hand. We enter the house, but it isn't what I expected. There's more inside than I might have imagined. It's a mansion inside, but the outside looked like any house in a regular family neighborhood.

"It's deceptively large," I mutter as I gaze about the foyer. I swear I've seen a home this large before, but I can't place it now.

"Do you like large houses?"

"No. It's weird, maybe something left over from my childhood. But I like townhouses. I like my house touching the neighbors'. I like knowing someone's there, so close. Just in case." I don't finish the sentence with "just in case you scream," but it's what I'm thinking.

He smiles like he understands, but I don't think he can. "You are different from any girl I have ever met."

"Why? Because I can kill you with my thumb or a paperclip?" I ask, and laugh. I don't know why I feel so free here. "Ask me any medical questions you like and you'll see I have my weaknesses."

"Have you killed people before?"

"That's not a medical question." I don't like the question, but I answer it; I know he knows the truth. "Yes."

"How many?"

A grimace spreads across my face as the words slip out. "Sixty-three that I know of, but there have been more. Some were group assassinations like bombings, so that's obviously going to bring the number up."

He coughs. "Sixty-three?"

"That's the minimum number."

"Does it hurt?" He has the slightest accent when he says *hurt*. I've never noticed it before. It's English though, for sure. He must be a Brit.

"Yes. The first few hurt. You watch them fall, and you realize they won't ever get up again. The ones done from a distance hurt the most. It feels dirty, like you cheated by using the scope. But I don't look for people to kill. I am given a name because they are doing something terrible."

"Is the pink mist real?"

Meaning, do I know what it looks like when a sniper kills a human being with a head shot from a distance? I'm not ashamed of killing bad people, but that is likely to show through if we do talk about it. I simply nod.

"How is someone so small so brave?"

"I'm not brave. I just don't have anything else. This fits. The holes in my memory make it easier to not care about things."

His eyes fill with emotion, and I see the pity everyone gets when they hear about my family or my childhood. "One thing I promise you, you won't remember much of this trip inside my head. The memories presented here are based on what I want you to see." He steps closer, sliding one of his huge hands down my cheek and making a shiver run up my spine. He bends and kisses me softly.

I don't know what my response should be, but I desperately don't want to forget it all.

He steps back and everything starts to fall apart. He waves as his skin and body flake away, blowing in the wind created by the void taking over.

I close my eyes and scream, but when I blink I'm back out. I'm in the same room of the lab, and Dr. Dash is staring at me from his bed, and he's holding my cat. I smile, but I'm crying on the inside.

A great realization has just crashed over me as I watch Binx jump down and saunter from the room.

Rory is in control. I am in a mind run.

Binx is telling me I am in trouble again. He is the clue.

There is no way Rory could have known what was in my head. He's creating a cage for me, a place I never want to leave from. He's making up lies and making me believe them.

But I don't act like I know. I smile at Dash and get up off the bed with the help of the techs. I walk across the room, looking for little Rory or the elevator.

I have to get off this floor. I don't know how much time has passed since I entered, but I can imagine Dash is pissed out there in the real world.

I'm in here and he's out there.

The hallway circles, just like the block did where I first met little Rory.

There's a part of me that fears I won't ever find my way out, but I have faith in the little boy. And the triggering of Angie's plan in his head and mine.

There's no way I am willing to stay in here forever, and he doesn't yet know I'd be happy to kill him to get out.

"Jane!"

I turn to see Angie hurrying toward me with a piece of paper in her hand. "We just got two perfect patients for ya and Rory to finish yer testing on. They will be yer first assignments. Exciting, eh!"

I gulp, remembering the first one we ever did. They were a male and female. She was a victim and he was the perp, possible Russian mob ties and human trafficking. The girl had been missing from a small town in Russia, possibly having been sold. She was seventeen, just a child. My head still cramps with what feels like a brain freeze when I think about the case. I tap my finger against my thigh and nod, smiling. "Okay, I guess—I'm excited." I can't remember my reaction. I think I was balls-to-the-walls amped about finding answers in the girl's head.

I don't feel that way now, mostly because I know what's in there. Now it feels scary and horrifying. I remember the way the girl was taken and the way she was kept. I can never forget the acts inflicted upon her just so she might eat and not have to shit in a can. The image alone of her losing her virginity scarred me for life.

But instead of being out of character and saving myself the misery of a second time in the dying girl's head, I turn and walk with Angie. "What happened?" I ask because it's what I would do. I don't want Rory to know I have snapped back in control.

"There was a car accident in Mexico, near Monterrey. Feds are bringing them both in right now by life flight. She's not stable, but he is. He's being drugged to mimic a coma; remember, we talked about this. It's not as easy as it is when they are in an actual coma. Rory will have challenges with this one. We need to ensure it's done with the utmost care." She hurries along.

I keep up, but I am bothered. I can't even pretend not to be. She's in love with him here; she's passing him into the program because of it. I know this.

Surely some of the weird stuff has shown up since Rory started playing in people's heads. And Angie let him in hers. I can't even imagine what that was like.

I don't really recall Dash's when I was in the real world. I only have Rory's twisted version of it, but I'm certain there was something about us playing cards and visiting a park he liked as a kid. Dash letting me in his head was soft and sweet.

We hurry to the lab, where a stretcher and a team of medics await. There's a girl on the bed and Dash is leaning over her, listening to her heart. He gives the man next to him a look. "She needs life support. She's going fast."

I stay in the background as they hook the young girl up. She's got blonde hair and a pretty face, from what I can see. She's thin, too thin, and leggy. She looks older than she must be, but the halter top and pink lipstick smeared with blood might be making that so.

She's a child. My skin crawls and my mind aches, but I watch and pretend I am excited and scared in an exhilarated sort of way.

I'm not. I'm upset and angry. Making a decision I shouldn't, I back from the room slowly, glancing about for Rory. The halls are chaos as the fat Russian mobster is wheeled along to the other room. Rory strolls behind him, looking smug. He pauses, giving me a look. "Ya ready for this?"

"Born ready."

"See ya on the flip side then," he chuckles, and continues strolling after his patient. But I don't go back into the room. I stay in the hallway, watching him get hooked up as the door closes. Then I hurry along the corridors, searching for the elevator or the stairs or little Rory.

I stop, letting my mind clear from the trap and the memories Rory is trying to create.

I close my eyes and take a deep breath.

When I open them I'm standing in front of the elevator. The hallway is dingy and gross again, except when I look back. Then it's clean and white and full of the people I am leaving in this part of his memory. Just before I step onto the creaky elevator, I see me. The memory, or the vision of me, is there. She walks to the room where the Russian girl is and gets hooked up. The door closes before I can see any more.

I press the next floor, staying inside the elevator when it stops, and I see it's Rory and Angie again. I press the next floor, a bit afraid of what's in his mind. He kisses Angie as she yells at him for something, but his eyes dart to me. I just catch it in the crack between the closing doors.

My heartbeat speeds up when the elevator stops next. I take a breath, shivering and cold suddenly. I know where we are before the doors even open.

Rory's standing at the door, in a white dinner jacket. His dark-blue eyes are lit with sarcasm and curiosity. He offers me a hand. "Hello, Jane."

I stay in the elevator.

"Ya know this is the floor ya were looking for. Ya know ya want to know why and how. So come on out, have a visit." He looks like Jack Nicholson in *The Shining*, grinning like a madman and talking to no one. I am the ghost in the machine, not a person at the party.

But I step forward, taking his arm. The brothel ski lodge looks exactly the way it did when I was here before, only now it's full of people.

"This is the time to visit a place like this—our season runs January, after New Year's, through to May. By June the snow is gone and the weather is warm, and everyone disperses for the rest of the year. We find not being here really makes ya miss it." Rory has gone mad.

He leads me down the hallway, stopping and smiling at an old man with a bobbing head between his legs. "I have to admit, the cells are fun, but this really is the Disneyland for horny men."

We reach the bar—he still has not touched me or tried to hurt me. The bartender gives me a wry grin. "Is she having a drink then?" He's got a thick British accent and a bit of stubble on his chin, but I would recognize him anywhere. He's the UK's bad boy of boy bands. His name is Winston Beauchamp. He's only twenty-five, if he's a day.

"She is having a drink with me. She does love a nice glass of dry red."

Winston nods, giving me another look. "Ya got two different-colored eyes, ya aware of that?"

I rack my brain trying to remember if this boy was ever at the lodge or if this is part of the game in Rory's head. I don't recall Winston's name being on the list of men who frequented the brothel. Were some people's names missed or is he trying to make me think that?

"She is. She's not a big talker."

Winston gives me a disappointed look. "That's a pity. She's got the sort of puffy lips ya like to see wrapped around the big chief, eh?"

Rory laughs and passes me my large glass of red. I lift it to my lips, not even caring if it's poisoned. At least if I do die here, the wine is delicious. I can't fault him for dreaming about amazing wine as a means to kill me. But I know I won't be dying in here.

"How and why? Am I right?" He asks after a moment of creepy staring.

I nod, scanning the sea of faces. I recognize too many to keep track of them all.

"That man there, right there." He points to an old man pawing a young girl. I know them both. The girl is Amanda, the younger version. And the old man is Old Dick, Amanda's adopted father. He pulls her down into his lap and speaks into her ear. Her lips tighten, but she agrees and gets up, hurrying from the room.

"Old Dick was the Russian's contact. My very first mind run, you remember that one." Rory says it like he doesn't care that I know this. "The girl in the accident with the Russian was coming here. They'd bring them into Mexico and cross the border at a certain spot. The Russian had been here loads, loved the place. He supplied all the European girls. When he was in that accident in Monterrey, the Feds in Mexico got there before any of the Russian's contacts. He didn't know he was under surveillance. When I did his mind run, my very first one, I got his version of this place and I knew I was working for the wrong side."

He gives me a look. "Ya know, our side never has any of the good stuff."

I don't know whose version of "good" this is. It's not mine.

He puts his hand on the small of my back and leads me down the hall, away from the bar, waving good-bye to Winston. "We never get to just do the things we really want. We save the world over and over, and no one even thanks us. They don't even care. The normal people don't even know we did anything. Here, every woman cares about whatever the hell ya want to tell her. This place is exactly the sort of place we need in our part of the world."

"You force sex on them. The girl whose mind I went into was a child. Like Amanda, and like quite a number of these girls."

"'Tis true. We have to cater to it all, and by 'all,' I mean *all*. Some blokes just like a young girl."

I try not to hear that last comment and change the subject. "How did you find the cells?"

He turns and gives me a blank stare, like he's disappointed. "The Russian. Why aren't ya paying attention?"

"The Russian knew about the torture cells?" I seem to be lost.

He laughs. "They were training cells. The girls were there a month before they transferred here. And only the girls who needed some coaxing and training went there. The eager ones came straight here. We can't have a bunch of upset little girls running around, can we?"

"So the Russian would drop off the kidnap victims at the cells? To Old Dick? That explains why I never saw the cells in the mind of the girl on my first run. She hadn't made it to the cells yet because she was in a terrible accident."

"Look at you, all Jessica Fletcher."

I choose to ignore him. "But how did you get Old Dick to show you the cells?"

His eyes sparkled. "That is the information of the season. Ya want this." He strolls into a room with a fancy four-poster bed and closes the door. He leans his back against it. "I followed him there and then I killed him. I made it look like he was badly injured in his tragic accident. Then I started using the cells for myself. He had a few girls in there, but they weren't my type. So I had them sent over here." He looks me up and down, licking his lips. "Ya, however, are my type. Ya were the moment I met ya."

"Did you ever love Angie?"

"She's a fiery redhead in a doctor's coat. What's not to love? Plus she was as gullible as they come and likes to takes things to the next level. I'm all about the next level."

I fill with disgust, staring about the room. "This isn't real. You can force me to have 'sex,' but you're not seeing me naked. You're not inside me. It isn't real."

He holds a finger in the air and paces. "Ya know the fun thing about ya, Jane? Yer very susceptible to the world we build. That's what happens when the past is shite and there are holes in yer memory. Ya let people fill them up." He laughs like he's got a joke on the inside I can't see or hear. "I like the fact ya get lost in here so easily. And I know it's what makes ya good at this mind-running business. Ya come in, all weak and confused, and within the first seconds of contact, that other person believes they are you and you are them. It's a real gift."

I feel like he's stalling or planning something by distracting me.

He continues. "But I am not susceptible like you. It's harder for me to become them, so I become their best friend. We kill together, we fuck together, we fight together, and we eat together. They tell me secrets and I tell them lies. I get my answers, just not the way ya do it. My version of a mind run is a mind fuck."

"So the Russian told you everything in the mind run, you killed Old Dick, and started up with the cells. And then the ever-disgusting children of Old Dick wanted to sell the place."

His lips are coated in saliva. He's getting excited. "Aye, I let them take me to their mansion there in the city, let her tie me up and shag me. The weird brother jerked himself off the entire time. It's a bizarre setup, that is. She's a fatty, but I find they always try harder. Anyway, I found the will and made myself executor. A very prominent lawyer in Seattle had a reason for it to all work out. He was a member of the naughty club. He witnessed the change in executor. I knew then that Amanda was my best chance to fix it so the cabin was mine. I'd seen her fucked enough times in the Russian's head to know she was a broken little bitch. I did all the things I needed to do to make her trust me. Once she contested the will, everything was tied up in the courts. I knew the judge, the lawyers, and everyone I needed to know to make it all go in my favor. I told Amanda my only fee was that cabin. It worked perfectly."

"Why are you confessing all of this?" I can't put together his plan or why he's telling me how it worked.

"Jane, I'll never leave this country again. I won't be tried in the public. I'll be locked away forever. I'm an Irish citizen, so I think it might not be easy to end me without paperwork building up, but they can't just attach me to the international courts for this. I was an agent in the mind ruins, that's top secret. So I will rot away or die in this coma they have me in. My best chance at happiness is right here in this room with ya. And here ya are. They sent ya right to me." He takes a step closer. "My own little fuck puppet, isn't that what ya called it?"

I flinch as he gets close enough to run his hand down my cheek. "Let Dash and Angie have each other. Stay here with me, stay in the warmth of this lodge. Every day will be a new and exciting one." He leans in, lowers his wet lips on mine, spreading his disgusting sloppy kiss across my mouth. "I love ya, Jane. Ya make me want to be a better man."

My knee comes up fast, driving into his groin. The moment I feel his stomach tighten at the impact to his balls, I shove him back and open the door. I run down the hall, hearing his laugh in a creepy echo throughout the halls, but I don't stop running.

I sprint until I end up back in the bar. When I look down, I'm wearing a genie costume. Several men glance over, giving me a weird look. It isn't the expression I expect. When I look down again, I realize the scars on my stomach are showing. My hands instinctively cover them.

Amanda and her adopted father, Old Dick, walk up the stairs to my back. I turn and follow them. I don't think there is anywhere to hide in Rory's mind. He's fully in control. My best bet is killing him in here.

12. ALL NIGHT LONG

The dark of the closet I am hiding in, trying desperately to focus, feels safe. But I doubt I am safe. I close my eyes and try desperately to see Binx. I call him to me in soft whispers.

The air is cold, so I know I'm still in the brothel in the mountains.

"Binx, please come to me." I whisper it again, but I don't hear his little feet on the hard floor.

Instead I hear a heavy tread. I take a deep breath, willing myself to see that it is not real. He can do whatever he wants here, including raping me, because it's not real. He is not touching me, nor is he hurting me.

But as the door opens, it's not Rory I see. It's Dash. He grins and I realize I have made him the bad guy in this mind run. Out of desperation and a lack of better options, my chip has kicked in my usual suspect. Dash, or rather Derek—the name I use with Dash's mind-run identity—has joined the fucked-up world of Rory Guthrie.

He reaches down, dragging me from the closet. "Found you!" He glances back at a large man with three young women trailing him. "You go on ahead. Rory said I could have this one." He slams the closet door and turns, not even speaking to me.

He pulls me to the door of the room with the Arabian theme, the one I recall with the girls dressed in genie costumes. The video I watched of the surveillance makes me shudder as Dash shoves me inside the room. His smile is wicked, evil even. Rory has let him in, not realizing the main reason Dash always plays the bad guy in the runs.

I cannot fear him.

Even now as he locks the door and cocks an eyebrow. "Remove my clothing, genie."

I look down, almost rolling my eyes at the outfit I am still wearing. It might have been a sexy outfit on a normal girl, but a woman who is ex-military doesn't usually have the flawless skin of a secretary or even an actual genie.

I walk to him, unbuttoning his dress shirt and loosening his tie. I drag it off and drop it to the floor. With him I can play this game, and right now he's a sight for sore eyes.

"Rory said I have to be extra hard on you. You're new."

I nod, not sure what that means, but it doesn't stop me from wishing I couldn't feel pain here. Because it doesn't matter how hard you tell yourself it isn't real; when it hurts, it feels as if it is.

He pushes me to my knees. With trembling hands I undo his pants and drag them down. I don't remove his underwear. I don't want to see him naked here. I don't want Rory to see him naked. I pull off his shoes and socks, stalling.

"Pull them down and put it in your mouth." The outline of his massive erection is not hard to miss. I hate that I know what Dash looks like naked and I am going to impose that on Rory's mind.

My hands tremble more, but I slip my fingertips into his waistband and drag the briefs down over the top of the erection that's sitting at attention and brushing his stomach.

He moves it forward, shoving it near my face. I close my eyes and pretend we are home and this is normal. I grip the shaft firmly, sliding my hand down before parting my lips slowly and placing them on the tip. His hand drops into my hair as he thrusts.

I struggle against his thighs as he pumps into my mouth, choking me and yanking on my hair brutally. I gag and sputter. No matter how hard I fight him, he forces himself into my mouth.

He pulls back after a moment, leaving me gasping for air. I realize then I have been tricked again.

He's got the subtle hint of a scar on his knee. I cringe as he laughs, and as fast as I was stunned by the sight of Dash, I am now stunned by the laughing face of Rory. His still-erect cock is bouncing as he steps, laughing and pointing. "I got ya."

I jump up, running for the door. With his underwear halfway down, he can't move as quickly as I can. I'm out of the Arabian room and running for the stairs when he finally screams my name, "*Jane!*"

My feet ache in the little genie shoes, but my pounding heart and dry mouth distract me. I'm certain I'm covered in a look of terror as I race down the stairs to the basement. I hurry for the room I never did see inside when I was in the real world.

When we took the brothel down, it was the room I wanted so badly to get into, the one I assumed held all the information on the brothel's history. The one room that would actually show all the clients and all the victims.

In my place, a team of hand-selected federal agents looked through the room in the real world, but Rory's memory of it might hold other clues to other crimes.

From the window in the hall, I can see the outside door is open. I rush for the door that leads right out into a blizzard and along the side of the building. The wall doesn't look the way it did in the real world. Here the wall is open, like a hatch, and behind the panel that was a wall when I walked past it is now a glass door. I pull it open, pausing the moment I step inside.

The gray hallway with the elevator.

I sigh in disappointment that I might never see inside the stupid room, but with a little relief at seeing the elevator again. I press the button to close the door, and drop down into the corner. It takes a minute to catch my breath and my heart. The cold dankness of the elevator feels like a warm welcome. I close my eyes and sigh into the dark.

The elevator jerks to life.

I lift my head, watching the lights on the panel glow. Somewhere in that moment I lose the worry. I stand, in my ridiculous genie costume, and lift my hands. When the door opens, I am going to kill him with my bare hands, or die trying.

I have avoided combat with him; he's stronger and faster and a better fighter. But I am far angrier than he is.

Coldness surrounds me as the numbers decrease and the elevator creaks and groans its complaints. When the door opens, I cock an eyebrow at the small boy tilting his head before me. "What are ya wearing?"

I lower my hands slowly and look down again at the ridiculous outfit.

"I never have seen a sister wear something like this before."

"No. I don't suppose you have," I say, forgetting to use my Irish accent, and offer him my hand. "But I'm pretending to be a genie, so I can grant your wish."

He looks confused, but he takes my hand and steps into the elevator with me. I squeeze, finding it conflicting to want to protect the boy and yet kill the older version of him. The door starts to close, but I slip a foot into the gap with a smile as I hear something—the scampering of little white feet across the broken gray floor. Binx climbs in and rubs himself against my ankles. Just as I'm about to tell little Rory not to, he picks the cat up. Binx doesn't squirm. He doesn't do a thing. He lets the boy hold him.

I press the very top floor, but I don't care to let big Rory control the destination. I look at little Rory and smile softly. "If you could pick one place in all the world that this elevator went, where would it be?"

"To the good sisters who love the little boys."

I smile. "Let's close our eyes then and imagine that place." I close my eyes too. "There's a stone house. It's very large. There's a large front stoop with a porch all the way around, surrounded by a garden like no other. The gardens are mounds of black earth with colors shooting from them in every shape and color—daisies and roses and tulips. Crawling vines with purple flowers that look like stars and bushes of lavender infusing the air around you with a beautiful smell. Large trees provide shade and dark-green hedges keep you safe. Inside the house are rooms, more rooms than you can count. There's wallpaper with flowers, and fluffy couches for when you want to read a book from the massive library. Every boy and girl gets their own special room. Everyone is loved. The sisters, all the kindest women, dress simply, but they are more than they seem. They will be waving and waiting for us on a sunny day."

I grip his tiny hand harder. "Don't open your eyes when the doors open. Focus really hard inside, instead. That's how the magic works."

His breath hitches and his grip on my hands matches mine. Though he's small and excited, he's also brave and hopeful. I doubt it's fear causing his hand to tremble—it might well be hope.

When the old groaning elevator stops moving with a jerk, I whisper, "You ready?"

The doors open and I smile when I feel the warm breeze. I crack one eye, grinning from ear to ear—it looks almost as good as the real thing did. To him it *is* the real thing. His smile is so big it takes over his entire face.

He grips my scowling cat and hurries out of the elevator, running onto the bright-green grass toward the women in soft-colored dresses. I step out behind him. Just as I leave the elevator, it drops behind us, crashing below.

I'm sure big Rory has heard, but I don't even care. I now know the secret to his mind: the little boy runs the show. He has been here longer. Big Rory scared him and little Rory shut him out. He shuts out most of the bad stuff. Except the nuns, but they are all he really knows. Better than being alone, I suppose.

As the boy runs for the ladies, Binx squirms from his hands. As he lands with a plop on the ground, he shakes and turns back, giving me a look. I walk to him, lifting him into my arms. He's my version of my cat; he will let me struggle-snuggle him.

The women surround little Rory, hugging him with wide smiles. He beams, practically glowing from love and affection.

He looks back at me with a wave and the scene changes.

13. SLOW IT DOWN

The house has morphed into the one in the French countryside, the one I use as a trigger to help me leave the mind runs. It's telling me it's time to go. My favorite nun is there, sitting beside me. She covers my hand in hers, just as she did when I was a little girl. "We are not ashamed of you, Jane." She says it so calmly.

It is one of my greatest fears, the nuns thinking less of me for the path I have chosen. "We know you have done the very best you could with the life you had." She lifts her weathered face and smiles. "But now you know what you must do." She turns into flower petals right before my eyes and blows off, out the open window. Yet the warmth where her hand touched mine lingers.

Little Rory sits next to me on the other side, stuffing in far too big a bite of mashed potatoes for such a small boy. "Just like my ma made them."

A peaceful feeling sweeps over me as I lean his way, whispering, "If I go, will ya be okay?"

He looks confused. "Why in God's name would ya want to go anywhere but here?"

The answer isn't there straightaway so I pause, giving it a moment of thought. "I don't belong here. This is yer place now. I spent my childhood here and now it's time for me to go."

"I don't want ya to go. I like it when yer here."

I glance about the room at all the other children and sisters. "But yer safest here. The big Rory can't come here. He doesn't like the light."

His nose wrinkles. "He never comes to where I am, and when I try to go to him, he keeps me away. We never see each other. Not since he let the bad things in."

I kiss his cheek. "Yer safe here." I get up from the table and walk to the bathroom. It looks the same as it did in our townhouse when Rory and I were dating, if you could call it that, in the last run.

I drop to my knees and fish the grate off the heater vent. I slide the box with the four-leaf clover on it from the hole and stare at it.

There are so many things I don't remember about my life before and the little glimpses only ever started coming when I did mind runs. No matter what terrible things occurred here in the minds of bad people, I learned more about myself inside the minds of others than I ever could have on my own. I can never begrudge the fact I came.

I lift the lid and whisper, "Tell me about the swans, the way the swans circle the stars and shoot across the sky."

Everything turns black—not the response I expect. Yet inside Rory's mind it never is.

Instead of swirling and the confusion that comes with leaving a mind, I sit in a darkness that echoes and yet is silent. The sound I hear in the echo is my own breath and heartbeat.

I close my eyes and submit to defeat. "You are better at this than I am," I mutter into the darkness.

"I know." Rory is here. "The best part about ya coming into my head this time is that I was able to turn the tables on ya. I was able to venture into *yer* head."

I flinch, realizing why it seemed like he wasn't aware of me inside him. He was, but he just didn't care what I found out. He was never planning on hiding anything. It was about finding things in my head. "You're lying."

"I'm not, Jane. Can we be more original than falling on the old ways of creating doubt and playing mind games back and forth? You've seen my darkest secrets—all the nooks and crannies. Ya know what kind of person I am, what makes me tick. So end the bullshit and let's be real."

I open my eyes to find we are still in the dark.

"I am going to take ya on a tour." His voice is confident and cocky. It can only mean one thing. He is about to do something dastardly. "Show ya the lies in your head."

"Lead away," I offer, refusing to fight about this. I am ready. The moment he makes himself vulnerable, I am going to gut him like a fish. I don't care if we die in here together.

A warm hand takes mine, floating me through the void. There's nothing but his warm hand through what feels like eternity. I squeeze and try pulling him to me, but it doesn't work that way. He controls everything. He pulls me along until we enter a tunnel—I can tell by the way my breath echoes against the closeness of the walls around us.

The same door I used to get into his mind materializes, surrounded by light. I feel weaker now than I did the first time I saw it. I was ready then. I'm tired now.

He's suddenly right beside me. "You ready?"

I nod, not understanding what I am ready for or what we are doing. He opens the door, blinding me with the light from the other side.

I wince and shield my face, struggling to see what's before me.

When my eyes clear and the brightness fades, I smile. I can't even help myself. It's my mom. I would recognize her anywhere. She looks exactly the same as she did in my faded and blurry memory, only now her face is perfectly clear. She waves and I run to her, no longer attached to Rory.

She hugs me and the smell is the same. It's home. Lilacs or some sort of flower. And her perfume.

She laughs and squeezes me as my father wraps himself around me. He is the perfect mix of deodorant and laundry detergent and the smell a man has that is his own. I close my eyes and drink them in.

It is the moment I have waited my entire life for.

Tears stream down my cheeks, and even though I know it is fake and a trap, I don't care. I know them.

I open my eyes and see her. She is me, only her eyes match and she is a child still. She was frozen as a child in my mind, never aging a minute more.

Andrea, my twin sister, smiles wide, reaching for me. I cling to my parents, not certain if the dream will end with a trap if I take Andrea's hand. Binx is there; he swirls around her feet, rubbing and purring. I take it as a sign from my mind that this is safe.

I step to her, wrapping my entire hand around hers. She takes my hand and flips it over, showing me that the pattern in the lines on our palms matches perfectly. I don't know what that means, maybe that she has lived a whole life with me, sharing in my experiences.

"We are the same person, you and I," she whispers.

I nod, looking down on her and wondering if we might have been the very best of friends if the accident had not happened.

I look back at my mother and father and smile, still crying silently. "Where did we live?"

They shake their heads. "It doesn't matter, Jane. What matters is that you are whole and happy. Your life is there, on the outside. This isn't real. It never was. And chasing us in the minds of others will never bring us back."

My mother's words burn inside me. They are true and yet they hurt more than anything.

Rory shakes his head. "Ya could stay here, with me. They are here, inside me and you. We can live here." He snaps his fingers and we are in a home with flowered wallpaper and fancy couches.

The house in France. Rory has been in my mind and seen all the little places I hid and kept to myself.

"Ya have saved me, Jane. I knew ya might. The moment I met ya, I suspected if one girl could save me, it was ya. I knew if I could get ya to love me the way I love ya, we could be happy, really happy in here. No one understands yer pain like I do."

I grimace, not believing his bullshit for a second.

Done with it all, I turn and hug my sister, whispering in her ear, "I miss you." She trembles a bit and nods. She doesn't speak, because I don't know what I want her to say. They say the things I want them to.

I let go and walk back to my parents. They wrap around me, whispering all the things a little orphan needs to hear. "We are so proud of you and we wish we had been able to stay. We love you, Janey. We always have."

I blink and the world fuzzes into a mess, everything blurred and oddly shaped. I let them go and walk to the cat, the one who has had my heart wholly since the beginning.

"If ya leave, ya won't remember them. They're in here, in my mind. Ya won't have new memories, just the glimpse I showed ya."

I nod, fully aware of the rules of the run.

He moves quickly, pulling a knife and sliding it along my sister's throat. "I will torture them, if you don't stay."

I bend and pick up my cat, shrugging. "Like you said, I won't remember this. This is a glimpse you gave me of a lie you made up based on my memories." A slow smile crosses my lips. "You cannot hurt the dead, Rory. Just like the dead cannot hurt you."

I snuggle into Binx, pressing my face into his fur and whispering my secret words, "Tell me about the swans, the way the swans circle the stars and shoot across the sky."

He screams, my sister screams, I can smell the blood mixing with the air as everything swirls and falls apart. I grip my cat and in a moment he's gone too.

I blink and the hospital-exam-room lights above me make it hard to see. Angie is there, worried and speaking, but I cannot hear the things she says. My hearing hasn't come back into the present just yet.

I lift my hands and pull off the headphones and the tabs stuck to my face. Hunger gnaws at me, but there is only one face I want to see—the man who was a monster in my brain for a half a second.

I need to see the real Dash.

I shiver, searching the room for him, but he's not there. Only Angie and a team plucking sensors. They each speak over me and yet to me, but I don't comprehend it all.

I take a deep breath and nod. This is the real world. I can taste the difference in the air.

14. BILLY, DON'T BE A HERO

The sidewalk traffic moves faster than I remember it. Everyone is in a hurry, and if you just sat and watched, you could feel like you were still in a dream.

"He's still not taking yer calls?" Angie asks over her giant latte.

"No." What is there to add to that?

"Has he been by the townhouse?"

I glance down, furrowing my brow. "He must have been by while I was at the lab. His stuff is gone. It was gone when I got home from the mind run."

She drums her gel nails, a new beauty thing she's doing since she's single. They click when she types like little tap shoes on the ends of her fingers. I sort of like the sound of them, but I know I would instantly have to pick them off. I don't like things that are so permanent. I've worn falsies and those long eyelashes for undercover missions, and the moment I got to undo all the hard work the makeup team put in, I breathed a sigh of relief.

"Did you and Dash date?" I finally say it. I've been plotting asking it for the two days it's been since I left Rory.

"No." She scowls, giving me a look. "Rory was a bad man, Jane. That's all that ya can take from that. The Russian is on the list of names that was found in the secret room at the brothel. Antoine found him. He was on there as 'G. Rusky.' Giant Rusky. His flights to Mexico with his cousins coincide with the dates at the hotel in the heaps of shite they found."

"They went into the little room? Did Antoine get to go in there?"

She smiles, but looks confused, like I was there for it all. "Of course. The whole team out west was in there. It was a gold mine of terrible things. The names and dates are shocking. Presidents and kings and princes and prime ministers and clergymen. Ya know that. It was awful. The names of some of the girls shocked us as well. Young starlets who then had a sudden surge to fame."

"Creepy."

"Truly creepy."

"Can I ask you the weirdest question ever?"

Her cheeks flushed with color. "I don't care what he showed ya in there. I don't care to know, I guess."

I want to ask her about being screwed in the office supply room while Rory choked her for pleasure. But she's right. It doesn't matter.

"Does any of it make ya think less of me, Janey?"

"No." I sigh and ask her the other thing I wanted to know. "What did he say when you told him I was in again?"

"Who?"

"Dash."

She shakes her head. "It wasn't me that told Dash. He showed up, angry and ornery, and that's how I found out he knew ya had gone back into Rory's head. He was livid with ya and said that ya had tricked him into believing ya were done. That if ya couldn't care about yer own well-being, he might as well not care either. But he did stick around long enough to help the engineers with some of the fine-tuning, and then packed his office. The engineers were the bastards who outed us to him. They called him to ask some advice before I came in with the plan. After ya were under, Dash told the president that he was done. He walked out and that was that. He never came back."

"Then he went to my place and took all his stuff." I glance down, hating myself. "The sad thing is, I never even really learned anything. Other than that good Rory ended when he started the mind running. He was clean before that."

She sighs. "I know." Her gray-blue eyes look riddled with guilt. "I never should have pushed him forward. Dash asked me not to and I didn't listen. I said he was choosing the girl and I was choosing the guy and that was that. I trained the girls and he chose who to promote from the pile. Well, all that was left at the end of the pile was ya. So his choice was easy. For me Rory was the one because we had been carrying on. I saw him as a troubled young man and a brilliant agent. I never saw insane."

"Did you have an affair during the testing?"

She nods, more shame filling her eyes. "Aye, we did. We'd had an affair from the very start. Second day in, we were hiding in the office supply room."

The room little Rory had showed me.

"Did you regret it while dating or only after we discovered he was actually evil?"

"Only when we discovered his hidden agenda. He'd been placed on special duty with the CIA and FBI, outside the operation we were running. His absences were fully explained. He never had an issue with his double life. I think he was the very example of what we were trying to avoid. He's the sort of man who takes on the personalities of the people he's inside." Her eyes are like staring out at the sea on a gray day.

"I'm sorry, Angie. I wish I'd known too. But I agree, I never saw anything that might have made me think he was doing what he was."

She shrugs. "He'll be in jail the rest of his life now. And batshit crazy to go along with it."

I furrow my brow. "What?"

"Oh aye, the president has deemed him no longer a person of use and has decided he will be dealt with in the military courts instead, totally sealed from the press and public. He will be placed in solitary and spend the rest of his days in the brig, I imagine. He never died from the coma, which would have been lucky for him."

I almost wince and I almost feel bad for not just killing him. But he would have killed me, we both know that. "That's a terrible fate, sitting in a cell going crazy."

"Not one he didn't bring upon himself." She looks like she might be sick just talking about it. "The girls in those cells earned him this fate."

"Yup." I don't want to talk about it. I get up and drop cash on the table. "Well, I have the rest of my debriefing to endure still, with the ever-lovely El Presidente. He is making me go through even the smallest of details."

"Disturbing and yet thorough, I like it." She gets up, leaving her coffee completely full. She hasn't been the same since Rory was arrested, she might never be, but at least she's amazing at faking it. "When is your last day?"

"The moment I am freed from the debriefing. They will have me on standby, in case new things come up. But I am being allowed to either return to active duty or retire and come back to the program on contractor status. I will be part of the mind-running training as a teacher. I can come and go as I please, based on contracts I'll have to renew every two months. In case it's too much."

"Wow! They never even offered me that."

I crack a grin. "You left crying and cussing everyone out."

She snorts. "Aye, I did. Damned project from hell."

"How's the new one going for you?"

"Dull as balls, but I can do the same sort of schedule as a contractor. Come and go, and work when I need to. It's all research at this level; they don't have any trials up and running yet. They don't even believe it's one hundred percent possible." That makes her laugh. Me too.

I wrap my arms around her and breathe her in. "Message me when you get back to Scotland."

"Come and visit me."

I nod, actually contemplating that as a possibility. I haven't been in ages and the idea of relaxing for a couple of weeks while pub-crawling with Angie is enticing.

She pulls away and I catch a glimpse of the tears on her cheeks. "Kiss that bugger of a cat."

"I will." I wave, but she doesn't see me. She's out the door before I can really get my hand up. I almost don't trust the quickness of her pace—faster than she normally moves. I can't help but question everything. How do I know that I'm really out of the run?

Dash left. That's how.

It makes perfect sense. I prove his reasons for leaving every couple of minutes. Here I am standing in a coffeehouse wondering if what I saw my friend do was real or not.

I fear that this will be the entirety of my life.

I stroll out, moving slowly on purpose to see how it feels. People passing me on the street give me a weird look.

I love the real world.

When I get home that night, I am spent. I have gone over every second of my time spent in Rory's head, including the forced blow job and the way I was excited about seeing the nuns from my childhood.

It's all surreal and confusing—there's no way I can catch up.

But the moment I get inside the house, the little pitter-patter of a fat cat's feet lift the corners of my lips. I drop to my knees and drag him into my arms. I know he wanted to rub against me, but I need to smell him and feel him against my cheek. I hold him tight until he stiffens and I know I'm about to be bitten. I place him down gently and run my hand along his back.

"I missed you too."

He purrs and arches, rubbing his body against my hand, until there's a knock at the door. Then he runs off, peeking around the corners.

I get up and open it, surprised to see Mrs. Starling. "How was the trip?" Her grin flickers, but rebounds as if to convince me that she's cool with the danger of my job.

"Great." *Fucking horrible* is what I want to say, but she's old and she never swears around me. And I cuss way too much.

"Dash came by. He gave me the key and asked if I could watch his royal highness, Sir Binxy Bears."

"Thank you. I meant to stop in the other day and say that, but I got busy."

She waves a hand. "There's a fresh lasagna in the freezer, and I popped a chicken Parm in the fridge today. I had a bit of a week of cooking to avoid the sadness over a death in the family, a cousin of mine."

"I'm so sorry." To my ears, my sorries always lack the genuine touch an emotional person might have.

"No. He was old. His time came, as will all of ours. I was just sad because it felt like I was facing my own mortality a bit." She offers a quick wave and nod. "Tell Dash I hope he enjoys London. It's beautiful this time of year."

She turns and walks back to her own house. I hate that she is alone and old. I close the door and stare at my cat.

"Fuck."

I realize then that I am going to have the same fate. I am going to be a quirky old lady with cats and no one to love me. I will be old and alone. It won't be today or tomorrow, but one day I will be her. But worse. She had love. She had a marriage. She had a man.

I had one for a minute, but I lost him. I lose everyone.

Being a hero is a lonely job.

I wish I could have been a girl in a sundress and a wide-brimmed hat at a polo match, laughing like the rest of them.

I sigh and think about walking to the bathroom to run a bath.

The two days of debriefing have at least created a distraction. Now in my little townhouse, silence occupies most of the space. And then there's me. Me, and the bed I have made—lonely and uncomfortable and not the bed I might have wanted now that I have it.

I force myself up, force myself to the kitchen, and force myself to heat up food I will force down my throat. I can bathe afterward. It'll make me feel better.

At every turn I expect him. Every moment I think I hear him. The hot chicken Parm, my favorite food, and the cat rubbing against my ankles used to be enough.

It all used to be enough.

But now I am here and Dash is gone and this is not enough.

I could settle and be fine with it. I could force myself to live with it. I could make my bed every day and sleep every night. I am a survivor. It's about the worst thing a person can be.

And I don't want to be that.

Dash is the first thing I want. I don't remember wanting a single thing the way I want him. Even Binx, who just showed up one day as a tiny, starving baby kitten in need of love. He foolishly showed up here, where love had never lived.

But I loved him in my best possible way. Sometimes it's more like a serial stalker sort of love, the kind where I obsess over him. Maybe it's not healthy, but I don't know any other kind.

Dash is the same.

He showed up and he saw the bed I slept in, the one I made myself. It was built by blocking everything out and pretending I was fine. And he didn't judge my bed and he didn't care that I was emotionally stunted.

He accepted.

And when he told me there was one thing I couldn't do, I shouldn't do, I did it anyway. Knowing he believed it would ruin our relationship. It would ruin me.

The mind run was a stupid gamble, but it did work out. I am freed.

I get up, grabbing Binx and hauling him to his carrier, the worst torture I can ever inflict upon him. He ate the cloth one Dash had bought him, so I got him a plastic one. I pick up my cell phone and dial the one man I can always count on to help me through everything, Antoine.

"Hello, Miss Jane. How art thou?" Antoine asks in the annoying tone he uses when he's gaming and I'm interrupting. That happens a lot, since he is usually gaming and waiting for me or one of his other agents to call in with a crazy request that has seconds to be solved.

"I need you to tell me where Dash lives. Where his big house is, the one he wants me to move to." I had literally forced him to keep it separate from me and refused to go to his fancy houses since I discovered they existed.

"Why do you want his address?" He chuckles into the phone. "Have you fucked that one up already, Spears?"

"You know it."

"I do. As heartbreaking as this is for me, I actually predicted you would blow this brutally. He is rich and fancy on a good day, and you are—you. How did it end?" he asks, but his mind is still midgame. He is talking and gaming, the very worst sin as far as phone etiquette goes.

"I went back into Rory's mind to end it, to find closure and see the end of the line." How does he not know this? Being part of the team, he should have known I was back in Rory's mind.

He pauses and his tone changes. "What?" He's alert and has paused the game. "I didn't hear you were doing that. How come no one told me? What did you find in there?" He sounds worried or angry.

"My family."

"Oh shit. Rory showed you them? How? I didn't think he could."

My stomach tightens. "Yup, he did." Wait. What? *Didn't think he could?* What does he mean by that? I want to ask, but he might clam up if thinks I don't know what I am pretending to know. He's big on need to know.

"And you want to go to Dash, even after all that?" He sounds worried.

"Yup. I need to talk to him." *What the hell is he talking about?*

"Are you going to kill him?"

I sigh. "No. Jeez. I want to ask him questions. It's going to be civil, I swear."

He returns my sigh. "The last time you said the word *civil*, I ended up bombing a building to cover your tracks."

"That was human trafficking." And, in my defense, it was Iraq, not the suburbs of DC.

"It was gruesome and you should be ashamed."

I roll my eyes. "And yet, I'm not. The address." I have one small problem with remorse. When I see someone has taken away another person's rights, through war or trafficking or slavery, I have no problem taking theirs. If someone ends up on my list of names, marks, or targets, then I assume they deserve to be there. It's a flaw. "I want his address." What hasn't Dash told me? My brain screams this is a mind run and I am unconscious somewhere right now.

"It's not close to the city. It's a bit of a commute."

"Then I want a helicopter and his address." I hope my tone suggests I am annoyed.

"Give me five minutes." He sighs and hangs up as I exit, locking the door. Binx gives me a look. I nod, sitting on the steps. "I know, buddy, but you have to stay in the carrier so you don't try to kill the pilot. Remember last time?"

He growls low. I'm sure the growling and hissing are entirely because he remembers the last time he flew.

I ignore the cat and rack my brain for the missing pieces Rory might have showed me.

What do I know?

I know I saw my family.

I know I didn't find any memories in there. They were Rory's invention, and I don't remember them the way I should with my own life memories.

I remember the run and that is all. Nothing new is there. Just as he taunted me there wouldn't be. I wouldn't remember anything new from inside his head; it was all his memories or ideas he forced on me. I didn't find anything in there.

But Antoine is the least dishonest person I know. If he says there are secrets in my head, there are. And Rory must have known about them. There must have been pieces of the puzzle I am interpreting as his, but they were mine. Details I gave Rory, not the other way around.

A car pulls up in front of the house after about a minute of my mind scrambling to make sense of the concept of new secrets. A man in a suit opens the passenger door and then the back door for me. I walk to it, noting the cut of his hair. He's military.

Am I in a mind run?

My cat, my pissed-off cat, uses his claws to tell me I am not. So I get in, putting Binx next to me on the seat. There's no trust left—I am scarred for life from the mind runs. I assume the military driver and passenger are a trap. Everything is.

"Evening, ma'am," the driver says.

I offer a nod and turn my head to the window. I watch them the entire time in my peripheral vision. Neither even looks at the other. One drives and the other one looks out the window, maybe watching me in his periphery too.

It's dark, and DC is almost still—it's not as bad as New York for some reason. To me, it's far quieter and more civil.

When the car stops and I see the chopper, I breathe a little better. I had planned out both their deaths, but I knew I would have been injured, to say the least.

I carry Binx to the helicopter, keeping in my line of sight the escort I had in the car who is now following me, all while maintaining one eye on the lone pilot.

He nods at me and the escort just behind me. I open the door and climb in, receiving a piece of paper the moment I sit. The escort gets into the passenger seat up front.

Binx looks terrified. I feel like an ass for bringing him, seeing his eyes so wide, but I didn't think it out at the moment I decided to come. My plate of half-eaten food is even still back home on the table.

We lift off after a moment and my eyes lower to the piece of paper. I frown seeing the address. I know the area, not well, but it's not what I expected at all. It's not far from here by helicopter.

I figured I'd be flying farther away from his parents' house, not closer to it. McLean is on the way to Middleburg. Not that I ever knew where Middleburg was before I met Dash.

The man who was in the car with me turns and shouts, "Do you need a weapon, Master Sergeant?"

I part my lips to say no, but I nod, not speaking. In that moment of noise and worry, I remember the words Rory said about the tour we would be taking. The one that showed me the lies inside my head— when he showed me my family.

I take the nine mil and stuff it into the back of my jeans like I'm Dirty Harry and not a trained assassin who knows not to stick guns in her pants. I have seen an ass cheek or two shot off by careless handlers.

"Thanks." By the weight of the gun against my waistband, I assume it's fully loaded.

"Ma'am."

We fly over DC, leaving the city and all its lights behind us. But we are heading in the direction of McLean, so we still see heaps of residential lights down below. I now know exactly where the house is, but I cannot imagine what it looks like. I pull my phone out, putting the address into Google. Nothing comes up. Google Maps refuses to be directed to the area, and the aerial is completely fuzzy. I can't help but wonder how much that costs.

I leave Google Maps and look at the "call" button. I touch it, staring at the number that called me the night of the dinner party. I press it, swallowing and wondering what I am up against.

"Jane?" Henry answers directly.

"Who is your brother?"

He pauses. "What did you find out?"

My insides tighten and I feel like I'm in a mind run again. "Who is your brother?"

"Get my father on my side and I will tell you anything you want to know."

"Why do you think your father would listen to a word I said?"

"I wasn't the only member of our family there, I was just the one who was dumb enough to not pay attention to the cameras."

I close my eyes, wondering if Dash was the other one. I am still scared the blow job from hell was real after a fashion.

"Tell my father I need him and he has to answer me, or I will out him and Dash."

I nod, even though Henry cannot see me. "Okay."

"My brother isn't just the dashing UN doctor you know so well. He's a memory specialist all right, but you were someone to him before you were ever in this program."

I bite my lip, trying to remember anything or piece together the puzzle. "Did he take my memories away from me?"

"I don't know that, Jane. But I know he knew you long before you knew him. He has spoken of you for several years, like a decade or more. He is a liar, Jane. A very good one."

I hang up the phone, not wanting to hear any more. I'm sitting next to the only person I trust and he's a cat.

The helicopter lands on the pad of what I can only call a castle. It's gray brick and completely castle-like. It must be more than ten thousand square feet, with a pool and a guesthouse. It's ridiculous and there's no way I know the man inside. The man who loves me and lives in my three-bedroom townhouse in downtown DC. They cannot be the same man.

The lighting around the outside is meant to mimic torches; it's perfect and yet frightening.

The man who gave me the gun looks back. "We will wait here."

I should tell them I'm fine and that they can go. But I have a feeling I might need a getaway vehicle in about eight minutes. I might also then need an alibi.

I grab my cat, my poor, traumatized cat, and climb from the chopper, ducking and running for the back door to the house. I don't knock. I just walk in, closing the door and placing Binx on the counter. He growls at me through the little slats. I swallow hard and leave him there, entering the dark butler's pantry. It leads directly into the kitchen, the main one—marble and ornate, of course. They always are in houses like this one.

Everything looks like an older lady lives here. I almost worry I don't have the right house as I creep through the shadows and round the massive circular staircase.

"I didn't expect you like this." His voice comes from a shadow in the corner, across a great room.

"Yes, you did," I say. We both know it.

"I expected I wouldn't know you were here. I planned on a knife to my throat in my sleep."

I want to die and I don't even know why yet. "I want to hear it from your lips."

"Which part?"

"All of it." My words are nearly a whisper. I drop to my knees on the hard tile floor and stare at the shadow he has become to me.

He doesn't move, just speaks like a villain in a movie. "We met a long time ago. I was an intern and you, the girl in a coma. You were in your late teens, we thought—me with all the knowledge of my early twenties."

Tears stream down my face. I refuse to give him the satisfaction of knowing he has broken my heart completely by lying to me.

"You had been in the coma for weeks when I met you—almost Christmastime. You were a runaway. No family, no one looking for you. No one. Just the doctors and nurses in the ward. A Jane Doe."

These are lies. I want to tell him that, but I sit on my heels and listen.

"I had worked there for a summer as an intern and then stayed on doing evening shifts for the fall and winter. I spent months that winter wondering what was going on in that pretty little head of yours. Through a family connection, I'd heard of a project for coma patients. I volunteered you and me for the program. When I arrived, I was stunned to discover the art of mind running. It was in its early stages."

I shake my head a little. It's my twitch in interrogations like these. I don't understand why he's lying to me. He certainly doesn't recognize this as an interrogation.

"The first few times we tried to get into your mind we realized whatever was in there was bad. Your world was dark and dank. There was no color, no stories, no life. We had been in the minds of a couple people each as test runs. You were the first person with nothing but a cell and dark hallways and doors that led nowhere. You never let anyone in but me. So we created a program to help you see nothing while I was there, just me and you. I have actually walked the halls of your silent mind. You were always a little girl in your head, crying in the corner. I couldn't see why you cried. The pictures were blank. Needless to say, I felt an affinity with you. Always. Sitting in the dark, speaking about nothing. I read to you, from books I had memorized. I spent my entire winter trying to coax you out of the coma—mind run after mind run—until it became dangerous. Yet one day it worked, and you woke." He pauses. He might be lying. I don't know what to believe.

He sighs after a couple of seconds and then continues. "Your head had been filled with things that were much worse than any of us wanted to know about. A girl on the streets living as a runaway always has the very worst memories. So we inserted a nanite, the very first of those memory bots we created. We made it wipe your memory, including your long-term memory, completely. We made you new memories. We created a past. Loving nuns and a fabulous childhood. A twin sister and loving parents stolen from you by a tragedy."

I look at the shadow he is and tilt my head. Can I see through the lies? Do I know him at all? Is everything a lie?

"You joined the military a year later—fully healed and ready to be part of the world. Being a blank slate made you an easy fit. And you were a natural at shooting and combat, I suspect from years of fighting for your life on the streets."

I look down at the light from outside sending shadows in the bands of light across the marble floor. I don't say anything. It's the best tactic a person wanting the truth has against a person wishing to lie. Human beings hate silence. Especially humans who lie.

After a few moments he speaks. "I finished my internship and I moved on to a degree in robotics engineering. The internship with the nanites had intrigued me enough. When I finished it all, Angela and I were placed in the program I had interned at. This type of neuroscience was still so young and fresh as far as the rest of the world was concerned. This lab had the technology and the secrecy and the funding to explore that little bit extra."

There is nothing but silence when he pauses. I can hear both our breaths gently caressing the air.

By the time he starts talking again, I have decided it is all lies. "When you signed up for the program, at the urging of your superiors, I was not part of that decision. I had begged them not to allow you in, knowing your old memories were a carefully built ladder. It could all come crashing down if they messed with it. Even so, they knew you were very susceptible to the bots and memory manipulation. They felt it was the best place for someone like you. I would not have chosen that for you. But you proved them all right. You really were the best at it."

I remember the urging of my superiors. I remember signing up and thinking I was on to the next adventure. But I don't remember him at all. "Why don't I remember the hospital or you?" I ask before I can stop myself.

"The chip was designed so that you believed you were at a military training facility for the first six months. It was actually a brain-injury rehab clinic. Then at the very end we tweaked your memories again, reinserting the new life we had made up for you. As far as you knew, you left the orphanage and joined the military."

The words ring in my head.

It might be true.

In my first run in Rory's head, I saw his face when I woke from a coma. He was the doctor. I lift my gaze. "Your face was the first one I saw, wasn't it?" It isn't completely a question. I know it's the truth.

"Yes."

I gulp, contemplating just shooting him and leaving. Footsteps startle me, pulling me from that idea. I turn back behind me to see the wolfhound. He's so huge for such a small puppy. He barrels toward me, sniffing and jumping. "Sirius!" Dash calls, but the pup doesn't listen.

I lift a hand, scratching his ears and his head. "Are all my reactions because of you and your lies about who I am?"

"No. We restarted you to be like any amnesiac. You recall how to chew or swallow or walk or what your personal choices are as far as favorites go. Those are instinctual, not memory based. They are who you are. We could not take that away. We took only long-term memories. The scars they created are still there. Sometimes I see them in your eyes."

I close my eyes and scratch the dog's ears, hating that I even feel the way I do about Dash. "Did you make me love you?"

"Of course not. When I met you again, you were a fully formed woman with skills that frightened me. You had grown into a soldier in those ten years. I had kept track of you, of course. But I wasn't stalking you. I had been engaged and broken it off and lived half a life by the time we were reunited."

"When you let me into your head at the end of training, you told me I wouldn't remember it. I wouldn't form memories of it."

"Do you remember it?"

"No. But I think Rory showed it to me."

He gets up, walking to me. The dog sits in front of me, snuggled in. I wrap an arm around him, hugging and needing an anchor.

Dash sits on the cold marble across from me. The shadows play with his features, scaring me with what I see and what I imagine. "Rory knew about you, about your past. Angela told him in a moment of intimacy. She called me straightaway to tell me she'd done it. I panicked and asked you to marry me before I'd even explained my family or any of the other things about me, or you. I wanted you to know I loved you more than anything and that was my way of showing it, in case Rory decided to tell you. I never wanted you to find out who and what you were. It changes nothing, and there's nowhere in your past that will explain who you are better than when we are together."

It is at least an attempt at trying to explain how he had handled his family so badly and why the engagement had come out of nowhere. It doesn't explain why he thought getting married would solve anything.

Technically, at this point, everything is likely to be a lie, even if it feels true. I don't care about anything else. I just want my one answer. "Did you go to the brothel with your brother?"

"No. I told you I didn't."

I heave a little, I can't stop it. He rushes at me, but I pull the gun, my hand shaking as I extend it and point it at him.

My hand never shakes.

"You made me a monster. I don't remember my life. You took it away and fed me lies and made me love you."

"I swear—"

"*Shut up!*" I jerk the gun. "Nothing you say will ever be the truth to me! You are a liar and you made me hollow and blank! I am a lie!"

I tremble everywhere, lowering the gun and getting up quickly. I hear the dog chasing me as I run for my cat, but I don't hear Dash. I grab the cat carrier and run out the door and across the grass.

The grass is damp and my feet push in hard.

I almost dive into the helicopter, but I stop. I need one answer. Just one. I turn and look back at the house, clinging to my poor cat in his carrier. Dash walks through the door, holding his dog. I walk back to him a little bit so he can hear me, but not too close. "Did you make up all my triggers?"

"The four-leaf clover is yours. The purple scarf, yours. The cat named Binx, yours. The rhymes about bullets made of blood and bone and the swans circling, they're yours. I don't know where they came from. The French house in the country was the one I took you to in my head. It was my grandmother's cottage for quiet time. You loved it."

I take a step back. "You took everything."

His green-gray eyes are filled with emotion. "I tried to take away all the bad and give you good in its place. I just wanted you to be okay."

My lip trembles.

"But I had no twin sister! No mother and father! No car accident! That was everything that got me through all this bullshit! Through basic and the military and being a fucking assassin! Goddammit, that is who I think I am! Who am I, if not that?"

"I just wanted you to be a whole person. No leftovers from some horrid life."

"Why did you care?"

"Because I lov—loved you. I-I loved you from the start." He stutters and walks toward me, but I step back. I turn and run away from him, climbing into the helicopter. I slam the door and stare at him, wondering how I ended up here. This reality is so much worse than the fiction of a mind run.

15. SHE TALKS TO ANGELS

The gun in my hand barely moves as I squeeze the trigger, hitting the man in the eye each time. I can shoot. That's normal. That's mine.

I chant these things a lot, making myself see the chanting in Rory's head was mine. I think more than a few things in Rory's head were mine. It's been weeks of me processing, and the longer I think about it all, the messier it becomes.

I have spent the last two weeks telling myself that talking to Rory is not the answer, even if I think he has answers. The man is likely to be even crazier than ever from being isolated in his own dirty little world for weeks on end. There will be no answers from him, only more annoyances.

I am done with being fucked with.

I put the gun down and pull off my safety glasses and earmuffs.

"You have a caller, Jane," the owner, Mr. Christianson, shouts to me from the door in the back of the shooting range. I turn and give him a wave, but I can't imagine who would be calling me here.

I put my gun in the holster and stalk over to the door. Through the glass I see he means a person calling *on* me, not a phone call. I sigh and open the door, immediately enraged seeing his remorseful green-gray eyes. I lean against the door when it closes. "What?"

"I need to talk to you." Dash looks upset, but I force myself to not care, just barely. "Please, just a quick walk around the block. Maybe minus the gun."

"Scared?" I lift my eyes, almost grinning at him, but I'm afraid he'd take it the wrong way. He's been calling and texting nonstop for the entire two weeks I have been avoiding all life forms beyond my cat and my loving neighbor.

"Actually yes. I am scared of you with a gun."

Mr. Christianson snorts and mutters under his breath, "Wise man."

"Fine. But remember that I don't need the gun," I warn before smiling at Mr. Christianson. "Thanks."

"See you next week, Jane." He eyes Dash as I empty my gun and put it in the lockbox. I carry it to my car, Dash's car, our car. I put it in the trunk and realize I should give the car back. "I'll give the car back as soon as I have a chance to get a different one, if it's all the same to you."

"I need to explain."

I turn and give him a look as I close the trunk. "Explain what? I think you did that."

"Why I left when you went back into Rory."

That makes me smile bitterly. "I know why you left. You knew he would show me and I would kill you."

"I hadn't changed his nanobot the way they wanted me to when you went in the first time. I had it limited so that he was unable to enter your world. That was a risk if we did the changes they wanted to make. The world was entirely his the first time, apart from a few similarities that you brought to the table. But the changes we made the second time you went in allowed him to enter your mind, with the understanding you would have more control. Suck him into your world a little. But that gave a skilled operator the ability to scour your mind and use things inside of your head against you."

"I get it. You were worried about what he ended up showing me, so you ran."

"I was worried he would hurt you, and I didn't run. I gave you space." He sighs, his attempt at not having an accent diminished. Dash-with-an-accent reminds me of something. "I gave you some room to be angry and hate me. I had planned on coming to see you on the third or fourth day, hoping you had calmed down a bit."

"Well, you didn't have to worry about giving me space, just breaking my heart. I'm dense enough that I didn't put any of it together. I thought you broke up with me due to anger, without actually breaking up with me. Rory was elusive and Antoine slipped up, so I had some idea that you had been lying to me."

He can't hide the surprise on his face. "You didn't know until you came to see me? Antoine gave me a heads-up when he got off the phone with you. I was ready for you to kill me. He believed you knew everything."

"No. That's why I asked you to tell me the story. I knew nothing."

A grin creeps across his mouth. "So deceptive."

"You mean for someone with no brain in their head? I guess."

His humor flees the second the words leave my mouth. "Jane, that is not what I think."

I shrug. "I never want to see you again, Dash. I just want you to pretend that we worked together once for a couple years and that's that. I don't want to see you and I don't want to hear you. And I don't want to know you. It's been lie after lie after lie."

"I fucked up." He never cusses.

I don't say anything else. I don't need to. I know what I know and I believe none of it. I am a Frankenstein brain-damage victim.

"I fucked up," he repeats, and for the first time I see just how broken he is. He is devastated. But I am too far gone to care.

"Do you really want the story, Jane?"

I shrug again. "I want the truth maybe. Not a story, Dash. You took away the only good things in my life and left me standing alone on the road. *Fucked up* doesn't really cover what you've done. Thus far I've learned that my best friend is a liar. Her ex-boyfriend is a pervert who has tortured and mocked me. The entire family I thought I once had is a figment of some doctor's imagination. My childhood likely contains more things than I can handle. I was the victim of something so bad, it left me brain damaged and in a coma. You never told me what it was, so I have to guess it was horrific. And the worst part, for me, is that the man I loved more than anything, the man who got me through every nightmare and saved me from every dark corner, was the biggest lie of them all. If you don't mind, I don't want to spend the rest of my fucked-up life dwelling on all of that." I am so close to tears that I can't bear it. I toss him the keys to the Mercedes. "On second thought, just take it now. Keep the gun." I walk away, crossing the parking lot of the gun range. "Good-bye."

"Jane!"

My heart clogs my throat and my stomach is quivering and threatening to come back up. I turn, as the tears I am desperately trying to rein in slip from my eyes. "You know the funny part? I brought my cat to your house because I was admitting defeat. I was wrong to go into Rory's mind. I was wrong not to respect you telling me it wasn't safe. And I knew it. I knew I was wrong and I missed you, so I was coming to beg you for forgiveness. That's why I came to the castle you call a house." I laugh at the irony and turn and walk away.

It's about the saddest moment in my life.

Not the death of my pretend sister. Or the painful loss of my fake parents. Not the pretend worlds I thought I lived in. Or the real minds I ran through.

No.

The saddest moment is walking away from that man. And my gun.

I catch a cab, wishing I still had a car or even my helicopter, to the military base no one knows is a base. I flash my credentials at the kiosk and am buzzed through.

A man greets me at the front door. "How can we be of service, Master Sergeant?" he asks with a salute.

I salute him back, and nod. "You have a prisoner here I wish to speak to."

"Prisoner?" He sounds confused. If the world knew some of the worst military criminals were kept in downtown DC, they would flip out. I nod my head at the wall that I know contains an elevator into the ground where the cells and extreme military guards are.

"Rory Guthrie. I need to see him."

His eyes widen. "We do not have—"

I sigh and pull out my phone, pressing a number in my recent calls.

"This better be good, I am a busy man for God's sake. Spears?"

"Sorry, sir. Can you just tell the officer in charge at the DC brig that I am allowed to see Rory?"

"I can, but why the fuck do you want me to do that?" The president's military years come back to him quickly in a decent amount of sailor talk. "Are you fucking kidding me, Spears? What is going on?"

"I need to ask him some questions for my own peace of mind. I'm sure you understand. You can record it for your records if you like. Something might come of it."

"Fine," he barks, and I hand the phone over to the officer in charge. He takes it hesitantly, his eyes widening and his mouth dropping. "Yes—yes, sir. Of course, sir. Yes. Thank—"

I take the phone back from the baffled man. "He hangs up on me all the time too."

He gives me a look. "Who the hell are you?"

I shrug. "That is the question of the day."

I turn and walk to the wall where the door is. It takes an eye scan to open it. I lean forward. I have been here before.

The light turns green and the wall slides away, sounding heavy and thick. I step into the elevator, again allowing a scan of my eyes. The man stares at me in disbelief. "Floor seven," he says as the doors close. I press the seven and we descend into the earth. The elevator dings after a second. I step out where two men with assault rifles stare at me with their guns pointed. I lean forward and scan my eyes again before they lower their weapons. They then salute.

I nod, saluting back. "Rory Guthrie, please."

They look puzzled, but one turns and walks to a door on the right. He scans his fingerprints and then his eyes. The door slides open, again sounding heavy. I walk to it, instantly shuddering when I see him.

Rory's behind Plexiglas in a bright-orange jumpsuit. He lifts his face, smiling wide. "I knew you'd be back." He looks sickly, as anyone would after weeks in a drug-induced coma. His eyes are shifty and his face is slack, as if he is drugged even now. Mind running has made a mess of us both.

I sit in the chair as the two men stand guard, listening to our conversation. The male and female prisoners in the cells are trained to the highest level; there is a reason they are kept under such strict guard. I lean back and sigh. "You set me up."

"Aye." He nods, sitting and leaning forward on his bed. He sighs and swallows funny, like his throat has thickened. "I did. I am sorry for that, Jane. I wish I had been there the moment ya realized ya were nothing but an urchin like me."

"You think I care about being an urchin?" I pause and then just ask the thing I want to know. "Why do you hate me, Rory?"

"Are ya kidding me?" His dark-blue eyes are hazy. I can tell they've been drugging him for a while. Honestly, if I were the guards, I would drug him too. "I don't hate ya, Jane. I love ya. I have always loved ya. I hated what they did to ya. When Angie told me what Dash had done, I was furious."

"You tormented me."

"Ya like it rough. I know ya do." He laughs and taps his temple. "I've seen what's in there, ya do remember that."

"I want to know what you saw in there."

He shrugs. "I didn't see nothing ya don't remember already."

I close my eyes and sigh. "What did you see?"

"What's it worth?"

"Nothing to me. But for you, it's a moment to redeem yourself for the horrible things you've done."

His eyes dart to the right and left. "I got nothing to feel bad about. I lived the life I was meant to with the cards I was dealt. I didn't have it all erased like a little bitch. I suffered through. On my own. Persevered."

His words don't hurt me. I didn't run from my past. It was taken from me on purpose. "I feel sorry for you, Rory. Sorry that you won't ever love anyone and no will ever love you."

He winks, but I can see the words have hit him. "Ya loved me for a minute, Jane."

"I didn't know you."

He laughs again and I can see he's crazy. He's gone. I get up, but he jumps to his feet giving me a desperate look. "They made me think Dash has a nano with your old memories. He had to collect them with something, didn't he, then? But I think he covered them up, and they still exist. Ya just need triggers to find them again."

"If he took them, then you really didn't see anything in my past."

"No. I might have lied a bit on that one." He shrugs, but I think he's having a second of clarity. "Blank slate in yer head. But I did see him in the rehab center, rebuilding ya. Some mushy shite in there. But you bitches always fall for the mushy shite. There's layers in yer head, Jane. They're trying to hide something from ya."

I lift my middle finger and then look down at it like I'm surprised it's there. He laughs and I walk out. I will do my best to never see him again.

16. CRASH INTO ME

Mrs. Starling hands me a spade and nods her head at the flower bed. "Now we turn the soil as deep as we can."

I dig it in and push with my foot, lifting and turning the dirt. She kneels and plants as I till and turn. It's the best-case scenario for her, and me. I get to work out my frustrations in life and she gets to plant a flower bed without the hard part.

"I sure do miss that Dash. He was a sweet boy. You can always tell by how someone acts when they don't know you're looking." She looks up at me and smiles. "Caught him talking to Binx once. He was going on about you. Told Binx he was going to work hard to deserve you."

I snap. "He's an ass and we're done. You need to get past this. It's been months. He's over it too, I'm sure."

She flinches, but the saucy old lady she is rebounds. "He was a nice boy, Jane, and you shouldn't call him an ass. Whatever he did, he's sorry. I know that. I see him all the time, walking by with that dog that's slowly turning into a horse. He's not over it."

"He walks by?"

Her eyes light up. "Oh, he does. All the time. Back and forth, talking to himself, and then off he goes again. Then I see him a few days later and it's the same thing. Twice every week for months now."

I gulp. "Let's just stick to the gardening." It doesn't dawn on me that she means to set me up so that he walks by as I am digging an old root from last summer.

"Dash, how are you? That dog is something," she says. "Hello, Sirius. Such a fancy name for such a goofy dog."

I freeze, hearing his voice. "Thanks, Mrs. Starling. He's a good dog." I stand and turn just as he says my name. "Hello, Jane."

"Dash." I lift a dirty hand. Sirius, who has indeed become a horse, jumps at me. Dash can barely contain him as he hurries over to sniff and rub against me. "Hey, boy!" I pet him, scratching his ears. I can't fight my gaze lifting to Dash. He smiles at me, but it's his hand I catch. He's got a wedding ring on.

My insides ache the moment my eyes lock on the silver-looking ring. Though I'm sure it's not silver, but instead made of some kind of titanium or platinum—another metal that is expensive and hoity-toity.

I can't help but wonder if it's the one that he matched to the rings he got me? The ring is on the correct finger, but then I realize it's the wrong hand.

Oh my God.

He is wearing the ring we should have been married in.

My chest tightens and aches, but I focus on petting Sirius and brushing off the dirt I've wiped on him. "Can we talk?" I ask, hating that Mrs. Starling is grinning from ear to ear about it, but the ring has me thinking.

He nods, and his eyes get a bit hopeful. He holds an arm out for me. I don't take it, but I can't stop myself from wanting to.

Four months has killed off all the hate. My heart has spent all this whispering that what he did was for the best. He took away the things

I didn't want anyway. But the common-sense part of my brain shouts that he lied to me for years. Years more than I am allowed to remember. I am thirty-four and I have known him for seventeen years.

Walking beside him, I can't help but still love him. I love his smell, the one I assign to all good men in my brain. They always smell like Dash. My father, kindly men, and cops I meet. It's all the same.

The memory of him on top of me and inside me haunts me, making me crave him in the dark of night. It's worst first thing in the morning when I swear I can feel him next to me. Sometimes my feet seek him out and I end up sleeping sideways on the bed.

It's fairly awful.

Seeing the ring on his right hand on the wedding finger makes me sick. I don't want to let him go and I don't want someone else finding his feet in the night.

"How have you been?" he asks, almost like we are going to go for the weather next.

"Fine." I don't want to know how he's been. I haven't been fine.

"I'm fine also." He laughs and looks at me. "I miss you. I miss everything about you."

"You miss me?" I glare. I can't even stop myself. "What exactly? All the things you put in there? I was essentially the perfect woman for a while. I was whatever you rebooted me to be."

He looks injured and I'm angry. Maybe we haven't changed in four months. We haven't even traded places. He looks exhausted still, if I stare and really try to see past the golden tan he's sporting. He's clearly been somewhere warm. Maybe out boating a lot. I always did hate boating.

"Can we start over?"

"No." It's a lie, but I will not yield. "I just needed an answer from you."

"I dropped your gun off months ago. It's back in the closet. I left my key with Mrs. Starling."

"You went in my house when I wasn't there? Or was I sleeping? Did you watch me sleep?"

"No." He steps back. "Please, stop. I'm not a freak, Jane."

"I think you are. I think you liked that I didn't know everything and you did." I don't believe my words. I just want to hurt him. And not because he hurt me, but because I am hurting and petty.

"You're wrong!" Rage fills his eyes. "If I could have forgotten too, I would have. You don't even know the things I have done."

"I can imagine."

He reaches for me, grabbing my arms, not violently, but assertively. "I didn't have a goddamned clue what you did for the ten years we were apart! I kept track of you—as in, I knew you were in Beirut or wherever you went on mission—but I didn't know what you were doing! I knew once upon a time you were a scared little girl who had been brutalized! Jesus! Do you want to know it all?" He runs his hands through his hair, grabbing it and tugging a bit. He leaves it sticking out all over. "Fine! Fine, goddammit. Fine! You probably were raped and then stabbed. Is that what you want to hear? Those scars on your stomach are not from a car accident. They're from a teenaged girl being gutted like a fish to remove the baby she had been carrying."

I gasp and he calms down a little and speaks with the deepest regret I have ever heard. "The police found you in an alley in the winter, bleeding out from head wounds and practically disemboweled. The cold saved your life—your heart slowed down, so you didn't bleed to death. No one knows who you were but me. I happened to be working that night, an intern at the hospital. There are police reports if you don't believe me, but it's all about a Jane Doe. You can Google the whole story. It was in '98 and you were found in New York. The Lower East Side. A teenaged homeless girl was attacked and her fetus cut from her. There's a reason you hate Manhattan."

I shake, trying to wrap my head around it all, but I can't.

He looks distraught. "You stayed in a coma for a winter. When you were stable, they transferred you to the brain-injury facility and I went with you. I had us both put there because of the remarkable things they were doing. I thought I could help you come back."

"No." I twitch and tremble.

"I stayed with you until you woke up, and my face was the first thing you saw. I have always been the safe person for you. Which was why I was always the bad guy in your scenarios, as you said. I feared it was some part of you realizing who I was. Which was why I agreed to let Rory be the bad guy in that one scenario with Ashley Potter and the girls in the cells. That played rather well for him unbeknownst to me."

He's rambling and I'm still stuck on pregnant teenager.

"I have spent my entire adult life protecting you from this," he continues. "When you signed up to be a mind runner, I tried to convince them not to use you, but they knew you were already susceptible to the process. And being military, you had the training to go with it. They convinced me that you would attribute most of the bad things to the minds you were in and not see them as your memories at all. And to be honest, they didn't give a shit about you either way."

He pauses, releasing me, though his hand still grips me. I have a terrible feeling he's going to cry. "I won't ever forgive myself for what I did, but I could not bear that you might wake and remember you had been pregnant. That you had been growing a life and someone took it. Or that you had had that terrible existence. Every day I walked into your room to assess you, and every day I was stunned by how perfect you were. I didn't understand how you had come to the fate you had."

My eyes fill with tears as I step back. Sirius whines and rubs against me. I part my lips as if to speak but I can't. I'm in shock. Absolute shock.

I don't have words. But I don't need them. He steps in, wrapping himself around me completely. He holds me, shielding me from it all, and whispers, "You are not that girl. We buried that girl. We let her die and let it end for that poor, sad soul. We created *your* past, for you.

You are strong and capable and a better person than anyone I know. You were an amazing spy and agent for the CIA and FBI. You have always been brilliant as a Master Sergeant and soldier. You are strong and capable."

I don't feel that way. I shove him back and turn, running away from it all. I push everything away, but he catches me, again gripping me. "Jane. What's the difference now? Your childhood was shit either way."

"I had a baby cut from my stomach, Dash!" I snap.

"Right. You were a drug addict on the streets. High as fuck. You got pregnant, likely sold it and then backed out of the deal, so the broker took the baby and left you for dead."

"The baby? Did anyone find the baby?"

"No. The investigators attributed it to black-market baby brokers. They believe it was either a pimp or a broker, but the baby would have been sold if it had lived."

"Did anyone ever come for me? Try to claim me?" None of this feels real, but I fear it is the real world.

"No."

"I'm Jane Doe? I don't have a name?"

He steps to me, huffing his breath. "Jane, let me give you one," he says and kisses my cheek, brushing his face against mine. I love his breath on the side of my face. "Let me make you part of my family."

I nod. I don't have another answer or the capability to speak. I lean into him, letting him surround me until he feels too big, like all the words he has spoken are falling in on me, smothering me. I push him back. "This isn't true."

"I am so sorry, but it is. I have all the proof you need. I can show you video footage of you as a pregnant junkie, Jane. I just didn't want to. I wanted to keep you safe from this."

He steps back in and lowers his face, pressing his lips to mine. He kisses gently.

I need it. I need to feel something other than this desperate pain.

I grab his hand and we turn back to the house. We haven't made it far, so we just walk back. Mrs. Starling jumps up and grabs the leash from Dash's hands. "Let me take him for a walk. He's such a good boy." She turns and leaves the gardening, taking the happy horse with her.

I ignore her and the dog and drag him up the stoop.

We crash into the foyer, kissing and tugging. I hear Binx running for me, but I am lost in the warmth of the kisses and clothing being pulled away. Dash slams the door and lifts me into his arms. He carries me to the bed, laying me back and tugging my dirty jeans off. He stops and kisses a scar along my thigh before moving up and kissing the scars along my belly. The ones that took something I never knew I had. Something I can't even feel because I have not even dealt with that yet.

His lips and tongue trace the spots that try to tell me I am broken and hurt and damaged beyond repair.

But then he slips his fingers into the waistband of my underwear and tugs it down, spreading my thighs and landing soft kisses along them. When he reaches the center, the warm place I desperately want him to put his mouth on, he pauses. "Did you miss me, Jane?"

I nod, impatient for the warmth of his breath and mouth to make me feel something beyond the sadness he has caused, anything. I want to feel something beyond the horror of my broken heart.

"I missed you so much." He places another gentle kiss on the inside of my thigh, so close to the right spot I swear I feel him brush against my lips slightly.

His hands move with his face, one finger inserting into me the moment his mouth encloses around my clit. He sucks and flicks and fingers. I cry out, instantly lost in the movements and pleasure.

I am not that girl.

I am me.

I am Jane.

Even if Doe is my last name now, it doesn't matter. It doesn't have to be a bad thing.

I am me.

I chant it a little, like a crazy person. It makes me laugh and I don't even care that I'm laughing alone like a crazy person.

I care that his finger is speeding up and my body is in a swirl of chaos. I care that his tongue is putting me over the edge. I care that I am about to orgasm for the first time in ages. And it's my favorite way to do it.

He sucks and flicks at the exact speed I like. He knows me. He didn't make me like this; I like it because it is who I am. My body knows I like it.

I clench with the buildup as he pumps his finger, maintaining his perfect rhythm. When I come, it's with a tremor the whole world can feel. I shake and shudder and grunt.

There's no recovery time for my overstimulated clit. He spreads my legs wide, sliding between them, rubbing himself between my legs. He pushes his cock in gently, breathing like he's already desperately holding on to control. Like I have bewitched him.

He slides in and out slowly, getting a feel for me, like we have never done this before.

And maybe we haven't.

In this honest place, the one where I finally know why, we are making love, not fucking. We are worshipping and caressing. Maybe he knows I need gentle.

He lowers his face to one of my nipples, sucking and stroking with his tongue. He shortens his thrusts, like he's not quite certain he is going to be able to keep going.

He's lost with me.

He clenches his teeth down on my nipple, speeding up the pumping to the point that his balls are slapping against me and his fingers are gripping a little too tightly. I pull his face to mine, sucking his tongue and biting his lip. He makes a face when he comes. It's almost a painful expression, but I love it. He thrusts a few times more, really twitching and jerking into me.

When he does stop moving, his breath has turned ragged and violent.

His weight atop me makes it hard to breathe, but in the best way. I don't feel like his words have fully hit me. I don't know how to deal with them. So lying here under him is a nice alternative.

I look down at his right hand and ask the question I know will hurt me, but I need to be hurt. I need to feel something normal people feel. "The ring is it—"

"It's ours. Or it was meant to be. Before we canceled the wedding of the century. Well, after I canceled the wedding. You sort of left that up to me, didn't you? I assumed it was canceled when you never returned a single call or text."

"Oh, right." I blush and look down. "I just didn't want to think about it. I didn't want to cancel and I didn't want to go ahead with it. I hated you as much as I loved you. I think I still do."

He kisses my cheek. "Surely you must see why?"

"Absolutely." I hate that we are back to that part of the story. But he doesn't press and he doesn't make me talk about it. We don't have to. We aren't those people who force talking.

I close my eyes and sigh, holding on to him like I never want him to go anywhere. "Can we let go of the fragile orphan girl? If you stop treating me like a feeble little bitch, I will stop acting like one."

"You don't act like one, and yes, we can."

"Thank you." I give him another look. "I will be needing proof of what you say."

"Do you want it now?"

"No. One day."

"You realize you agreed to marry me on the street there, and I am holding you to it." He rolls out and off me, and lies on his side.

I cock an eyebrow. "I want to wait on the wedding and the whole "getting back together" thing. I don't want to rush this."

His smile falls. "Why?"

"Because I don't trust you, Dash."

"Everything I do is for you, Jane."

"While I understand why you did everything, you have to see that you have been lying to me for years. Even though it was for a good reason, and I get that, it still has not made me want to trust you. And," I look down at my belly, "there are other things I have to adjust to."

"You were a drug addict and a kid yourself." His gaze has followed mine to my stomach.

"I know. And I shouldn't care about what I did when I was a stupid teenager, but nothing changes the fact that I had a baby with a person who is now a stranger to me, maybe a rapist or a John, and then, to add to that craziness, someone stole it. I should be saving that for a particularly low point when I need to cry and do the whole "wine-and-sorrow" thing women do. And while being a teenage runaway with a baby and a drug problem is not a past I really want, I need a bit of time to let it all sink in. I can't move forward until I move past, as clichéd as that sounds."

He winces, but he agrees. "It sounds fair, Jane, not clichéd. I have had seventeen years to adjust to all of this. I won't rush you. I mean it. I just don't want to be apart from you. I'll sleep in one of the other rooms, but I want to be here with you."

I want to tell him that it's okay, that he can sleep with me, yet I pause. I don't trust him, and trusting someone means turning your back when you're sleeping and at your most vulnerable.

I want him to earn his way back. Earn his way back to the place where I trust him enough to turn my back.

At this point, I don't feel that way. "I'm scared that either this is a mind run or you are testing me in some way. That none of this is real. Or that there is something so much worse hiding out there in the world. Something you are preparing me for."

He gives me an astounded look. "Jane, what could possibly be worse than what I have told you?"

"That it's all lies and you are judging my reactions. That you don't actually love me and that this is part of the project."

He leans back a bit. "Okay, that is much worse. I would never lie to you about that. But I have lied about everything else, so I can understand. I don't expect you to. Just know I am on your side." He leans back in, kissing my nose. "I have always been on your side."

I close my eyes. "It doesn't feel like it."

"Then I will not rest until it does."

I believe him, and that makes me uncomfortable too.

17. HO HEY

Antoine's voice hovers in my ear. "The package is a man with brown hair. The informant says he's got a tan jacket and he's carrying a bouquet of flowers. The cyanide is in the flowers."

I signal, glancing down at the girl I have partnered with, Cami. She was my choice. I've never made that decision before; Rory was always the one who picked new team members. But I am the senior agent now, so I get a say in whom I train. I chose a woman. Mostly because I think more women are needed in undercover work. We are always unassuming. People think of spies as men.

I motion to her that I am going to sneak thirty yards and peek around the corner of the building to see if I can see him yet.

She acknowledges. Her doe eyes and chestnut hair complement the location of this mission. She's tanned like she belongs in the desert. Like the people who live here.

Her mix of any number of ethnicities makes it easy for her to blend in wherever we are. In France she can get mistaken for a Sardinian or a Romanian. In India, with her makeup done right, she looks like every girl in the temple.

Here in Bahrain, she wears the traditional abaya and sports smoky eyes as if this is her lifelong jam.

I on the other hand manage to rock the Asian tourist look, mostly because I let Cami do my makeup. She's pretty good at it. She's also remarkable with a knife, a sniper rifle, and eleven languages.

She's essentially my new favorite person. Especially because she's twenty-three and fit as a fiddle.

I remember being that girl, but it's a little painful to see Cami so young and so strong, as I am now so much older.

Especially because my memories stop just before her current age. I was almost nineteen when I signed up for the military. Before that is a haze of lies. I wish they weren't there—the lies or the memories—but unfortunately they contain years of hard work and experience too.

So I am stuck with all or nothing.

"How hot is she in the abaya?" Antoine asks in my ear alone, making me smile.

"You don't even have the ability to comprehend just how hot. She is ridiculous."

"She speaks Portuguese. Did I ever tell you how much that turns me on?"

I smile wider as I creep across the stone roof to the corner. The man with the flowers comes into sight seconds later. "I got him."

"If you shoot, someone is going to find those flowers and die from the cyanide. I was thinking maybe you could—"

"Shhh. Do I tell you how to search the Internet or poop in a tube sock properly so you don't have to leave your mom's basement?"

"I love it when you talk dirty to me." He chuckles in my ear as I tuck my gun and sprint across the roof. I leap across a catwalk between two buildings and jump down onto a balcony. I toss a support up into the rafters of the building next to me and attach a rappeller to the rope. I add a second knot as I attach it, for the extra heavy weight.

"You got this, Jane?" Cami asks with a very British accent. I know Antoine is dying. Every time she speaks he pees his pants.

"Got this," I confirm, and the moment the man is close enough, I drop down, just hovering above the ground, snatching the flowers in one hand and him in the other. I head-butt him and press the retrieving button. The rappeller lifts us back up. The man's nose is bleeding and he struggles, but I wrap my legs around him and squeeze. When my hands lose him, my lower body doesn't.

He shouts obscenities at me, but the moment we are on a balcony again I place the flowers down carefully and then punch him hard. He cries out as I grab my scanner and check him for cyanide. He has none hidden away, so I grab the flowers and press the button again.

He scrambles to grab at the flowers, but I kick him in the face, knocking him back again before leaping for the railing of the next balcony. When I get to the next level up, I unclip and start the long and painful process of jumping from one balcony to the next and climbing the railings. It wouldn't be so bad if I wasn't bent on not stirring the flowers up while hurrying to the rooftop.

Using the same skills, Cami has made her way to the roof as well and is holding a rolling suitcase.

I try to catch my breath as the wind twists my hair. I glance up at the chopper overhead. We have made it just in time. I walk quickly, dumping the flowers into the special case as Cami closes it. I nod at her as I hurry past to the ledge on the far side of the roof. Cami grabs the case and jumps onto the chopper's ladder, climbing up as it flies away, as if it never stopped near the building at all.

I jump down the other side of the building, landing on the highest balcony. The way down is better; there is a fire escape. I spotted it earlier when we were plotting how to get away with snatching a man from the street. I had needed somewhere to stash clothes.

I strip and get into my business suit and put my glasses on, brushing my hair smooth with my fingers and folding my Asian tourist name tag over my lapel. I drag off my comfy shoes and slip on the heels to go with my suit.

Leaving the clothes I had worn moments before in the same spot as my stashed clothes, I rush down the stairs to the concrete. When I get back on the ground, I smile and laugh into my Bluetooth, switching to Mandarin when I tell Antoine I have delivered the flowers he ordered.

"Your flight is ready. The Lord and Lady are expecting you in eight hours. So you had best make this flight."

"Did someone grab the trash?" I ask about the man I left bleeding on the balcony.

"Yes. It has been taken care of. I found my uncle a very nice apartment in the city there. Right in that building we were checking out."

"Excellent."

He's quiet as I hail a cab, so I say, "We aren't ever going to talk about it."

"I know." He swallows hard. We haven't talked about it since I found out exactly who I was. I can hear the gulp in the earpiece before he speaks. "I'm sorry. I just needed you to know. It was for the best, your best. Trust me, Jane."

"Whatever. I still don't want to talk about it." I click along in my heels on the concrete to the taxi that has stopped, and nod. "Airport, please." The driver nods and drives as I speak to Antoine. "I still want the proof. That's all I'm going to say."

"It'll be on the plane. Waiting for you." There's a hesitation in his voice. "I'm glad you're back."

I laugh. "You don't sound glad."

"I am. You run the smoothest op in the entire world. I swear it."

"Thank you. But I think a lot of people would disagree."

He chuckles. "They don't, Jane. Everyone knows you are the best."

"I think we both know there was one who was better." I hate to admit it. I hate to remember him as anything but a monster.

"But we shall not say his name, so that he will not rise again." He makes an uncomfortable joke, likely in reference to one of his video games.

For me, though, it might be a bit early to joke about Rory, even if that's how we attempt to deal with everything.

The cabbie takes a turn, like I don't know the city. I point and say in perfect Arabic that he needs to take me to the airport or I will gut him like a fish. His eyes widen and he turns and gets back on the road I need to be on.

"Getting dodgy again?" Antoine asks.

I smile. "Yeah, but you know me."

"Right, not a fan. I never feel like the Arabic countries are the right choice for you and Cami."

His words bring about a hearty chuckle. "Because we are clearly delicate flowers."

The driver eyes me up. I slice my finger across my throat, showing him how I will kill him. He flinches and drives faster.

"Well, let's not get out of hand. Obviously I didn't mean delicate. But perhaps just female. Delicate or not."

I sigh and look out the window at the beautiful scenery passing me by. "You just have to avoid the sketchy-looking people. Those show up in every city. The minute they get a little aggressive or sneaky, you leave or force your way out. Either way, it ends there."

"Is Bahrain bad? Because I feel like India would be the one where I would avoid being a girl."

"India is not so bad." I remember them all so well. "And Bahrain is a cakewalk, compared to almost everywhere in Africa. There, you're guaranteed to get murdered."

"I know I worry about Cami being there."

That makes me smile. "You like her a lot."

"I do. And I intend on asking her out this weekend."

"She thinks you're cute." I throw him a bone. I shouldn't, but I have to. He is the sweetest guy in the whole world. Even if he lied to me for years.

When I get to the airport, I nod at the cabbie. "Try that shit again and I will find you."

He gives me a dirty look. I toss cash at him, American cash, and hurry to the front doors.

"Is it a private plane?"

"Yeah, in the hangar you hate. Cami is already on board, waiting for you."

"Chat in a bit." I disconnect and smile sweetly to clear customs.

When I get to the hangar, I hurry on board and strap in, nodding at Cami and a guy I don't really like. His name is Dwayne; he's the overly confident and annoying surveillance guy Rory handpicked. I find him creepy and sexist at the best of times. But I relish the fact it drives him nuts that I have the president's ear. When that doesn't get me by, I spend every moment we are together fighting the urge to throat-punch him and tell him exactly why I have the ear of the president.

I pull up the laptop in my seat and lay it down as we taxi. We need to leave right away. We have a case full of cyanide and have just assassinated three men.

When I turn the computer on, I see Antoine on FaceTime. He grins, giving me a cheesy look. "You come here often?"

I roll my eyes. "It better be here." Neither of us wants to see my past, but I know I won't ever believe Dash if I don't see the proof for myself.

His smile fades and a worried look crosses his face. "You sure? Jane, the things in your past are bad. I wouldn't want to know."

"I want to see."

"Okay, then." He vanishes as the FaceTime ends and the screen fills with documents.

One is a newspaper report out of Manhattan of a seventeen-year-old homeless girl found naked with her belly cut open. Her baby had been stolen. She had been assaulted and was in serious condition.

The next is a video link. I click it and watch as I, a young pregnant me, walk into a store. I buy food—a sandwich. There are sores on my face and my hands shake as I count change on the counter. I resemble a junkie; there's no doubt. The way I eat as I leave the store makes me think I hadn't eaten in days. I glance up at the camera, clearly aware of them. It's me. There's no mistaking the girl as me.

I look like I am dying of starvation and on drugs while being very pregnant. A man follows me out. I back the video up and watch the man in the video. He's watching me. I can't help but notice the way he stares at my belly.

When the screen-me leaves, I catch a glimpse of his face. I don't know him and yet he seems familiar.

The next link is a police report. I click it, immediately seeing the handwritten account of Jane Doe.

Seventeen, approximate age.

Caucasian.

Female.

One hundred twenty-eight pounds.

I grimace at the thought of being that small nine months pregnant.

The next lines catch my eyes.

"Victim is easily recognized by other street people. They say her name is Andrea, no last name. She's a runaway from Atlanta. One girl bunks with her at a shelter for homeless kids. Says the victim was due in a few weeks and that the baby was being given up for adoption. Says it was legal, but none of the agencies know of her. Spoke to one agency in the Lower East Side. They said the street kids sell their babies illegally. Lady at the adoption agency said she has seen this before where the seller went back on their word and decided to keep the baby. It's a theory the buyer might have taken the baby."

I stare at the words sell their babies. My eyes cross, but I don't stop staring.

I click the next link and find a doctor's write-up of the damage— the stitches and surgeries and lacerations and prognoses.

I should have died.

But I didn't, not really.

The words might as well be a language I cannot read, because I do not know the girl in the report. I do not know her, I do not remember her, and I do not know what it would be like to be her. I cannot even comprehend what it means to have a child.

I see it there in that moment. Dash gave me a second chance. He bought me a second chance. My medical bills were paid. I was sent to the best brain-injury clinics and centers. Every single document that comes next is a shocking revelation that Dash has been caring for me for as long as he said.

I dug myself into a terrible hole and he pulled me out and sheltered me until I was strong again.

I had a family, but I left them?

I chose to starve on the streets, and sell my body and my baby, over going home?

How bad was home?

Or was I such a bad kid they kicked me out for drugs and stealing?

The possibilities are endless, and I can see why Dash took it all away. Whatever happened to me, happened to a different girl. I am not her.

I am me.

I would love a baby and care for it and treat it better than anything in the world. I would love to be married and be normal, but I don't think that will ever happen for me.

Maybe this right here is the me that I am choosing to be.

The only thing that makes everything else right is the knowledge I am not that girl. Andrea or Jane Doe or whoever I was.

She was my twin sister.

We were identical.

But now she is dead. She died in an alley.

I am free.

All I can do is pray that the baby is okay.

18. ADDICTED TO YOU

While the past is exactly what Dash said it was, the horror and reality push back against my desire to know about any of it.

However, the car ride to the house in London, after the plane ride, goes much better.

Nichols, Dash's family's loyal driver, picks me up from Heathrow and even lets me ride up front, after much persuasion.

"How have you been?" I ask. I genuinely like the man. He is gentle and kind and thoughtful. And he is far more intelligent than either of Dash's parents.

He nods and smiles. "I have been well, miss. Thank you for asking. How have you been?"

"Very well." I contemplate sparing him from my nosiness, but I can't. "Did Henry ever have his court date with the international tribunal?"

"No, miss. He is scheduled to be tried along with the other men next month. International courts take much longer, and the evidence is just so extensive." He doesn't have to tell me that.

"But I thought he was being tried in the military courts?"

"No. The last I heard from Lord Townshend was that none of them are being tried by the military. They had hoped the American military courts could prevent the media from hearing all the details. But the crimes aren't localized to one region; this is widespread and global, so the United Nations is demanding an international tribunal."

"Oh God." I wince, realizing I never did tell Henry's father to help him. "Has Henry got a lawyer?"

"No, miss. He's been cut off completely. Been given a barrister from the UN who is meant to do the job."

"That's not very good."

"No, miss. He's a foolish boy, but cutting one's children off is not the way to handle a situation like that."

I nod and glance out the window at the stunning neighborhood of old row houses and mansions made into apartments. We are in Hyde Park, a wealthy section of London. "Is the house nearby?"

He chuckles. "No, miss."

I sit back and relax, thinking about everything, when it dawns on me I haven't sent Antoine the e-mail I had composed on the plane. I link my phone, creating a hotspot, and send it. It has the picture of the man who followed me from the store on the video. I can only hope Antoine finds him.

I would very much like to repay the favor he once bestowed upon me.

I may not be able to mourn the loss of the baby I never knew, but I can fucking well avenge him or her. That is the one motherly skill I possess.

We drive for what feels like hours but has been closer to an hour, then he turns into a driveway and slows the car. I cringe as he drives up to the house that is not a house but can't stop from laughing nervously. "A castle? Do they own anything but castles?"

"My dear girl, honestly." He sighs and shakes his head. "You must learn to Google the family better."

"I do. Their houses never show up on Google Maps."

He gives me a look. "In today's technological world, you can't get a few pictures of these places?"

"I never really think of it until it's too late. And by then we are driving up and I'm doing my orphan stare and reliving scenes from *Annie*."

"At least they can't ever say you were a—what is that American term? Gold digger!" He snorts as he gets out, pointing at my door. "You open that and never sit in the front again, young lady."

I lift my hands innocently, wishing I wasn't wearing a work outfit. A pantsuit isn't exactly Lady Townshend–worthy.

"Your friend Miss O'Conner is here," Nichols says as he opens the door.

I haven't seen her since the big reveal. I nod. "That's good. I'd like to see her."

"Come now, we are already late." He escorts me to the massive front door of the English castle I am absolutely going to be exploring in the morning when it's light out. Even in the dark it is incredible.

"This is bigger than the house in Virginia."

"Far bigger," he laughs. "This is the Townshend Castle. It is a very fine home with a lot of history. The family has owned it for hundreds of years. The smallest section was built in the fifteenth century and the largest addition was built in the seventeenth century and expanded again in the eighteenth and nineteenth centuries. It is so large it is continually under renovation. The original castle was a quadrangle in shape for military defense. It was a fortress, which is why it is allowed the term *castle*. It's situated on thirteen thousand acres and has a total of one hundred fifty-three rooms."

"Holy shit." I glance about the massive front entry and wonder if they have turned it into a museum or if the museums are all built to mimic *it*.

"I assure you, my dear, if there was shit here, it would be holy."

We both laugh at his joke as the large wooden door is opened for us and Nichols stops dead in front of it. "Have a lovely evening, miss." He bows and leaves me there.

I step inside, wrinkling my nose as always.

"Yer the only girl I know who dates a prince and hates it."

"No. The rest of them hate it too, they just don't have the balls to say it. And he isn't a prince. Trust me."

"Och, come on now." Angie rushes over, wrapping herself around me. "He's rich enough. And I do suppose ya have balls big enough for everyone." She kisses my cheek. "I have an outfit for ya in the bathroom to the right. Slip down there and wash up. Ya have a splattering of something there." She pulls back, giving it a look. "That blood?"

I wipe it and shrug. "Maybe."

"That's disgusting." She tilts her head to the right. "Off with ya."

I hurry down the hall to the bathroom, which matches the house—huge and marble and over the top. I pull on the simple black dress she left on the counter and then put on the lipstick beside it. After folding my clothes and placing them in a neat pile in the corner of the room, I give myself a once-over.

The dress is perfect and the makeup from Cami is still fresh looking. I wipe the random splatter of blood from the side of my face, hopefully without disturbing the makeup, before washing my hands and leaving the room. By the time I get back down the hall, Angie is gone and Evangeline has replaced her. She smiles wide. "Miss . . . Jane. How are you?"

I hug her. It seems like the right choice. She is awkward for the first second, or maybe I'm awkward. But neither of us melts into it.

"Jane."

I turn to see Dash. "Hey."

"I didn't know you'd arrived." He walks to me as Evangeline disappears back into the scenery. When he hugs me it's different—all encompassing.

"How was Bahrain?"

"Good." I pull back and look up at him. "What's my story?"

He furrows his brow. "What do you mean?"

"Why was I on a business trip? Am I a doctor, still?"

He laughs. "No. God, no. I explained that you are actually a very important young woman with a very important career and that everything you do is top secret."

"You have told them the truth?"

"Not the whole truth. They don't know you are the patient I spoke of years ago, with the memory issues. They think I met you at work. And as far as your job is concerned, I only told them that it is sensitive in nature and military in description. That it is a matter of national security and you aren't able to speak about it." He lifts his right hand in the air. "But other than that, I am all about the truth now. There may be some omissions, but there's not a single lie in this room."

I bite my lip, knowing that's not true. I wince and spill, hating that he's working so hard at being honest and I am the one who's lying. "Except one."

"One?"

"Your brother. He called me awhile ago looking for my help with your father."

Dash looks confused and annoyed, and yet he manages to keep his tone calm. "Henry called you awhile ago and you didn't tell me about it?"

"I am telling you."

"What help could you offer him?"

I blink and blurt, "He implied another family member was actually at the brothel and that whichever of you two it was, you were smart enough to avoid the cameras."

"The log books?"

"Every name is named. I can only assume there is another Townshend name on that list they found in the brothel and Henry is suggesting he be helped before the entire family is implicated."

Dash wrinkles his nose. "Crikey." It's the most English thing I have ever heard him say. "My father went there as well?"

I can't even stop the smile crossing my lips. "Yeah. Unless it was you."

That pisses him off. "How many fucking times do we have to discuss this? A girl crying into the pillow as I hold her down isn't really my thing, Jane."

I lift my hands. "I know. I'm just pointing out your father and you were both sort of implicated."

"Well, it wasn't me. I clearly don't think human trafficking is acceptable. And I don't pay for sex. Jesus, I have some standards."

I pull his face to mine and receive a wooden kiss. One that suggests he is going to be angry with me for a while over the accusation.

"I can't believe my father would be so angry with him for it and act so indignant about it, and yet have gone himself."

"Henry could be lying."

"He could indeed be, but on the other hand, perhaps my father thought going was not such a big deal. The men at the club did start it out as a place for men to live out their fantasies. In their eyes it might have been legitimate prostitution, given that the women got paid. My father would hold with that easily." He wraps an arm around my shoulders. "Let me take care of this. I will speak to him."

We turn and walk into the castle proper. He grins wickedly when I look at him. "I know. 'It's a fucking castle, Dash,'" he says, trying to mimic my voice.

"It's ridiculous." I can't help but laugh at the way he does my voice.

"It's a family heirloom of sorts, nothing more. I don't live here and I don't believe in the pomp of this place. I like our life, Jane." He kisses my cheek and squeezes me into him. "Did you happen to notice the house in McLean at all when you were there? It's half the size of this, if not a third."

"No, it's not. I did see it's larger and fancier than I expected, but my heart breaking on the tile obscured everything else."

"Indeed." His voice deepens with remorse. "Well, I was hoping that you would contemplate coming to see it again. And maybe staying there, just overnight or something like a weekend. Binx likes it."

I turn. "You've brought my cat to your mansion? When?"

"Last month when you were in Libya for those ten days. I couldn't keep the two of them at the townhouse; it's not enough room for his highness. He felt that Sirius was in his space. So I packed them up and went to the country. They loved it. And Evangeline came to give me a hand out there, as my parents were in Monaco for the week. Binx loves her. And I mean, she is so very pretty. It was a great week."

I don't know how I feel about another woman, besides Mrs. Starling, being with my cat and my man.

He points. "Got you."

"That's not even funny, Dash." I swat him. "Letting another woman snuggle my cat is a surefire way to annoy me."

"What about me?"

I cock an eyebrow. "What do you mean?"

"You get mad because the cat is being loved by another woman, but not if I'm loved by one?"

He's completely joking, but I have to push it. "What are you? Fifteen?" I laugh and nudge him. "You are free to love whomever you want. Binx is my prisoner."

He chuckles and nods. "That is true. He's got a look about him like he's counting the days in captivity."

"He is." We walk into a large foyer that leads to a great room. Of course it isn't just dinner; it's a gala, as usual. I sigh and squeeze up next to Dash. Angie glances up from the man she's speaking to and gives me an approving nod.

Dash's mother and father both look our way from the group of people they are talking with. His mom laughs, maybe too loud and too excitedly. It's as if she's trying to fill the huge room. I almost glare back at her, but Dash whispers in my ear, "You should know she's very threatened by you. She acts like this because she can't compete with you. I swear to you, she isn't a bad person. She is quite self-conscious."

I lift my brow and my head, giving him a dubious look. "You don't have to lie. I don't care anymore. She makes me uncomfortable because she's so different from me. But I don't care if she hates me." I don't tell him that even a wicked mother-in-law is better than no mother at all. He'd think I was warming up to her, and I may never. I have just made up my mind to tolerate her and this bullshit way of life. It is all for him, after all.

He kisses my cheek, pressing his warm lips against me. "I love you, more than I know how to share."

The exact thing I need to hear.

We stroll into the room, greeting people. I see their eyes search for the ungodly engagement ring I sported last time we met with them. But I don't wear it anymore. To me that promise of love and forever was broken. It can't ever be repaired and I don't want it to be.

I want something new and fresh. Something that suits us. The us we have become.

This room full of people offering false smiles and fake hearts is not us either.

But it is him, and if I want him, I have to suffer through them. His arm around me or his hand at the small of my back feels better than anything in the world. There is nothing like being loved by someone willing to go to every length for you. He has already committed crimes and paid for things I don't even know about, to protect me.

I smile wide and shake hands, doing the same thing for him.

It's something I want to do.

It's part of the girl I am.

The one I want to be.

19. TATTERED BANNERS AND BLOODY FLAGS

My flats don't click the way her heels do. I am little next to her. But Cami looks up to me in every other way. She wants to learn the art of being a spy.

Cami gives me a smirk. "I know who Dash is. I know who his family is. I mean, everyone knows of them. It's like knowing who Sir Richard Branson is."

"I don't even want to talk about this." I roll my eyes as we round the corner of the building in downtown Taipei. It's been months since the last time I was at their castle, and I am still a little shocked one of his houses has friggin' turrets.

She laughs. "I figured. After knowing you and seeing what a Yankee you are, I was a bit surprised that your man was actually a Townshend. It's shocking, I won't lie."

I give her a look. "Are we done with this conversation and that little bit of judgment you are throwing down? Because the woman we are actually looking for is across the road from us, and I figured you might want to start tailing her so I can sneak inside her apartment and take a quick peek. I mean, we can totally stand here all day and chat about how ridiculous my life is. I like a sturdy Jeep and he likes Bentleys. I like hot dogs and he likes veal and game hen." I wrinkle my nose. "Game hen just makes it sound wrong."

She laughs and shakes her head. "The target is moving south. I will be over there if you need me."

I nod, still scowling. "How's Antoine?"

She glares back as she crosses the road.

"That was uncalled for, and I think you were a bit hard on her. She can't help but fan-girl over Dash. They all do. He's the next lord of the manor," Antoine torments me in my ear. "She was a tween when he was first an eligible bachelor."

"Shut up."

"Do you incorporate the mansions and castles in your sex games? 'Cause I feel like I would—lord of the manor. Do you play the kitchen wench or the girl in the dungeons? They have dungeons, right?"

"Like I would." My mind wanders the corridors of his words. I can barely speak and the discomfort twitching through me is actually visible.

"That was too much, wasn't it?"

I shake it off and scoff. "No. I just hate you." I don't think he can understand how inappropriate it was. That I haven't entirely shed the mind-run damage.

"You love me. Now go left and laugh aloud again. We have a situation. The man in front of you is quite a bad man. When you glanced at him, the facial recognition went crazy."

I glance at the chubby man and nod. "How much time do we have on the assignment?"

"Not enough. But I can remote-access his cell phone if you get close enough. Maybe he keeps a schedule. You know, that thing I tell you about all the time."

I laugh again, but this time it's a bit forced. "Then people could get into my schedule the way you do. I don't like being surprised by tech-savvy spies."

"Keep your voice down. He speaks English. He actually lived in Chicago awhile back. Did his degree there. He moved home and kept it honest for a few years, but now he's back. His uncle is a drug lord and runs some of the gambling in Macau."

"Yikes."

"Right. The man in front of you is known as Cheong Lou."

"Isn't that a fried noodle dish?" I mutter with my head low.

"In some variation. He must really like it. We don't have intel on that."

I sigh. "I feel like one of us is working a lot harder than the other."

"Oh, I know I do." He chuckles.

"Right, if you need to believe it's you, that's fine."

"This guy is actually on Interpol's list for most wanted in Macau. If you can make the kill in ten seconds or less, then do it. We need him gone, no matter what. It will actually start a small war there, which I know the CIA has been wanting for some time."

"I never trust anything they actually want."

I follow the chubby man into a building, pausing as he walks to the elevator. I turn and take the stairs, grateful I'm in flats. "What floor?"

"Nine."

I take a breath and kick it into high gear. When I get to the ninth floor, I am sucking wind, but I force my breath back to normal as I hurry along the corridor of the office building. My sunglasses and wig make it impossible for me to be recognized by the cameras in the halls and stairs.

When the elevator opens, I bump him back inside and shoot at the same moment. The silencer keeps the noise level down. I press the fifteenth-floor button and step back out. Mr. Lou falls to the floor. His eyes roll into the back of his head and I turn, hurrying back to the stairs.

I run for the exit and take the direction opposite to the one I need to be going. I circle the block before entering an older building. Ripping off my jacket and wig, I leave the building from a different door as a different person.

I circle the block again, but walking slowly and texting, like all the other people on the streets.

My slight ethnic look blends me in well here. I look similar to a Taiwanese girl, but maybe one who had some surgery to look more Western. It's something I have come across here a lot.

Breast enhancement and Western-style ass padding are advertised on every corner. The girls are beautiful here; they don't need to look Western.

But I am biased. I think women in Asia are stunning. I always have. I *think* I always have. It feels like something I have always thought. When I see a woman from Thailand or Bali or the Philippines, I can't help but admire her beauty.

"That was well done. I have wiped the security on the cameras in that building. They will be very shocked when they open the doors to that elevator."

"No one has found him yet?"

"No." Antoine laughs. "But of course, two old ladies are walking into the foyer as we speak. So it'll be those two sweet old ladies."

"You shouldn't assume old ladies are sweet. You never know."

"That's true. One day you will be an old lady."

"Exactly my point." I hurry to the place I was meant to be going from the very beginning. It's an office building with a bar downstairs. The man who owns it is an Australian who loves Taiwan. I imagine it has more to do with the fact he loves the women. Possibly because they are more forgiving than women in the West.

I enter the bar, smiling at the owner, who smiles back with lips too big for his face. He's got the ruddy cheeks of a man who spent a lot of years in the sun. His forehead is shiny and missing the blond hair the back of his head has.

"This guy is fugly as hell," says the voice in my ear.

I smile wider, trying not to laugh when the unattractive man turns to face me. "Hello, love. Can I help you?"

"I was wondering if you had any job openings?" I smile as I lift my sunglasses to the top of my head and bat my lashes.

I don't look completely Taiwanese, so he doesn't check me out the way he does the girl bending over the counter. "We don't. But you should come back in a couple weeks. We are losing some girls to college. You got bar experience?"

"I worked in a bar in Manhattan for a while."

His eyes widen. "Manhattan. That's impressive." He chuckles like he's mocking me maybe. "Then what brings you here?"

"My boyfriend is an engineer."

He nods, wiping the counter and still staring at the girl bending over. "Of course he is. They all are."

"I know. It's weird. So many factories here."

"My favorite is the BMW factory. Nothing is made how it should be anymore."

"Jane, you have three minutes before she is back." Cami whispers in my ear.

"Do you have a washroom?" I ask sweetly.

He winces. "Customers only."

I lean against the bar and tilt my head. "Shot of whiskey." I slap some cash on the bar.

He smiles at my haste and pours a shot, spilling some on the counter. I slam the shot back and place the glass down.

"Bathroom's in the back." He nods his head at the door I already know is the bathroom.

I walk slowly, sauntering until I reach it, then I hurry inside. The cameras freeze the moment I pass them, making it seem like I am in the bathroom. But I bolt back out, running to the back alley. I rush to the row of apartments I am trying to get to, climbing up onto the railing to the fire escape. This is the only way into this building without having to cross through a guard house.

I doubt anyone will even see me, thanks to the lines of laundry everywhere. They extend from each back deck where there are also crates of things Americans would have a stroke about. Food and extra dishes and a dog or two. All on the deck, getting covered in the pollution from the city.

I climb like a madwoman, swinging and jumping and pulling myself up. When I reach the fourteenth floor, I climb onto the balcony and enter the apartment. It is the only balcony that doesn't have laundry or anything on it.

When I get inside, I sigh and try to catch my breath.

The one thing I'm seeking is the computer in front of me in the barren apartment. There's also one camera set up on a tripod. One bed. One rack of clothes, all schoolgirl outfits and other varying forms of young-girl apparel.

I slap a strip of magnetic metal on the back of the computer, a sleek remote access for Antoine. The system is set up with outstanding security. We had to make it inside to get at it.

I turn but stop when I see a photo on the desk. I blink and look closer. The girl is young, maybe fifteen. She's got dark hair and pale-green eyes, filled with real tears. She pouts in the picture. It's a random Polaroid.

That draws my eyes upward to the cameras and the minimal furnishings. It's a den of slavery.

"She's in the building," Cami mutters.

"Okay," I whisper back.

Antoine whispers as well, "I am in too, and Jane, I might add, the cameras are everywhere. That tripod is nothing compared to the other shit here. I am talking everything, including a piss cam from the bar downstairs. That ugly fuck is in a bunch of pictures."

"I don't want to know." I speak through the acid burning in my throat.

Something about this is familiar. "Have you ever run facial recognition for me over the Internet, searching for porn?" I whisper it, but the words feel like they were shouted. They hang in the air.

"Yes."

"Did you find anything?" I take a breath. I know the answer.

"Yes." Humor has vanished from Antoine's voice. He sounds like he wants to talk about it as much as I do.

"Do you think it's why I ran away, or were they taken while I was a runaway?"

He pauses. "Before you ran."

"Are they gone from the web now?"

"Yes."

"Do you have a street address?" My heart is racing with panic and plotting, but I need to do this. I need it. I have to see where I came from and what brought me to this moment. It's part of letting go and moving forward and being a clichéd mess.

"Yes." I can hear the sadness and nausea in his voice.

"Send it the moment we get on the plane. Fly me to the place I came from. I don't want details."

"Okay." Antoine sounds like his voice is cracking.

"She's on the floor," Cami whispers. I'm grateful she doesn't hear Antoine and me speak.

I pull my other gun from my right holster. It's one made for assignments like this where you don't commit murder and leave a body behind. Even if this isn't the mission I am meant to be on.

I can't control myself.

When the door opens, I lift and pull the trigger. The dart hits the woman who has just entered in the eye, causing an instant seizure. Her other dark eye lands on me as her lips part to scream but the poison in the dart put her in shock and then she's dead. I pluck the dart from her head and stroll to the bathroom to wrap it in toilet paper and flush it.

I flush a second time just to be sure it's gone. She will look like she had a massive aneurysm.

Cami is there a moment later. "I thought we were keeping her alive. We haven't found out who is doing the abducting and trafficking."

"I fucked up." I don't offer anything else. Antoine remains silent as well. We turn and leave through the stairwell, running down in complete awkward silence.

At street level, we leave the building as if we don't know each other. The plan is that we will meet back at the airport. But that plan is gone. She is catching a commercial plane, and I am taking a private one to the place I am from. She just doesn't know that yet.

20. ELASTIC HEART

Maybe it's the flight from Taipei or the mental exhaustion of the past months, but seeing this house I feel something—a twinge of sadness.

I grew up poor, I expected that. Something about running away and being a drug addict and hooker made me think I might have already had low standards.

Walking through the neighborhood to get to this small and run-down house was a bit disappointing. The houses are all dilapidated, but it is just a plain low-income area. But the house itself is much worse.

It isn't dirty.

Just soulless and dull, like the light of day might never actually reach inside of it.

The walls haven't been painted in a long time and the roof has spackle on it, making the ceilings feel even lower than they are. Everything about the house is small and damp.

The whole town has a dampness to it. It's not anywhere I have ever been before and it's not somewhere I will ever be again.

There are no pictures of me on the walls. Not one. I expected that too.

But there are pictures of a woman with dark hair who might be half Filipino, or maybe half Thai. She is pretty and demure looking. Actually, she is beautiful. She's about fifty in the most recent ones. She poses and smiles the same in all the pictures.

Not what I expected.

The man in the photos is older than the dark-haired lady, maybe sixty-five in the most recent photo. He's white and looks like the sort of pervert who would frequent Thai brothels. The sort who might bring a purchased wife over from abroad. I don't think I look like either of them, but I might look like a mixture of them.

"Where is she from?" I ask softly, knowing the eye in the sky is still with me.

Antoine mutters back, "Her father was an American soldier during the Vietnam War. Her mother was full Vietnamese. She grew up in Taiwan; her mother was a maid. She came to America when she was twenty to be an au pair. She met your father then. He was forty and she was twenty." He stops short and I don't ask for more. I don't want to know her.

I am a bit surprised I am a quarter Vietnamese, though. It's sort of fascinating. My grandfather was in the American military too.

I turn my focus back to the house, noting there are brightly colored items about, lending a surprisingly cozy feel—elephants and doilies with swirling patterns and lamps that look like they might have been bought at a garage sale.

I examine room by room, while my insides burn. Everything about me is begging me to leave this house. I ran from it once for a very good reason, I can sense that now. My entire body has gone numb except for the burning sensation.

My heart is so constricted in my chest I don't know if it's actually beating normally or pounding and screaming that we, the version of me that was here and the version I am now, ran once and it's likely there was a reason to do so. And that reason might still be here.

But the warrior in me shakes her head. She wants to stand up and show them what we have become. That we are no longer scared little girls running away in the night.

I am separate from her, that sad little girl. She is like the twin sister I never had.

When I get into the bathroom, I flip open all the cupboards and drawers, looking at the normal things they have. They are not monsters as far as the contents of the house go.

"Jane, I know you want silence, but I need to know if you're okay every couple minutes, all right? I don't want you to freeze up."

I nod. I know he can see me in the mirror. I never removed the camera or earpiece. I want him to see it all, I don't know why. I guess so I am not completely alone in the horror show.

I sit on the toilet and stare at the wall, absolutely stunned by what I see. There's a picture of a beach house and sand. And written in the sand is "Tell me about the swans, the way the swans circle the stars and shoot across the sky. Tell me about the angels, the angels in your heart that remind you of the beauty in a day."

I swallow hard. Every time I peed I stared at those words until they burned in my brain to the point that even memory removal couldn't take them away. I glance at the door. "Maybe I shouldn't be here," I whisper.

"I already said that twice," Antoine whispers back.

My stomach threatens to empty itself as I stand on shaky legs. My heart begs me to leave the house, but my head rules, as usual. I turn and walk through the bedrooms, shocked at the lack of bad things. Jesus on the cross hangs in every bedroom. Dirt on the screens dims the old windows, but the rest of the house is immaculate.

I turn to leave, but as I pass a door, my inner alarms go off. I turn and face it, grabbing the handle and twisting. There are stairs behind it. Basement stairs.

Bad things are always in the basement. It's so clichéd.

I take the stairs like I am in a trance. I am, I suppose. When I get to the bottom of them, my breath hitches.

It's unfinished and mostly concrete down here. Everything is gray and dank. It smells just like something terrible is about to happen. It is nothing but dreary, dim lighting and doors that lead nowhere.

I realize I might have actually been showing Dash my life. The gray, dank space is what I knew.

Canned goods line a wall at one corner. Jars of peaches and pears and beets and beans. They all have dust on them, like she canned too much.

A washer, dryer, and hanging rack are in another corner.

The back wall has a couch. It's old and rotten looking, but I walk to it anyway. I walk so blindly I almost stumble over cords leading to a door in the corner under the stairs.

I know this door.

I know this gray, dank space.

I lower my gaze to the electrical cords on the floor and follow them to the door. The tiny windows provide almost no light and they are clear across the room, but I don't need much light to see this place and know it.

I lift my hand to the doorknob and hold it, trembling and begging myself not to open it. In my head there's a ring of light around the door, as if there were light inside the room. But my eyes do not see what my head says is there. Courage or stupidity takes over and my hand turns the knob.

It takes a second for the door to open, as my arm has joined the idea that I shouldn't see inside. When I do open it, I gag, heaving at the sight of the plain room. There is nothing in there but the tail end of the cords. However, my head is suddenly full of memories that fill the empty spaces of the dank basement.

The memories were never taken; they were blocked. I see that now as they all fill the empty space. Time spent in this horrid little room takes space up in my brain. The small room is the trigger. It is the memory bank I have sought for so many years.

I drop to my knees, still heaving and somehow now sobbing.

"Jane," Antoine whispers. "I'm here, Jane. It's okay."

I don't share what I see inside of my head, the things he cannot. Because I know deep down he has seen them. He has seen the photos my own father no doubt loaded on the Internet so his disgusting friends could see too. I would have been long gone by the time the Internet was around, but the pictures would have been there—here.

I close the door, turning around and leaning against it.

The song fills my head. The one I believed had come from Samantha Barnes. But it's not hers, it's mine.

My childlike voice fills the empty space in the dank room. I am singing it, alone in the corner with the Barbie he gave me. She's so pretty. Her name is Andrea. And I am singing the song to her. I don't know where I heard it. "Listen, listen to the wind and stone. Listen, listen to the sounds of old. Listen, listen as my hopes are drowned. Listen, listen to the sounds that bullets make of blood and bones. Where will you run today? How will you ever get away?" My voice cracks as I sing it.

With my tiny little fingers, I tie the purple scarf around Andrea's throat, making it fluff exactly the way my mom always does with her scarves.

I lift her up, looking her over. She's so pretty. I wish we were twins, Andrea and me. I named my Barbie that because of the beautiful girl at school. The girl with the blonde hair and the pretty face. She's exactly the sort of girl I wish I were. Her eyes match.

Even though my mom tells me that eyes are sisters and not twins, I wish my eyes were twins like Andrea's.

"Penny!"

We both look, me and the little version of me. My mother is there, with her dark silky hair and beautiful face. Her eyes are haunted, dead like fish eyes.

"I told you to clean your room before your dad gets home. You know he likes it clean." Her accent is thick, but her English is good.

The little version of me puts the Barbie in the room with the door. There are other things in there now, in my old memories. A camera on a tripod and a Polaroid picture that shows my face with tears in my eyes. My different-colored eyes. The pale-blue walls make me cringe. I hate powder-blue paint. I hate powder-blue walls.

I get up and follow the memory to the stairs.

Little me, little ten-year-old me, climbs the stairs. A picture on the wall catches my eye when I get to the top and open the door. It's of me and my mom at the beach. She's wearing a purple scarf and sunglasses. She looks happy, but in the reflection of her glasses I can see him. He's holding the Polaroid camera. That was the day she was singing it, "867-5309/Jenny." She sang it in the car. It was her favorite song.

I hate him.

Penny, the little girl I am not, walks into the kitchen and sits. Her mom is making a drink. A tequila sunrise with maraschino cherries. She pops one in her mouth and ties the stem off. She hands Penny one and Penny tries. She can't do it. I can't do it.

She leans across the counter and sips her drink, letting Penny have a sip too. "One day, my lucky Penny, me and you are gonna be happy. One day." She winks and sucks back the drink too fast. She takes cash from her pocket and leaves the room. I leave Penny at the table and follow our mom. She walks down the hall to my room. She pulls down the four-leaf-clover box and places cash inside it. She tucks it back into the nook in my closet.

She turns, stopping when the front door opens. Penny is watching from the hall; she and I are standing beside each other. We both see the look on her face. We both feel the same dread.

He's home from his trip.

Penny loses all the sweetness on her little face, and I force away the memory.

I close my mind off and look around the gray, dank house.

All the pictures of me are gone. Penny is gone. She ran away when she was fourteen. I remember sneaking out the dirty window. I remember the way my fingertips smudged the dirt as I opened the window and climbed out, taking the box of money with me.

It had seemed like so much money, but it didn't last.

The rest is history.

The attack is still blank, and I don't want to recall the other things. I don't need to remember living on the streets. Whatever the trigger is for that, I am fine without finding it.

My father was a pedophile and my mother was an immigrant who never stood a chance at getting away. She wasn't strong as I was. I pause at the doorway, as I am about to leave.

"Where is my fath—the man who lives here?"

"Dead. He died a few years ago."

I have a terrible feeling I know the answer but ask anyway. "How?"

"Stabbed in Atlantic City. He was there gambling."

"Did you have him killed?" I ask. It isn't something I would put past Antoine, not in a situation like this. I would kill someone like that man without even a slight provocation.

"It wasn't me." He leaves it there, offering nothing else. I wonder if it was Rory. If he had ever done me a kindness like this one.

"Is she alone, then?" I don't want to call her *mother*. She was not my mother. She was Penny's mother and even then not much of one.

"Yes. She still works as a housekeeper at a hotel. She's been there for years."

"Is she happy?"

"I don't think so. She has a simple life. She is alone all the time."

"Tell the driver to go. I want to walk for a bit," I whisper as I leave the house, leaving it in the past where it belongs. The few memories I have of it are bad and I want them gone. The way they were before.

But like always, there are a million things in my brain that I want gone. If I get rid of those, everything else goes.

My career. My love. My friends. All I will have is the distinct feeling I know that black-and-white cat and I love him. Beyond that I will have nothing. Nothing good or bad.

It's a big decision to make.

I had hoped to enter the house and kill the monster. I'm a little disappointed by the fact I am not going to get that opportunity.

"You all right?" Antoine asks in my ear.

"I will be." I walk along the broken concrete of the random street in the random town. Not Atlanta. Not Andrea. Not at all who I thought I was.

I make it off the block when I see him.

He turned out not to be what I expected either.

When I walk to him his face is twisted, not just in anger but also in disappointment. Maybe in me or maybe for me.

I click off the camera and the earpiece. "You killed him, didn't you?" This is the piece of Dash I have been missing. This is the darkness inside him. He has taken a life against his oath as a doctor and against his nature as a human.

Dash looks down, pressing his lips together. "I didn't know the details. I never lied to you. Antoine came to me and I wanted to be able to say I didn't know your name and I didn't know who you were. I wanted deniability. I didn't even know where this house was until recently. I swear."

"I'm not mad."

He sighs. "I had to do it. You know that, right?"

I nod, but I'm a little worried about him. "Have you killed other people?"

"His blood is the only blood that stains my hands. It was a terrible thing to do, but the pictures were too much. I couldn't do it. I couldn't let him live. I am not strong enough. I went to confront him. Antoine traced his credit cards. I only wanted to confront him about your fate. But I got so angry—" His hands tremble and his eyes turn dark, scary dark. His brow is so furrowed I don't know that it will lift again. The haunted look in his eyes makes sense. The things he has done for me. I realize then the darkness inside my lover's heart was put there because of me.

"None of it matters now." I step into him, pulling him to me. "Thank you, though."

"What for?"

"Taking it all away. I wish it were gone again. I wish I didn't know." I think about the story I made up for Samantha Barnes and realize I must have known all along. I must have had an idea.

"Taking it away doesn't work. You are a naturally curious person. You solve the crime no matter how hard I hide it. You solve the crime and I look like an asshole for hiding shit from you."

I laugh weakly into his chest. "I want to go home. I want to forget all of this."

"What about her?"

"She was Penny's mother. She's not mine." I link my fingers into his.

"Penny?" He looks confused. He honestly never knew my name.

"That was my name."

"I hate the name Penny. I like Jane."

"Even Jane Doe?"

He chuckles. "We gave you a proper English name. Spears is very respectable. He was also the doctor who first operated on you when you were found."

"I think Townshend will suit me more."

He pauses, looking down on me. "You do?" His eyes fill with hope and whatever is left over from talking about him murdering a man in cold blood.

"I love you, Dash. I have always loved you. I will always love you. Even if I were to get my memories wiped again, I would find you again. Every time."

He smiles but says nothing. He kisses me softly and whispers, "Then let's go home."

I have a feeling "home is where the heart is" will become something of a thing for us. He has likely moved us into the big house. The mischief in his eyes suggests it.

We walk to the car he has down the road.

Walking away from something bad and toward something new.

21. MARRY YOU

The big house is not my type of house. But I like the pool. I drop my robe on the sun chair and jump in. The cool water refreshes. I swim with the huge wolfhound running laps around the deck. His whine means he's contemplating coming in.

"Sirius, go lie down," Dash commands. The dog tucks his tail and finds his huge pillow, his docility a ridiculous sight.

Not like the black-and-white cat that ventures out from under the table and chairs to give us an indignant look. He strolls the deck, fishing his white toes in the water. It makes me smile until Dash pulls his T-shirt off and walks to the edge of the pool.

Then I sigh.

Perfection.

Binx runs when Dash dives in, swimming underwater to me. I try to swim away, but he is a much stronger swimmer than I am. He pulls me down to him, wrapping himself around me. We surface and his wet lips find mine.

I encircle my legs around his waist and cling to him. "My mother says the wedding is still going to be the wedding. We are not getting off without the hoopla."

I laugh and lean back, letting my upper body float, but my legs stay wrapped around him. "I figured. I'm not going to fight it. Dash, marrying you is the only part of the entire day I give a rat's ass about. The rest she can have."

"Are you happy, Jane?"

I stare up at the blue sky and wonder if anyone has ever asked me that question. "I am."

In the sparkle of the sunlight, a star fills my gaze. I lift my head and cock an eyebrow.

He's holding an engagement ring over my head. It isn't the same as the one before. It's old and larger, the sort I would never have thought of as an engagement ring. "I don't know how the hell we ended up here. How this worked out even after everything fell apart. I only care about going forward. I want every day to feel like this one. I know they won't all feel this way. I know we'll fight. I know we'll disagree. I know my mother will always be an issue—"

I laugh, cutting him off.

He smiles at that one too, blushing a bit. "But I also know that if we can make it through what we have already, those other things are nothing. I have never met a woman your equal, Jane. I have never met someone who manages to survive the way you have, but then live and live well. You evoke my respect and my loyalty without ever saying a word. I used to think it was my job to protect you from everything. But now I see you don't need that. You are a hero in your own right and I love you even more for it."

My heart is racing. Not because he's saying fancy things to me. Not because he's proposing. But because for the first time ever, I feel like he sees me. I slip my fingertip into the circle. He pushes the ring onto my finger—of course it's a perfect fit.

He is a perfect guy. They don't actually screw things like this up. The advantage to having yard surrounded by woods and no neighbors for miles is that you can celebrate an engagement in a pool.

You can kiss until you don't think your lips can take one more. You can rub and touch until you both need to exit the pool for a beach chair. You can make love in your backyard with no one watching you.

If ever there was a moment for slow and passionate, this is it.

He lays me down on the chair and slips between my legs, dragging my bathing suit bottom down. He enters me before we have contemplated more foreplay. It's too desperate for that. When he's inside me, he flips up my bathing suit top to expose my breasts. Our breath hitches together as our bodies writhe in the sea of bliss.

When we finish, we lie there a moment longer, holding on to each other and the moment we have made magical.

"Every second from now on will be the best in my life," I whisper and kiss his cheek.

"For me too." He scoops me up, carrying me inside to the shower. Water pours down on us, massaging us almost, it's so intense.

I walk from the shower, staring at the large oval ring with the diamonds all over it. It's too fancy and too expensive for me, and yet I love it. It's different.

Like us.

I take a quick picture of it and send it to Angie. She texts back and I can only imagine the series of sounds she's making—*ochs* and squeals.

She sends a picture too, of a guy looking down. I recognize him immediately and carry the phone to Dash. "Who is this guy? I saw him at your parents' place."

"That's a cousin. His name is Charles Jardine. He's from Scotland."

"Of course he is." My roll my eyes. "He and Angie are dating, I think. She sent me this picture. And from the background, I'd say that is her house. She has flowery wallpaper like that."

He leans in, looking at the floral wallpaper. "Maybe, but that particular paper is in my mom's bathroom upstairs."

"Oh, dude. She had sex in the bathroom at that party?"

He chuckles. "Apparently." He points at the black underwear on the floor behind poor Charles, who doesn't realize she has snapped a photo of him as he looks down at the buttons on his shirt.

I press her name on my phone and stroll into the kitchen to find food.

"Och, that is some ring, Janey. Ya must have nearly shit."

I laugh. "I was in the pool, so no."

"Ya filthy thing. Shitting in the pool over a ring." She laughs harder.

"So Charles, huh?" I don't want to talk about shitting in the pool.

"Oh my, that is some lad, that is. He's a rugged man from an area just outside Edinburgh. It's been a pretty fantastic two weeks." She sighs. "He's exactly the sort of man I need. Exactly what a man ought to be—successful and weird, in the right ways. Not the scary ways, though. He folds his socks when he takes them off."

"That is weird." I can't help but smile for her, even if she is just in the beginning stages. "It must feel nice to be dating again."

"It feels nice to be shagging again."

I laugh. "And that."

"That is the important stuff." She sends me another picture, making my phone buzz again. "I sent a picture of the family home. He's right rich, Janey."

"Not everyone thinks rich is important."

"Tell me that again when we're sixty years old and taken care of. Everyone cares about rich a' some point. His clan is well known in the country. His family owns a shipping-something-or-other."

I open a yogurt and spoon some into my mouth, thickening my words. "But you know love is more important."

"Love is everything." She yawns. "And I have to get back to work. We are starting some test runs soon. I'll let ya know how the poor subjects fare."

"You know how they'll fare."

"Aye, I do. I know they'll think it's remarkable and amazing. I remember when ya first went in. Ya thought the sun and moon set in me arse."

"I still do."

"Kiss the cat and the dog and Dash." She laughs and hangs up.

Dash walks in wearing nothing but pajama bottoms. "Is she well then?"

"She seems to be. She is pretty happy that he's a Scot like her and he's rich."

He nods and takes my yogurt, eating a big bite of the small cup and passing it back nearly empty. "Can we hire a cook?"

I wrinkle my nose, almost prepared to say no, but then I glance about the huge house. "Yeah. I think we can."

"Can we hire Mrs. Starling?"

"No. Weirdo. She has her things she does. She doesn't want a permanent job. And no Evangeline, not since you made the creepy joke."

He grimaces. "I would never hire a young cook. Cook's position can only be filled by an old, patient lady. She has to be motherly and cut the crusts off your toast."

"Oh my God. You are kidding, right?"

"No." He grins, drinking the orange juice right from the carton and licking his delicious lips. The side with the large incisor sticks out a bit, making me want to suck it.

I blink myself out of the Dash daze and mutter, "But then they'll be here all the time, and then we can't have sex in the kitchen or living room or random stuff like that. Is that what you want?"

He pauses, holding the jug. "Is that an option?"

"If we lived alone, it could become one."

"Okay. But one of us has to learn to cook properly."

I shrug. "We can just have sex in our room, then."

"That's probably the right idea. It's not sanitary to have one's bare arse on the table or counters anyway."

"No." I step toward him, taking the jug of juice from his hand. I take a big swig and swallow it as he plants juicy kisses on my neck.

"What's the plan for the day?"

I press my lips together and think. "I have to talk to Antoine and Cami, find out where we are in the weapon-slash-drug lord situation in Panama. And I have to figure out how we can find the asshat who is trafficking the girls in Taiwan. I screwed that one up."

He leans back. "You made a mistake?"

"Never. I just killed someone before I got the intel from them. But I wouldn't change a thing." The image of the Polaroid haunts me still if I'm not careful to keep the memories in check.

He looks concerned. "Why did you go back to active duty?"

"I needed it. It makes me feel strong and in control, and I needed to feel that. Everything was spinning out of control in my head, and going back fixed it. I knew I was done with the mind runs. I can't help in that project anymore. And you and I were not in the place where I was feeling good about ditching my pension." I take another drink.

He takes the jug and sips from it. "But now?"

"Now, I don't know. I need to finish off the projects I have going. I need to catch the bad guys. It's my gig."

"You mean kill the bad guys," he scoffs, and his eyes turn haunted for a moment.

I lean in, kissing his orange-tasting lips. "Sometimes the world is just a better place without those people. We don't use warrants. We don't worry about rules and laws. We just take away the bad people who are making the world a worse place. It's the best unit for me. Every mission is about stopping something heinous. Half the time the friggin' CIA knows about whatever we are hunting, but they let it run because they need a bigger fish. The bad guys die. The good guys are freed from the situations they have found themselves in."

"When will you be done saving the whole world?"

"I don't know. I can't save it all, I know that. I can only stop the few things I know about."

He leans in and kisses me once more. "Can we talk about the possibility of retirement? For us both?"

I wrinkle my nose. "Why?"

Dash looks hesitant, but he says the thing plaguing him. "The baronetcy comes with things—demands and expectations. My father is stepping down. His name is on the list after all. He knew it. He thought by distancing himself from my very guilty brother, he would be left alone. He is actually pompous enough to believe that his title will earn him clemency."

I cock an eyebrow, pausing all my judgments and thoughts. "Are you serious?"

"He's an idiot. That much is true. But you have to remember he's the last of a dying breed. The men and women born in the forties and fifties were still quite the gentlefolk."

"I expected your father to be a dipshit. Have you met him? He grooms more than any single woman I know. He fake-tans. It's weird. The part I'm asking about is the title. We really have to take it on?"

He nods, as concern crosses his brow.

"I'm the worst person for this. I am actually the worst-case scenario. I am no Princess Di. I am the exact sort of girl families like yours run from. You can't expect me to take a title from your mother?"

"She becomes the dowager, Jane. We have an obligation to my family. You will be Lady Townshend. You will be my wife. I will take this title and we will be responsible. That is what is happening."

The lump in my throat burns, but I don't argue. Accepting who he is to the world is half the battle of accepting who I am and who we are.

"You will be a beautiful bride and the world will call you humble and sweet."

"Assassin. They will call me assassin if they ever find out."

"A sharpshooter is not an assassin. And you forget I have blood on my hands too."

I step close to him. "How is your baggage worse than mine?"

My question elicits a laugh as he plants another orange-flavored kiss on me. "My baggage is lifelong. Yours was fairly solvable. It isn't hard to walk away from terrible things. But to walk from a thousand years of lineage is pretty impossible. My family came to the UK with William the Conqueror. My great-great-great-great-great-great-grandfather was King Richard the Lionheart's first cousin, and his father had been in the line of succession as a prince. My entire family has spent their lives as part of this. Sometimes they were in and other times they were out. Depending on the king. Most recently we were out and bought our way back in, very typical for the times. One thousand years of tradition. I cannot help but be proud, Jane. It's who I am."

His words, the ones I have been chanting all along, sting when they're thrown back in my face.

"Then it's who I am too." I nod, against my better judgment. I have no desire to be in the spotlight. Yet I would rather be a branch on his tree filled with great and terrible things, than be on the tree I belong to. Starting over with him is insane, but I want him and this is who he is.

He leans in, kissing me softly again. "We take it day by day. My brother and father will be cleared of this. They won't be charged. They will plead out and testify in privacy that they have witnessed what they have. But on the off chance that there are damages assessed later in civil court, they are both stepping away from the baronetcy."

"And adding me and my past to it, that seems like the right choice?"

"You are an orphan named Jane Spears who lost her family in a tragic accident. Kindly people in an orphanage raised you. You have a brilliant military career and everyone who knows you loves you. You are a better candidate than any one of my family members."

I give him a look. "You created that lie."

"It's the truth. Check the records." His green-gray eyes sparkle with humor and hope.

"No one will ever dig up Penny, the hooker who was left for dead?"

"No one but you and me and Antoine. No one else knows. It's been seventeen years. Records of minors are sealed, and besides, no one knew your name. The moment you looked at the documents, Antoine destroyed them. He had to actually dispatch a team to burn handwritten records. The pictures are gone. There is no record of you existing. Antoine stole the pictures from your mother's house. She doesn't even have a school picture of you, and the yearbook photos only go to thirteen. After that you were gone. At thirteen you look like any kid with a bit of an ethnic bloodline. Trust me, this has been wiped. It was only ever saved for you to see if, at some point, any of this came back to haunt you or you remembered anything. The files can't even be retrieved now." He kisses my cheek. "Your name is Jane Spears, Master Sergeant. You have created this life that you have."

I step back and process all of that. It makes sense, even to my doubting brain.

22. WEDDING DRESS

I hurry up the steps to the door and look back at Angie. She shakes her head. "I think ya might be off base by being here. Ya pissed Georges off by canceling the wedding. Lady Townshend said he was very angry."

I disregard her words—I love France, I always have. We have been here on missions a few times and it's always made me happy. I love pastries and coffee and late dinners at small bistros.

I open the door and walk in, mesmerized by the beautiful dresses. I was so out of sorts in Manhattan, no wonder I didn't notice the dresses. But here they are laid out simply and the design is the art. There is no fancy shop and fancy staff. There is one lady. "Bonjour!" she greets us and smiles.

I smile. "Hi. I'm Jane Spears."

"I am Celeste." It takes her a second to realize who I am, but when she does, her eyes widen. "Spears? You are here for za dress. You came for it?" Her English is still understandable through her thick accent.

"I did. If that's okay."

"But of course. Georges was certain you would come." I love the way she speaks—with the accent of perfect Parisian French. She hurries to the back and returns with the massive dress bag and hanger. She nods at the changing room. "We are very ready for your fitting."

There are no ladies or underwear or anything. I hurry to the room and step in. She comes with me, obviously. I undress, feeling less awkward with her than I did with the other ladies. She is efficient and fast at helping me into the dress. She doesn't coddle me or gush. She doesn't give two shits about who I am. This is a job and I appreciate that.

It's nice not having Dash's mom here either.

As the saleswoman clasps the last hook at the top of the back, she spins me around and straightens everything, fluffing out the dress. She smiles and steps back. There are no mirrors in the room so I have no notion of what she is seeing.

She opens the door and walks out, into the main area. Angie lifts her hand to her lips. Tears fill her eyes. I walk out, swishing the entire way. When I turn, my lips part as tears fill my eyes. "I'm a princess," I whisper like a moron. But I can't even help myself. I am a princess. For once I am fit for the social class I am marrying into.

The dress has a white satin choker round my throat—then sheer material down the chest to the heart-shaped neckline. Lace and pearls cover the sheer fabric of the bodice so my skin is visible, but the design is so heavy that the scars are not.

The bottom puffs out like a ball gown. The design of the corset is continued down the middle of the pleats in the front, and the firm pleats continue around the rest of the skirt in white satin and lace. She lifts my hair, revealing the back. The pearl buttons start at the choker and go all the way to the skirt. The sheer material is also heavy with design in the back so the scars are covered in the same way.

I am covered head to toe, but I feel beautiful and sexy. "It's perfect."

Angie walks to me, nodding. "More than."

The French lady smiles. "Georges will be so pleased. He made it perfectly. It's *magnifique*."

I smile wide, suddenly eager to wear it in public. It's a feeling I didn't expect. I want Dash to see me in it and for him to be proud to be marrying me.

She leads me back inside, starting the daunting task of undoing the buttons. "Your scars are very thick. You have been at war? Georges said it was war."

"I have. I have been at war a few times."

"Zis one here, it's bad." She runs her nail along the thickest of them on my back. No one has ever touched my scar that way before, out of curiosity. I don't show them to people because I don't want pity, but she doesn't have that in her tone. She sounds like she admires me.

I remember the moment I got the scar and smile, lost in it for a second. "I was twenty-two when that happened. I was in Afghanistan and a man had worn a bomb into a building. I followed him, stalking him. I was just trying to figure out where the remote detonator was for him to blow the building. The moment I had him in my sights, a man leaped from a doorway and stabbed me in the back. I broke his neck and managed to kill the man with the bomb before he detonated it. I defused the bomb, but then I passed out from loss of blood. I woke up in the infirmary. The Afghan people had saved me. They knew I had saved their lives. So they carried me out to my team and told them what I had done." She doesn't feel sorry for me and that makes me proud of the scars. Proud of them in the way a man would be.

She looks over my shoulder. "You are very brave for a girl."

I laugh and nod. I love that statement. We're all girls in a shop like this.

Her cheeks flush. "I just mean—"

"I know. It's true. Not a lot of girls show how brave they are."

"But we are all brave, you zink?"

A peaceful smile crosses my face as I relive all the moments that equaled heroism in my head. They do not all belong to me, but they start with a small girl climbing through a dirty window. "I do. I have met the bravest girls in all the world. Girls who died to save other girls. Girls who would kill to stop a monster. Girls who turned and ran into the fight instead of away from it. I have met them all."

"And you are all of zem?"

My wide smile returns. "I guess so—well not the girl who died obviously. But I have been in the position to have to be all of them. That changes you. You cannot escape who you will become when it comes down to your life or someone else's."

"I believe zis is true." She pulls the dress down and lets me step out of it. I pull on my clothes as she bags it up again. "We will ship it to za wedding. Georges is invited, so he will dress you."

"*Merci.*" I smile.

She bows slightly and carries the dress from the room.

We leave without escaping the French way of hugging and kissing strangers. She waves after us as we hurry down the street.

"I hope ya get an amazing cake. English cakes really are some of the best, but wedding cake is always shite."

That puts a look on my face. "Really?"

"Shite."

I nudge her the way Angie always nudges me. "How are things with Charles?" I say his name with a snooty affect.

She sighs and says his name like she is saying her very favorite thing. "Charles. He is amazing. I could love him. Easily."

I think she already does but doesn't want to be the first one to say it. It isn't like she hasn't been burned before.

My cell phone rings, and when I pull it out, I wrinkle my nose. "Hey?" I don't know why Antoine would be calling me.

"I have something. I don't know what you want to do with it, but I have it."

"What do you mean?"

He sounds funny. "It's a name. That facial recognition program, I ran your guy from the store, the one who followed you out the night you were attacked."

My insides tighten. "Yes?"

"His name is Denis MacDougal. He's a baby broker. His face didn't flag in the system, because he's never been caught. But he has been under surveillance for a while for tax evasion. So he flagged with the IRS. I have an address. It's in Montana."

My mouth is dry but I manage to speak, just manage. "Send it." I look at the text on my phone. "Get one of the ladies to book me on a plane home to Missoula. Have Cami meet me there as well as the ground team for backup." I hang up the phone and turn, giving Angie a look. "I have to go home."

She pouts. "We need French lingerie for yer wedding. It's a must."

"The dress actually comes with it. I tried on the lingerie in New York. Remember?"

She nods, but I can see she is not really recalling. Her memory is not detailed like mine is. "No. But I trust ya remember. Ya remember everything, and that would have scarred ya for life."

I laugh, still unsettled by the phone call. "Yeah, it did." I hug her and flag a cab. "I will see you in London, then."

"At the church!" She sings her words, knowing I hate that.

I get in the cab the moment it stops. "You'll be all right, right?"

She waves me off. "I'll get the Métro back to the hotel and see ya in a few weeks."

"The airport, *s'il vous plaît*."

The driver nods as I dial Dash. I don't want to keep things from him.

"Hello, my love." He sounds more English now than American. It's a bit funny watching the layers of lies peel away.

"Antoine call you?" I ask softly.

"No." He sounds confused.

"He called me. He found something in Montana."

He pauses. "Montana? I can't even imagine what it is. Is it something to do with Rory? Please lie and tell me it has nothing to do with Rory, or his past."

"No. It's a broker, someone avoiding taxes who has been under the scrutiny of the IRS."

"Are you lying and telling me this because I told you to?"

I laugh. "No."

The cabbie's eyes watch me in the rearview. I smile at him, not letting myself suspect he's also a spy and listening to me for something other than jollies. The paranoia of the mind runs has got to end.

"A broker? Is this code or did you actually want to invest money or something?"

"He deals in babies."

Dash is silent for another moment. "Dear God, how did he find him? Antoine scares me sometimes."

"I know. I'm headed there now. Ground team support and all."

"Jesus, Jane. This is serious. Are you going to take him down with people watching?"

"Yes. I will take him like the scum he is, like any other mission."

"Only this one is personal."

"Very." I nod, and look out the window as the city passes by. "So I have to be careful."

"I will meet you. Let me get Mrs. Starling to pop over to the house and stay here with the kids." His words make me smile as I hang up and look out the window some more.

I'm glad he's coming. He can't come to the mission, that would give away too much, but he will be there for the after part. And I won't be alone.

23. A DOG'S LIFE

Do we have any idea of ETA?" Cami speaks into her mic, but gives me a look before she glances around the bush we have been hiding in so the surveillance guys can do their job.

Dwayne, the giant wanker, as Cami calls him, murmurs into the earpiece, "We got movement, but I can't trace what it is."

"So what is the plan?" Cami asks.

I bite my lip, looking at the dark farmhouse in the middle of the huge field. The bushes and trees we are hiding in are the only real cover. The two military guys behind me standing guard are huge and might be seen easily, but I don't want to go in without them. I don't know how I will react to such a personal mission.

I nod my head at the small house. "We take the house silently—take him into custody if that's him that they are sensing in the house. We wait for Antoine to verify his identity and then we hunt down the evidence. There's no warrant and we are interrupting an IRS investigation, so we need to be silent and fast and efficient." I turn and look at the two men behind me. "Cami and I will go for the home office;

you two search the entire residence. I don't want a couch cushion left unturned. Check for hiding places, wall paneling, and heat sources."

Cami lifts one of her perfectly manicured eyebrows. "IRS isn't going to be pissed at us?"

"They will be if we don't hand them their case on a platter."

"Then we better get the platters ready."

Antoine laughs too hard at the cheesy joke. I roll my eyes, but Cami smiles. "Like that one, did ya?"

"I did," he says softly so we can all hear.

She grins at me, but I roll my eyes. "Focus. We have one shot at this. And he's been a career criminal. He is ready for this. He's ahead of the game."

Cami nods, no longer smiling at all.

"You are good to go. There's no movement," Antoine mutters. "Dwayne is showing the person inside as localized to one area."

I make a forward motion and we all burst from the bushes, where we have been sitting for an hour waiting for the sun to completely go down. Criminals get amazing sunsets in Montana.

If it weren't for the night-vision goggles, I wouldn't be able to see a damned thing. It's blindingly dark. We enter the farmhouse from the back door after disabling the alarm with the weird magnetic thing Antoine tried explaining.

A dog barks, but I can tell it's confined to one room. I would bet my money on that room being the one we are seeking. "We'll take care of the dog. You guys search." I grab the fire extinguisher off the wall next to the oven and carry it with me as the two men leave and start the search.

"What's that for?" Cami whispers.

I lift a finger to my lips. The movement detected in the house was not a man, but a large dog. I nod at the door we have just come in. "Be ready to open that."

Cami stares at me, not saying anything. I carry the extinguisher to the room with the barking dog. I crack the door, spraying the extinguisher at the massive beast. He cowers, pissing on the floor. In the dark I can smell it and also see it with my night-vision goggles. I spray again, making him whimper. I kick the door open wider and step back. He runs past me. "*Now!*" I shout and Cami opens the door. The dog runs yelping from the house.

"What did you do to him?" She asks like she's upset.

"I scared him. I didn't hurt him. I don't like hurting animals. But this is a dog whisperer in a can. It always scares the piss out of them."

She looks at the puddle on the floor and nods. "I see that."

"The dog was holed up here, which makes me think this is the room." We both start searching the small office. I place the remote access pad on the computer.

Cami finds something and holds it up. "A list of names and dates. It doesn't say anything else." I stare for a moment before finding the date with a name next to it. *Wendy 11/27/98*. That is two weeks after the attack on me.

This is the man who attacked me. "Take a photo and see if the timeline matches other abductions."

Cami takes the photo and sends it directly.

"Got it. Hold tight and give me a couple minutes. I made a list of baby abductions a while back." Antoine sounds excited.

I give Cami a look, and whisper, "This is the very thing I adore about working with Antoine. He's obsessive-compulsive when it comes to fine details like these. And a genius with numbers, patterns, and probabilities. I like competent people."

We spend the next several minutes checking the office thoroughly.

Cami looks at the doorway. "How much more is there to look at?"

"The other two have it." I point at the computer. "It's likely he doesn't have anything here. Antoine will be in his bank records and from there we might find the answers we are looking for."

Antoine confirms what I have just said. "His bank records have been pulled by the varying teams following him. He has a few suspicious deposits early on. Back in November of 1998, for example, he deposited twenty-five thousand dollars over the course of a month. Several small deposits. I think he thought that he could escape the eye of the IRS with small deposits. Like he could say he sold several things. Or something like that." Antoine speaks like he is distracted by something else.

"In '98 did he escape their notice?"

He pauses before speaking. "He did. He wasn't flagged for four more years. He slipped away somehow. There are no notes on the account because it's so old. He went under the radar again for a while, but got noticed last spring making some large purchases, too large for his income. They've been building a tax evasion case against him for several months and are going in for the kill. I think that's our best bet for a trial too. Black-market baby sales won't get him a lengthy prison term. That lawyer who got caught a couple years ago in San Diego got five years and served one. But tax evasion in the United States is worse than killing a cop."

"Maybe we should take care of the problem."

"Ha!" he shouts, ignoring my idea. "I got it!" He chuckles into our ears as we stand there awaiting the news so we can formulate a plan. "His bank accounts aren't in the United States. When he caught the eye of the IRS in 2002, he started using offshore accounts under different names, that's why they lost him in the system. His incomes there all have names on them, weird ones like Rose or Kennedy or Jameson. And they are all wire transfers. I bet he thinks he's invincible because he uses offshore accounts. All I have to do is link those accounts to his ones here and the IRS will have him. The names of every person who transferred him money from 2002 to today are there. And he has a lot of money, far more than he can account for. If the accounts are linked, then I can prove the money came from people who adopted. The list of baby abductions only has four matches, but the people who adopted the babies will have records of the adoption. They might not even realize they went about it illegally."

I sigh, annoyed that I won't have the answers I want, but then Antoine speaks softly, in my ear only. "The largest deposits he made in November '98 were several checks cashed from a lady named Wendy Cassopolis. She lives in Maryland. She has a daughter who is seventeen named Whitney Cassopolis. I have just texted you the address."

"Do we have enough to get this guy?"

"We have enough for the IRS to get him. I can fudge some shit and make it look like he hid his trail a little, but not nearly as well as he thinks he did. The moment I finish these changes, they will have him. The adoption dates will match the payments and he will owe at least seven hundred thousand in back taxes."

"He cut the baby from one girl, Antoine. Cut her baby from her belly."

"There is no way to prove that unless you remember."

It's disheartening but I agree. "Okay, let's go then. Tell the team to get out of here before he comes home."

Cami interrupts me from the doorway. "Should we get the dog back?"

"No. Let him know we are coming for him." I close the door to the office and walk from the house, putting the fire extinguisher back on the wall.

The four of us stalk quietly across the field. The dog is nowhere to be found.

I wish the man had been there. I wish I had killed him.

When we get to the trees we were hiding in, we run for the road as a team, back to the vehicles and the rest of our company.

"No movement, Master Sergeant," one of the guys says in my ear as I approach. "No surveillance detected either."

"Odd," Cami says and climbs into the Humvee, catching her breath and giving me a look. I have to wonder if she suspects there is something more to the story about why we are here. She's a smart cookie and we never work a lot of American soil. Add to that the fact we never work cases like these, and I have to assume she is suspicious.

We always work the ones in which no one cares about a trial or evidence. We are the branch of the government that shoots first and answers questions later.

I sit in the front passenger seat on the way back to Missoula. And maybe it's the scenery in Montana, the openness and huge skies, or maybe it's the fact I am nearing the end of something, but I am nostalgic.

I am lost in the ending of a person who saved me.

The Humvee stops outside my hotel and I nod at Cami. "See you soon. Don't forget to get the reports on this filed. Make certain we have something special to give the IRS so they don't come looking for answers."

I stroll into the hotel, leaning against the wall as the elevator goes up, and in the mirror opposite me I stare at the different-colored eyes I have. I can't help but wonder where I got them.

When the elevator dings, I stroll to the door I have been daydreaming about entering all day.

He opens it before I even lift my hand to knock. He grins and flashes that crooked smile. "Why, hello."

A soft sigh falls from my mouth when I see his face. He is like going home, no matter where it is. He offers me his hand and a look. "How was it?"

I drop my hand in his and let him lead me inside. "Well, it was a bust in one way and not in another."

"What do you mean?" He closes the door and pulls me to the bathroom of the fancy suite, where he has already filled the bath.

"I think we found what we were looking for, but I don't know if the evidence is enough. I don't know if he will suffer the way he should." I can smell the scented salts and start to melt in anticipation of the feel of that hot water.

"Did you find anything about the child?" he asks as he peels my shirt and pants from me, helping me into the water before he undresses and climbs in after me.

"Yes." I turn and lie back on his chest, relaxing into him and the huge tub. "The woman who possibly adopted my daughter is named Wendy Cassopolis. She lives in Maryland. Whitney is the girl's name. She's seventeen."

"What's the bad part?"

"He wasn't there, the broker. His house was eerily calm. No heat sources except a damned dog, no hiding places, no nothing. So we searched with a fine-tooth comb, and barely came up with a way to frame him for the crimes he has actually committed, but covered up."

"What a disappointing way to end it. I suppose you wanted to break his neck?" He dunks a cloth in the water and squeezes it, pouring water over my chest.

"Yup, though I like knives better than neck-breaking. But I would have done that."

He lifts a finger as a disappointed tone fills his voice and his body tenses. "Wrong answer. I want to hear that the only thing you wanted was to see him cuffed. Which you will. Even if Antoine has to make something up about it all and frame the man, he will see time for what he has done."

It isn't comforting. Not like watching the man bleed all over the carpet and his eyes lose the light of a soul.

That is a fine ending for a foul man.

But I keep that to myself.

24. ALL OF ME

I glance about the scary church they call an abbey from the bench against the wall. The whole place creeps me out. "What's an abbey?" I ask softly.

Cami gives me a cockeyed look. "Why do you think I know that?"

"You're British."

She rolls her eyes. "Funny. I think it means something big or important. Like more than a regular church."

It's massive and in downtown London, so that makes me dislike it even more.

I don't love cities. I would go back to Montana in a heartbeat. In fact, I intend on going back to Montana to snuff out a heartbeat.

I swallow, realizing I just plotted murder in a church that is so important they call it a different name.

I run my hands under my pits and wince, feeling the sweat building up again.

My only saving grace is that the noise of the traffic doesn't filter in here. The large doors keep everything out. I can hear my heart beating like it's trying to escape.

"At least you aren't getting married in here. This place is intense."

I nod, agreeing. We are in the church next door to the one I am getting married in.

We could have gotten married in this one, as Dash is a member of the Order of the Bath, but he knew I would be intimidated to get married where all the royals get married. I know Dash is trying to spare me the intensity of a wedding from hell, but he doesn't realize the one we are about to have is just about as bad as I can imagine. In his mind Saint Margaret's, Westminster, is a small church.

To me it's imposing and called a cathedral.

"You all right?" Cami asks in a whisper.

"I am about to have a stroke just thinking about going over there. But I'm good." I nod and lift my brows, hoping someone is thinking about getting me a paper bag.

"You looked really weird last night at the practice. Angie and I think you might need a Valium or some Ecstasy."

I nod again. "Valium might not be bad," I mutter as I gawk, mouth agape and all. The art and the vast columns in each row are intensely beautiful, and they do bring about a spiritual feeling in me, a pious feeling. The ceiling may still make me cry. I can't stop staring at it. It is someone's version of heaven.

Angie walks briskly to me with a glass of water. "Why are ya sweating again?" she asks and hands me the water.

I drink like I have been in the desert for a hundred years. "He knows I hate being the focus. I hate being center stage. I wanted to elope in Vegas."

She wrinkles her nose. "Saint Margaret's is a lovely church with proper stained glass and columns. It's stunning. Ya won't get that in Vegas. Ya won't get that organist in Vegas either. She's mighty good."

I sigh and wonder what the deal is with that. "Why do people care who the organist is? People have already complimented me on our organist."

"It's a thing apparently," Cami offers weakly.

"Look, the royals are showing up in droves out there," Angie squeals softly.

My stomach tightens as I look and see the hordes of fancy English people showing up. We are across the way in Westminster Abbey, awaiting our moment to walk across the garden to the front doors of Saint Margaret's.

I take a deep breath and remind myself I will have Antoine, Mrs. Starling, and three guys from my early years in the Marine Corps to sit behind me, and Angie and Cami next to me. Serving as real seat fillers on my side, however, are members of the Secret Service, since the president of the United States is the man walking me down the aisle.

That makes me laugh a little as we watch hundreds of people milling about outside. The guests all have ornate hats. People keep calling them fascinators, but they are hats, with feathers. It's another thing to add to my Google list.

"This is over the top and silly. We might as well be rock stars. I can't believe the president is walking me down the aisle."

Angie cocks an eye at me. "The president isn't even a big deal here. He's the least famous person, besides me and Cami. So far I have heard that ya are the next American sweethearts. Ya are apparently the kindest girl in all of America, saving animals and helping old ladies with their gardens."

I glance up at Angie with an exasperated sigh. "They talked to Mrs. Starling?"

She rolls her eyes. "Would ya try to put it into perspective? This is making ya as famous and fabulous as Dash is. He is coming up to yer level now."

I cover my eyes. "Oh my God."

"Don't touch zat face!"

I jump up and lower my hands. Angie snickers and I tremble, trying not to notice the sweat under my arms.

"I told you no sitting!" Georges barks and goes over the dress again. He tugs at it and swipes his hands along the pleats. He's seen me completely naked, completely terrified, and now completely ready. He lifts my arms, and the girl who did our makeup but never speaks spritzes something under them. It smells like lavender.

"You are like svan princess." He's on edge as much as I am but he's better at hiding it.

Cami and Angie look beautiful in their lavender and lace dresses. The other bridesmaids flit back into the main entrance of the church, holding champagne and laughing with smugness in their voices. They all still hate me, I think, despite my orphan story.

Lady Townshend comes with a flute for me. Since she discovered I am actually the greatest American girl in the entire world, she has been kinder to me. My being walked down the aisle by the president is about the best part for her.

Another girl hands a flute to Georges as Lady Townshend lifts her glass. "To the greatest designer in all of Europe, or the colonies."

Angie snorts but lifts her glass. Georges interrupts. "And to zee most beautiful bride I have ever dressed. She is beautiful on zee outside, but more so on zee inside."

Lady Townshend agrees wholeheartedly. "Yes, indeed."

We all drink to my outer ugliness. Cami winks at me and Angie beams. But Dash's cousins all act like I don't exist. Even the horse-faced ones.

"Let's get zee show on zee road." Georges claps his hands.

"Yes. Quite. The organist will start in two minutes. So let's all line up and take our places." My future mother-in-law leans in to whisper, "Please do try to walk calmly, but try to get across the grounds to Saint Margaret's with haste. Don't pause for the crowds or ham it up in front of the cameras." She says the name of the church as if it's some random shop, before she leaves us there, heading for the door.

Georges shakes his head. "I vill see you in zee church." He hugs me without really touching me and leaves abruptly.

I walk from the room, following the parade of lavender and lace across the grounds.

People clap as they see us leaving the grand abbey. I blush and try not to see them all as I make my way to the Secret Service, who are waiting in the wings of Saint Margaret's for me. They grin and nod, saluting me. I salute as well, looking insane in my wedding dress as I of course catch a glimpse of the cameras stealing this moment for their papers.

One of the guardsmen walks me to the president, who is surrounded. They part like the sea for me, enveloping me in the circle.

As usual, the president is on his phone, but the moment he sees me, he stops and smiles, hanging up. "Spears, you look fabulous. I need to congratulate you on making some positive headlines for the American military." He leans in and chuckles. "And really nice work on making Europe like one of our own. Even the French have nothing bad to say about this wedding."

"You're welcome, sir." I feel weird saying that since it's my wedding day.

The moment I clasp his arm, I have to struggle not to get emotional. I wasn't prepared to feel excited about any of this, but I am now that we are down to the wire. I glance down at the white roses in my hands. "Thank you for doing this, sir."

He nudges me, and when he speaks, I know he means what he says. "This is my absolute pleasure, Spears. You are a hero and you deserve to know that your country is your family."

My eyes water until he points and shakes his head. "I think that little Frenchman will kill you if you cry. Man up."

"Yes, sir." I press my lips together, leaning and looking through the crowd at the ladies in lavender, who are completing their last few steps to the front of the church, escorted by the men who are walking them down the aisle. The organist changes her song to signal it is my turn, and suddenly I understand the hubbub over the whole thing. The music fills the old church, vibrating through us, even though we are still waiting outside.

I don't want everyone to be staring at me, but I don't get a second to think about it as the president starts walking us forward, through the massive doors. His hand trembles ever so slightly as we walk.

"Look at Dr. Dash's face, Jane. That is a man in love if I ever saw one," the president mutters softly.

I'm panicking a bit from the sea of faces in front of me, but the moment I look up and my stare reaches those green-gray eyes, I am captivated by it all. I forget every other person here.

As far as I am concerned, it is just the two of us. His look says it all.

I swear he wears every second of this insane journey on his face in varying expressions. His lips tremble but he doesn't cry.

I'm sort of glad he doesn't. I think I might not like that.

I don't cry, mostly out of fear of Georges' retaliation should my mascara run.

When we reach the end, the president gives me a slight peck on the cheek and whispers, "You got this, kid." He shakes hands with Dash and walks to his seat on my side, surrounded by his agents.

Dash squeezes my gel-coated fingertips that hide the broken nail I got two weeks ago when a mag wouldn't slide in nicely. His fingers tremble the way the president's did. I'm worried that my hand doesn't, but the moment I saw him, I knew I was making the right choice. I am making the right choice.

He is my future. He is giving me a name, a real one.

He is giving me a family, a real one. Even if they are crazy.

He is love.

Staring up into his green-gray eyes, I get lost.

I say the things I'm supposed to and put the ring on his finger after I let him do the same to me. And when it's all over and the man says we can kiss, I'm a little afraid I won't remember any of it. I spent it floating on the green-gray sea in Dash's eyes.

But when his lips press against mine, I don't care. Someone must be recording this.

"You are so beautiful, Mrs. Townshend," he whispers into my cheek as he holds me tightly.

I exhale and the world stands still, just for me and the love I have found.

25. NO ANGELS

Through the scope his face is not what I expected. He doesn't trigger anything in me. What he did to me must have erased the memories on its own.

I was likely high and he probably knocked me out, hence the head wounds.

His chubby face bears a thick mustache that makes it seem even more round. His eyebrows are bushy and he has muddled eyes, maybe brown or hazel.

He's walking the dog that hates humans and fire extinguishers. I take a breath and sigh it out slowly, squeezing the trigger. The pink mist fills the air behind him as he stops walking and falls back. The dog starts barking.

I exhale and let go of the things I carried around due to him. It's a small gesture to the child I never got to give birth to. It's a small bit of vengeance for the hundreds of babies he sold.

It is wrong to kill people, I know that. But it is right to remove a plague. People like him are a plague.

I push my sunglasses up the bridge of my nose and get up.

It's exactly the sort of end I need before beginning again with Dash.

I walk back down to the Jeep and jump in. I don't bother taking the rifle apart just yet. I drive with the wind in my face and the feeling of retribution snuggling me like mental illness might. It justifies what I've done.

Some might have said live and let live. But I am an "eye for an eye" sort of girl.

That is an opinion I hold dear to my heart.

A person who cuts someone open and steals the life she had inside of her deserves whatever end finds him.

I can't have been the first girl he did it to. Maybe just the first to live. And I know I wasn't the last.

I can't help but wonder if I had changed my mind on him and decided to keep the baby. That is the thought that plagues me among everything else. Had I chosen to let that baby be the difference in the world for me? Had I decided enough was enough? Three years of living on the streets and doing terrible things was no longer feasible with that baby. Maybe I was about to change my whole life. Maybe I was pregnant from a boy I loved. More likely I was raped or someone paid me for the privilege of sex. There was no way to be sure.

But those maybes are long gone, dead with the girl who had them.

Her end was not fitting and this redemption was earned. She had been a victim her entire life.

I am the strength she never had. The strength she never had the chance to have.

My mind whispers, about her crawling from the window in the night and running away. And wanting to keep the baby. Maybe I have always been strong. I just didn't know it when I was young.

Either way, the bad man is gone. One more weight has been lifted from my shoulders.

I head for the car I am meeting, the one that will take the rifle and machine it into something a little different.

When I land in DC again, I don't go back to our house right away when I leave the airport. I drive to the brig no one knows about. I lift my ID, knowing I won't have it after today. The guard at the front kiosk gives me a look.

"Master Sergeant—" I begin.

He salutes and chuckles, interrupting me. "I know who you are. My wife made me watch your wedding on TV. What are you doing back here?" he sounds baffled.

I lift an eyebrow. "Believe it or not, there is someone in here I have to say good-bye to."

He passes me through the gate and watches as I drive on up to the parking spots.

The young guard at the door grins and lets me walk in after seeing my credentials. "I saw your wedding on TV. It was pretty cool to see one of us marrying one of them." He nods at the window next to his head like he means someone specific.

"Thanks. I was hoping to see Rory Guthrie."

He winces and looks down. "We aren't allowed to let anyone see him, Master Sergeant."

"Do I have to phone the president again?"

He lifts his face and wrinkles his nose. "Yes."

I pull my phone out and press the capital *P* in the directory.

"Dammit, Spears. What in Sam Hill do you want? I am in the middle of a very important—"

"I am sorry, sir. I just want to say good-bye to him." I cut him off.

"You need me to patch you through again?"

"Yes, sir."

He sighs, clearly fed up with me. "Hand the guard the damned phone." I pass the phone to the young man, who winces the entire time and hands it back, pressing the button. "You know the way."

"Sorry." I nod and bite my lip, walking to the elevator.

I flash my creds to the guards at the elevator and on the seventh floor. They aren't the same ones as last time, so they give me a strange look. "Rory Guthrie," I say with authority.

The door to his cell slides back, showing him in his Plexiglas confinement. He lifts his gaze as the door slips into the wall. A sick smile crests his lips as he sits up and nods. "I knew ya'd be back."

"No, you didn't."

"I did." He's turned paler in captivity—in a way that is unnatural. He sniffs and wipes his nose on his hand before he yawns and stretches.

I sit and look at him, wondering why I am here. He twitches and jerks, clearly strung out and suffering.

"What did ya find, Janey?" he asks like he is sane, but I can see that he is not.

"My grandpa was in the American military too."

He winks. "Knew ya had skills for a reason." He coughs and sits back. "How's Antoine?"

"Good. He's dating a girl."

He chuckles. "Our boy is all grown up."

"I'm retiring. Soon. I'm going to call the powers that be after I leave here and start the process." I lean forward and tell him the thing I need to. "I forgive you, Rory."

His cheeks flush a small amount and he laughs like he doesn't understand. I'm sure he doesn't. I stand up and nod. "I hope your life doesn't drag on in here. I hope you get a terrible sickness and it doesn't take too long to die," I say softly and leave the area. He's silent until I get back on the elevator and then he screams, but I don't listen.

I leave and head for the next place on my list, getting a pilot and a helicopter at the far side of the base.

It takes a couple of hours by helicopter, but when we land I jump out and shout at the pilot, "Keep it running." I run through the field and across the road into the old cemetery.

Her grave site is easy to find. I was probably the last person here. On the day she was buried, Rory, Antoine, and I were the only people at it.

I sigh when I see her, not happy, but peaceful. I drop to my knees and brush away the dead leaves and pick at the long grass so I can read the name better.

Samantha Barnes.

She was the first mind run in which bits and pieces of my real life mixed with hers. I sit quietly for a reflective moment, feeling like she is one of the few people who ever met me, the me that's inside of me. I know I shared it with her before anyone else, except Dash of course.

Her mind run still torments me in the dark places of my mind. A serial killer who took the lives of children so she would have someone to love her. All she was ever looking for was acceptance. I know that feeling.

"I just wanted to say good-bye. I don't know when I will be back. And I guess I wanted to thank you. From you I learned how to let love in. I learned how to forgive myself. It wasn't easy, but you know that. You know it better than anyone." I sigh and glance at the grass. "I think you felt like no one ever loved you. I think I felt that way too. But maybe in the dark, we loved each other like sisters. I think I will love you for the rest of my life. I hope you found something inside of me that took you to a good place, and I really hope the rest of your time is spent there. It's a place Dash made for people like you and me. It's a place where people like us find love and acceptance. And maybe one day I'll see you there." I stand, knowing I have one more place I need to see.

But the pilot can't take me there, so I get him to drop me in Charlotte, North Carolina, at the airport.

I dial my phone as I walk to the counter to get a ticket.

"Where are you?" Dash sounds annoyed.

"North Carolina."

He sighs. "You're working today?"

"No." I smile. "Not really. I am going to Seattle quick. I'll be back tomorrow. Meet me at the airport in Baltimore?"

"Fine, but there better be a bloody good explanation when you get home."

"There will be." I sigh. "Kiss Binxy for me."

"Not a chance. I will feed him and possibly risk a pat on the back or behind the ears."

"Go for the side of his face and brush upward along his whiskers. He likes that the most." I hang up and laugh as I head for the ticket counter.

I catch the last flight to Seattle, arriving around midnight Eastern Time.

When we land, I book my return flight so I have a four-hour stay and head for the car rental.

The drive to Tanner is a short one, only forty minutes. I head right for the cemetery where I know she's buried, next to her grandfather and her aunt. Almost all of Ashley Potter's family is still alive and well. I park the car, overlooking the dark cemetery, and push my seat back. It doesn't take me long to pass out completely.

Birds chirping and cool morning air wake me from the slumber. I hadn't intended to sleep all night and have missed my flight home, but I must have needed it.

I get out of the car and stroll up the dew-covered grass under the canopy of the swaying trees to where her grave is covered in fresh flowers and tended, the exact opposite of Samantha Barnes. She was a true victim in everything. My ex-partner, Rory, tortured her in a cell before he murdered her. She was strong, strong enough to survive his version of death. Strong enough to hang on to allow me to run her mind and bring him before a form of justice.

She is still one of the strongest girls I have ever met.

I sit on my butt and speak softly to the angel engraved upon the headstone. "I'm so sorry."

This isn't something I have ever done before her and Samantha. But I feel the pieces of them floating around inside me still.

A chill shivers through me as a thousand pictures roam my mind, just behind my eyes. "I forgave Rory yesterday. I let it all go. But the one piece hanging on is you. I'm so sorry." Tears flood my eyes at the images of the girls in the cells. "I came to apologize for not seeing it soon enough. I failed you and the other girls. I should have seen him for what he was. He was my partner. This is partially my fault and I won't ever forget that. But I came to ask for your forgiveness. I don't know if I believe you can hear me or not. I won't pretend to know anything. But I am sorry." I get up and offer a small wave. "Thank you for teaching me that letting go is better than forgetting. I don't need to forget, I need to let go and forgive."

I turn, just as a breeze ripples through the trees, shaking them and their leaves. It's warm and comforts me. Even if it's just a breeze and nothing more, it is a sign I am on the right track.

The flight back to the East Coast is painful after missing my flight and sleeping at a graveyard. I am tired of flying and twitching like Rory was.

When I arrive at the airport finally, Dash awaits me looking none too pleased, but I don't care because I am dying to kiss him. "What were you doing in Seattle?"

I bite my lip before I wince and answer.

The names I say make him shudder and anger flashes in his eyes. "You know if anyone saw you—"

"I know."

"You are not Jane Doe anymore. You have a name and a reputation."

I lean in and force him to kiss me. He wraps his arm around my waist and sweeps me out the door to the car. "You ready?" he asks.

I nod, kissing him on the cheek.

"What did you do to him?" he asks.

"He was going to get away with it. The charges were never going to be what they deserved to be. He was able to pay all the back taxes, so his sentencing would be minimal."

He gives me a sideways look. "No more of this, Jane. I am not kidding."

"I know," I repeat and shake my head. "I don't have anyone else on my list."

"The fact you *have* a bloody list is insane. You sound crazy." He sighs as we walk out to where Nichols is waiting.

"Mrs. Townshend, how are you?"

"I am well, Nichols. How are you?" I hug him, it's my new thing. I am the queen of awkwardly hugging the staff, as Dash's mom calls them. I don't melt into people but I am trying.

He chuckles and pats my back like a grandfather might do. "I am well." We get in and butterflies dance in my stomach.

Dash leans in, kissing me again and breathing in a deep breath of me. "My cousin asked Angie to marry him today."

"Why did you tell me?" I gasp. "She's going to kill you." My phone buzzes seconds later. I lift it so he can see it's Angie calling, almost as if she heard him tell me. "Hello?" I stare into the screen as I answer the FaceTime.

"*Jane*! He popped the question!"

"Oh my God, what?" I try very hard to be surprised, but she knows straightaway.

"Did Dash tell you? What a fucker."

I snort and ogle the ring. "Congratulations." She wiggles her fingers on the screen, hardly even showing me the massive rock because she's moving so much. It's so big I catch glimpses of it anyway. "It's beautiful, Ang. I love it."

"I am getting married, Janey!" She sings it, but I don't roll my eyes.

She blathers on for a few minutes before hanging up. I give Dash a look. "You ruined her surprise."

He looks apathetic. "I honestly didn't think you would care."

"I don't. But she does. She really cares."

"I gathered." He places his hand over mine.

When Nichols is in the driver's seat and Dash and I are alone at the back, I mutter, "I retired. For real."

"What?" He sounds surprised and dubious. "Really?"

"Really. It was too much. The president wanted me to be some poster girl for the military and I was pretty much finished with training Cami to take over for me, so I just said I was done. She's trained.

The rest is going to come with experience. Antoine and her are quite the pair. She's all balls and he's all tech."

He snorts.

"Sorry. Anyway, I'm done. I am officially honorably discharged."

He leans in, kissing my cheek. "Congratulations, my darling. That is wonderful news."

"You know you can just start using your accent again for regular conversation, not just when you're drunk and angry. I don't mind, I promise."

"I think my American is quite good."

"Right, but you still speak like a Brit so it comes across as fairly girlie with all those 'my loves' and 'darlings' and 'lovely.'"

"Girlie?" He cocks an eyebrow and furrows his brow. I sense I might have ventured into dangerous waters.

"Not like *girlie*, but like sort of a—oh, what do you British people call them? I know I heard Nichols call the gardener that word. Nancy! A nancy!"

He looks aghast as he glances over my shoulder at Nichols. "Do you think I'm girlie?"

"Hardly!" Nichols scoffs in the rearview mirror. "No, sir. You are anything but."

Dash sniffs and nods, puffing his chest out a little bit.

I roll my eyes. "Fine, keep saying 'darling' and 'wonderful' and 'fabulous' with your little English affect but not in an accent. Dudes must hit on you when I'm not there."

He lifts one brow, pursing his lips. "I mean, not a lot, but it happens. I assumed it was because I am always dressed sharply."

I laugh and kiss his cheek. "I love you."

"No, you don't." He smiles.

I close my eyes and lean against him, enjoying the scent of deodorant and soap and him. It's the best smell in the world. I toy with the cat necklace on my neck and enjoy the peace of the drive home.

26. AM I WRONG?

The next day brings a new drive—the last one, I hope. I can barely breathe, I am so nervous. When we arrive, Nichols parks and I jump from the car, running up the hill. It's sunny and windy, a perfect day for what's about to happen.

I don't bother with the blanket I know Dash is going to want down. He hates lying on the grass without one.

I dive onto the grass and lie on my belly, pulling out the scope I used to kill a man from half a mile away. I point it in the direction of the group of kids standing in a circle. I look for the girl with the chestnut hair spilling down her back. She is stretching and getting ready to do group yoga. Her Facebook status had mentioned this.

She is fine.

I watch her face as she turns. She has two dark-blue eyes and the chestnut hair. She has a subtle look of ethnicity and puffy lips. She is beautiful. Tears threaten my eyes as I stare at the girl. I point. "The brunette with the navy-blue shirt on. Man, look how tall she is. That's not even fair. She must get that from the other half, not me. Lord knows it wasn't me."

He takes the scope as he settles next to me. A slow smile crosses his lips. "She looks healthy and happy, Jane." I nod, swallowing the lump in my throat. He offers me a look. "She looks like her life is pretty good."

"Antoine checked for me. She's healthy and happy. No therapy and she has a brother. He's adopted too. They don't know they're adopted. The mom and dad are hardworking people. They think they adopted legally. It's a normal life, I think. It appears to be. Her room is cute and her journal is clean of anything horrid."

He gives me a different look. "What the hell do you and Antoine do in your spare time?"

"Important stuff." I snatch the scope back so I can continue to stare at the girl who lived. Of all the things I have ever made happen, she is the best. She gets into position and starts her sun salutations.

"She is perfect." I turn and look at Dash. "Okay."

He cocks an eyebrow. I don't even have to explain; he knows what I mean. "Really?"

"Let's do it. If my eggs are normal and your sperm is normal, we can use a surrogate, right?"

He nods, fighting a huge grin. "Only if you're sure." He doesn't sound sure.

"I can't be sure about anything. But I don't want to be sure. I want to live and experience. I'm tired of being scared and planning everything and worrying and wondering. I'm tired of survival mode." I don't bother trying to convince either of us I can be a mother. I am counting on the fact he can be a father and help me along.

"You killed a man only a few days ago—you don't want to think about it a little longer?"

I laugh. It's probably the wrong response. "No. I am not like you. I can kill a man and not even bat an eyelash at it. If he deserved it. That man deserved the end he got. In fact, I spared him the end he deserved. The only reason he didn't die horribly is because his terrible actions saved me and her. She was adopted by good people and I—well. You found me."

"That's very sweet. In a serial killer sort of way." Dash gives me a look. "But you can't kill people when you're a mom."

"I retired."

"Before or after you killed that man?"

"Both. I sent the final e-mail on the plane ride from Seattle, Washington."

"Where is the gun you shot the man with?"

"Montana. I met Antoine's friend, who is going to machine the barrel so it's never recognized as a murder weapon."

He lifts a hand. "I don't want to know any more."

I lean in and kiss his cheek. "Maybe you're right. Maybe we should think about it a little longer. I mean, Sirius is still pretty young and Binx is pretty old and sort of mean."

He kisses me back. "Sounds good."

We get up and I walk away from the girl. I don't take another look.

She isn't mine. I might have made her, but she has been formed by someone else. Her thoughts and feelings and likes and dislikes are all part of the environment she has been raised in.

I can only be grateful that she has had the chance to become that happy girl I saw down there.

We walk to the car, in the sunshine and soft breeze, and I can't help but be grateful for every second of it all.

Had I woken up on a bed missing a baby and craving drugs, I might not have had the remarkable life I have had thus far.

The depression he saved me from is massive.

The life he gave is unfathomable.

But the life I made for myself, figuring out who I was, is the greatest gift I ever got and I gave it to myself.

And yes, I have had to make peace with who Dash is to the world and whom that makes me. I am the girl who has tried not to be noticed. But I have to adapt to be with him.

The same way he once had to make peace with a cat that stole the bed and my heart long before any man might have.

The same way he has to make peace with the leftovers from the mind runs and distrust for the lies.

We are finding our way, and while it's not easy, it's worth it.

It is a fabulous end and beginning.

As I get into the car, Nichols hands me an envelope. He smiles and closes the door.

Antoine's writing sprawls across the front. I open it, pulling a single picture from it. It's of a handsome man with a nice smile. The picture is old and faded. But there is one distinct feature I cannot help but stare at. The man has a dark-blue eye and a pale-blue one.

I bite my lip, staring at the words scrawled along the bottom: *Master Sergeant Phillip Bergamot. 1935–1962. Died Honorably fighting for his country and freedom.*

"I have his eyes," I whisper as Dash kisses my cheek.

"That's not all you have from him."

My lip lifts as I let it sink in.

My past is what I choose it to be.

ACKNOWLEDGMENTS

Thank you so much to the team at Montlake, who have helped me in every way. I have grown as an author and as a self-editor. Working with you on this trilogy has been amazing. Thank you to my agent, Natalie Lakosil, at the Laura Bradford Literary Agency. You are the very best and always patient with me and my bizarre ability to hide under a rock for great lengths of time. Thank you to my husband and my children for allowing me to sink into a dark place while I wrote this. I needed to disgust myself and creep out everyone around me just a little to get there. Thank you to my loyal readers—you are the reason.

ABOUT THE AUTHOR

Tara Brown writes in a variety of genres. In addition to her futuristic Born Trilogy stories and her nine-part Devil's Roses fantasy series, she has also published a number of popular contemporary and paranormal romances, science fiction novels, thrillers, and romantic comedies. She enjoys writing dark and moody tales involving strong, often female, lead characters who are more prone to vanquishing evil than perpetrating it. She shares her home with her husband, two daughters, two cats, and a wolfhound.